ENHANCEMENT

BLACK MARKET DNA

ENHANCEMENT

BLACK MARKET DNA

ANTHONY J MELCHIORRI

CHAPTER ONE

Fulton, Maryland
October, 2058

URLED INTO A BALL ON the cold concrete floor, Christopher Morgan thrashed about in pain. He yelled out as two prisoners plunged knives into his sides. Wrapping one arm tight around his abdomen, he swung his other at the men in a desperate attempt to bat their knives away. Blood trickled out between the fingers he'd pressed to his side, and his arms shook. Pain struck like lightning, over and over again, coursing through muscle and skin. His gurgling cries joined the shouting voices exploding and echoing against the prison's walls.

With two outstretched arms, a hulking bear of a man tackled Chris's attackers. The three men rolled in a wild tumbleweed of slashing appendages.

Chris writhed in agony. He needed to run, to escape, but he coughed up blood as he drew himself up to one knee. Bright white lights seemed to flash before his eyes as he tried to yell out, his voice catching in the blood bubbling in his throat.

1

Choking and coughing, he crumpled to the floor.

Red lights reflected on solid steel prison doors. Distant voices called out, "Lockdown! Back to your cells! Lockdown!" A squad of men clad in black riot armor rushed into the frenetic mass of prisoners.

Like a disturbed beehive, the rioting inmates fought and screamed. One raised a shiv already wet with blood. "Come and get it, you pigs!" He rushed the guards, and a dozen other prisoners joined the charge. Climbing over riot shields and swinging shanks, they crashed against the guards.

Chris cowered. His nerves screamed, and he shivered in fright. He scooted backward and leaned up against a concrete column, pressing one palm against it to steady himself.

A gruff voice barked at him, "Are you okay?"

Cuts marred the man's face, but Chris recognized Lash's perpetually bloodshot eyes.

Blood covered Lash's arms. It matted his black hair to his mahogany skin. For a brief moment, the strobe of the emergency lights over his body made him appear ephemeral, ghostly. The man's attempt to protect Chris sparked a glimmer of hope in him despite the chaos.

He might yet survive.

"Lash?" He coughed until his thick red saliva dropped onto the front of his already crimson-stained shirt.

"Man, you ain't doing great. They're all dead but you."

Chris coughed again. "Who?"

Lash looked away, back at the mass of guards and prisoners, his fists clenched and arms cocked back defensively. Despite the aggressive stance, Chris thought he could see a glimmer of fear in the hulking man's eyes.

He reached out to Lash's tensed arm. "Who?"

Lash pulled his veiny arm away. Chris watched him scan the crowd. Most of the prisoners had been sequestered by the guards to a corner of B-4. The rest of the convicts had retreated to their cells. Still, they hurled curses at the guards through their small, barred windows.

Chris struggled to stand and pulled himself up as Lash eyed him warily.

"Don't you go anywhere, man." Lash inched back. "Gotta keep my eye on you."

The two attackers that had plunged their makeshift knives into Chris's side lay motionless just a couple yards from Lash. Chris watched their bodies for any sign of life or a renewed attack.

His vision going hazy, his body going numb, he blinked. He couldn't succumb to shock. He needed to stay aware, alive. He needed medical attention. Using the column to support himself, he stood up straight again. "Help!"

"Sit down," Lash said. "You're going to kill yourself."

When Chris ignored him, Lash pushed him down hard with one bloodied hand. Lash's hand dug into his shoulder and he felt a pop of a new, jolting pain. He could not resist the force behind the other prisoner's effortless movement. The man didn't even look at him as Chris slammed against the ground. "Stay put until the white coats get here."

Waves of pain traveled down from where Lash had crushed his shoulder and through his aching sides. The fellow convict seemed to want Chris alive, but the man could underestimate his own godlike strength and kill him with a grip like that.

Banging their batons on the cell doors, guards ran along the catwalks to quiet the prisoners. Just yards away from Chris and Lash, a brilliant flash of white light from a stunner felled the last batch of rioting prisoners. Agonized cries accompanied the thuds of men seizing and falling to the ground.

"That's just fugging cruel, man!" a man barked from a cell. "Did you see what those fuggers did?"

Besides Chris's attackers, several bodies sprawled across the ground in unnaturally bent positions, as if they had been hit by a semi truck.

Lash still stood protectively over him.

"Thanks," Chris said.

Lash laughed, a deep, disturbing growl, but didn't turn around. He appeared no more relaxed, though the mobbing had been put down.

Chris frowned. "Why are you laughing?" He coughed and wiped his mouth with the back of his hand. Blood smeared across it.

"Shit," Lash said. "I ain't saved your ass yet." He turned around. "You're bleeding like a mother."

Chris let his eyes close. "A mother?"

"Open your eyes, man. Don't die on me."

"I won't," he said. He tried to obey Lash, but Chris's vision faded. His sides throbbed. Raised voices, clanging metal, coppery scents, flashing lights, and cold cement blended together in a muddy confusion of sensations. "I promise."

White coats headed toward him. Two guards grabbed Lash's arms and bent his wrists behind him. They secured the inmate and pushed him to his knees. He didn't struggle. Three white coats bent over Chris. "Open your eyes. Open your eyes. Keep 'em open."

He smiled. Maybe. He thought he laughed, too. They stabbed something into his arm, and something else squeezed his sides.

"Don't let him die," Lash said. His expression seemed to be one of concern. Worry; sympathy, maybe. Something that looked unnatural on the inmate's face.

Chris watched Lash while the white coats barked at him and moved him to a stretcher. Lash stared hard, mouthing quiet, incomprehensible words. His eyes glistened as the two guards escorted Lash back to his cell.

"Open your eyes. Keep 'em open. Stay with us."

His vision wavered and he tried to focus on those words. His life had been saved. He wanted to live. Pain, exhaustion, and loss of blood weighed on him and pressed his eyelids closed.

A steady beep persisted in a slow rhythm. It echoed in Chris's ears. His arms felt stiff and his head pounded. Brilliant orange light blinded him. As his pupils adjusted, he recognized the source of the light through his blurred sight.

A window. Outside.

The sunset filtered in through small, wire-reinforced windows and illuminated the dust particles floating in the air. A white sheet clung around his body in a tight mold. As his vision returned, so did a slight pain in his sides.

He squinted out the window. He'd never had such a view from his prison cell on B-block.

Of course. The riots. He winced as he recalled the intense pain that had coursed through him with each stab. He remembered Lash's strange heroism and how the white coats had rushed in during his final conscious moments. They had brought him here.

He lifted one arm and brought his hand up toward his chest. No searing pain like before. Just an uncomfortable soreness as though he had slept on his arm and it was now recovering from numbness. Restored blood flow rejuvenated his sense of touch with a prickling sensation. The sheets, pressed and stiff, felt almost luxurious compared to the scratchy synthetic-blend blanket in his cell bed.

Forming a tent with his arm, he peered under the sheet at his bandaged body. No dried blood stained the white dressings on his sides. He wondered how long he had been unconscious, how long he had been healing.

"You awake?"

Chris rotated his head to the right. Long black hair framed a woman's oval face. A real woman. His heart beat quicker and he fought to calm himself. "Yes."

"Great. Should be a day or two before we send you back to your cell." The white coat's voice was dry, monotonous. No waste of bedside manner on a prisoner.

"What happened down there?"

"Damned if I know. I don't concern myself with inmate squabbles."

"What the hell happened to *me*?" Chris probed the stiff patches against his skin.

The doctor examined a holoprojection on her comm card. "You suffered internal bleeding, hemorrhaging, but applying air-blown fiber anticoagulants fixed that right up. Same stuff we used on your dermal lacerations. Those fibers will itch like crazy as your skin heals. It's going to be tempting, but don't scratch that stuff until it falls off. Like a scab, you understand?"

Chris nodded. He understood all of it. The intricacies of the blood-clotting agents and wound-healing technologies paled in comparison to the more complex genetic enhancements he'd worked on prior to prison.

6

"Also, you've got subcutaneous hemorrhaging in both eyes. Nothing to be alarmed about. The redness will clear up in a day or two."

"It'll be a like a bruise, right?"

"Yep," she said. "You've taken a couple of punches before?"

Chris didn't respond. Extreme pressure had popped a blood vessel the last time he'd suffered a subcutaneous hemorrhage. Looked and sounded far worse than what it actually was. The "extreme pressure" had been caused by vomiting after a night of heavy drinking. Would've been far better to have been punched.

"There's a cup of water on the bedside tray."

"If I need something, is there a nurse call button?"

The white coat scoffed. "Real comedian, aren't you?"

"Relax, doc. He's a newbie," a raspy voice said. "I can make ya laugh, though. Tickle ya in all the right places."

The white coat rolled her eyes. She exhaled, ignoring the other patient.

For the first time, Chris turned to see a row of beds parallel with his. A scarred, middle-aged man lay in the next bed. Where hair should be, tattoos wrapped around his bald head. Chris vaguely recognized the fellow inmate. The inked man resided in B-block but not in B-4 with Chris or else he would've known the inmate's name, would have seen him in the cafeteria or the gym, at least. Maybe the library. On second thought, this fellow didn't appear to be a frequent reader.

"If I'm going to be here for a couple of days, can I at least get a book?" Chris asked.

The white coat raised an eyebrow and walked away. The scarred man watched her until she turned the corner. He whistled.

"I'd stab myself to get another look at that one." The man made a vulgar gesture with one hand, and a grin revealed the mismatched set of yellowed teeth in his splotchy gums.

Chris tried to adjust the bed to a sitting position. The bed's electric motor whirred and emitted a jarring squeak.

The tattooed inmate laughed. "Only the finest for Hotel Fulton."

Pulling himself upright and grunting, Chris leaned against the whitewashed stone walls behind him. "Can you tell me what happened out there?"

"Kurt."

"What?"

The tattooed man grinned again. "The name's Kurt, from B-5, man. Ain't you got any manners?"

He shook his head. "Sorry. I'm Chris. B-4."

"No shit." Kurt's grin disappeared.

Chris shrugged. "What's it to you?"

"I mean, I recognize you. You're one of the new guys."

"Been here for almost eight months. Hardly new."

Kurt glowered. "You won't be new when you've been here for five years, or sixteen and a half, like me. You should know that, man." His chest puffed up and his chin stuck out. He sounded almost proud of his prison residency.

Chris looked back out the window.

"Your name was one of them on the list," Kurt said.

"The list? What list?"

"I don't know, man. I wasn't supposed to see it." Kurt frowned. "Shit, I probably shouldn't even be saying nothing about it to you." He chuckled. "I got a big mouth, that I do."

Intrigue filled Chris with a thousand desperate questions clamoring for his attention. "Why was I on the list? Who else was on it?"

"I don't know, man," Kurt said, his voice sharp. He turned away. "I shouldn't have said nothing. Besides, there's gotta be another Chris in B-4. Maybe it ain't you. Ain't an uncommon name."

"There isn't. I'm the only one."

"Sorry, man," Kurt said. "Even a newbie should know better. Say too much, they cut your throat. Maybe you said something you wasn't supposed to."

Chris recalled his past several months in the prison, racking his brain for anything he had done to offend anyone or endanger his life. He had mostly spent his time reading books from the library when he wasn't working on the circuit-board assembly line making his fifty cents an hour or scribbling in his paper journals.

Maybe he'd pissed someone off on the outside. But he'd never ratted anyone out. In fact, he'd been convicted because someone had ratted on him. He'd gone down for manufacturing and distributing off-label genetic enhancements without knowing who had given him to the authorities.

Everyone from competitive athletes to thuggish gang members had been customers of his black-market enhancements. The money was good. But, like any high-risk, high-reward endeavor, his business had come with a price— one that had nearly cost him his life.

Kurt fiddled with a silver coin. It spun between his fingers as it vanished and reappeared. He saw Chris watching him and grinned. "Just started sleight-of-hand tricks with coins. Inspired by Shadow."

"Shadow?"

"You know. *American Gods*. Neil Gaiman." Kurt turned back to the coin. He watched it flip in and out of his own hand.

Maybe Chris would've seen the man in the library after all. Too quick to judge. "Shadow say you gotta learn something in prison."

Guided by Kurt's gaze, Chris watched the coin flip between the inmate's fingers until it vanished. Kurt turned and looked alarmed until he presented it in his left hand. "It's all about misguiding your audience." A smile spread across his tattooed face again. "You a God-fearing man?"

"Not really."

The coin spun between Kurt's fingers again, back and forth, until he palmed it. He opened his hand and rotated his empty palm. "You might wanna pick a religion. Just because you didn't die this time don't mean they gave up. Gotta make yourself right with your god, make peace with yourself if you gonna die for something."

CHAPTER TWO

AS A COUPLE OF STERN-FACED corrections officers escorted Chris back to his cell, he peered into the other barred windows of his fellow inmates. He caught Lash's eyes, red and intense, through one window. Lash met his gaze but made no gesture of recognition, no greeting or acknowledgment. Haunted by Kurt's words, Chris wondered if Lash was a god. Or maybe an angel sent down by a protective god. He could not fathom any logical reason why the man would have protected him.

Before the attack, he had never looked at Lash with anything but fear and avoidance. He never spoke to the man, since he was too afraid of saying or doing the wrong thing. Lash seemed like a vicious dragon, coiled in muscle, ready to strike out when threatened.

Rumors had spread that Lash had been sentenced to life for a series of murders in which he had rendered the victims limbless. And rumor also said that he had needed no other weapon than his own hands.

Still, despite the ease with which Lash could bench press a bar loaded with weight plates, he had rarely lived up to his reputation and impressive physique. Chris knew of no incident in which the man had attacked anyone that hadn't first come after Lash.

He wondered what had caused the inmate to come to his rescue. As far as he knew, he had never done anything to earn Lash's sympathy. He'd never lavished the man with flattery or bribes like other prisoners to warrant favor.

"During recreation, you stay in your cell." The guard secured the electric and manual locks to the cell. His boyish face and smooth skin did not match his deep voice. Chris wondered if the mismatched attributes had resulted from biological enhancements. "Library visits will be restricted as well, unless you're escorted."

He recalled Kurt's warning in the infirmary. The threat to Chris's life still hung in the air like an infectious disease, and the guards knew it, too. Invisible but deadly. Symptoms could rear up at any time. Another bout and he might not make it. Lying in his bed, riddled with confusion, it took him far too long to realize that his cellmate Vincent was gone. It wasn't lunchtime, recreation, or work shift. The small collection of paper books, a private journal, a rotating holo of his deceased wife, and a jar of pencils sat on Vincent's small desk.

"Here it is."

The door locks clinked open and a guard pushed another man into the cell. The prisoner held a box filled with belongings.

Chris sat on the edge of his bed. "What's going on?"

"Vincent's dead. Frank's your new cellie." The guard slid the cell door closed and locked it.

Frank, wrinkled and round, placed his box on the empty bed. "Hey, guy's still got all his stuff here."

The guard shrugged. "It's yours now." He walked away.

Wrinkles creased Chris's forehead. A mixture of apprehension and dread replaced the confusion as the words coalesced more clearly. He repeated them in his head. "Vincent's dead. Vincent's dead."

Though his cellmate had claimed to have murdered a man in a crime of passion, Vincent had never intimidated or alarmed him. Chris had never worried about his belongings with Vincent in the cell, nor had he been afraid to close his eyes at night. He might have even called the fellow inmate a friend.

Frank shoveled through the small collection of Vincent's old books and shook them out over the floor. Finding nothing of interest, he picked up a journal.

A sudden protective instinct flared in Chris. "Wait. That's mine." He stood up and tugged on the journal latched in Frank's hands.

"Guard said all your dead cellie's stuff is mine."

Chris yanked it away. "This wasn't Vincent's."

"Let me see."

Chris shook his head and stashed it away next to a couple other journals he had filled with pencil and charcoal sketches. "It's private."

Frank shrugged. Though he stood a full head shorter than Chris, he narrowed his eyes and stepped forward. "If you're hiding anything in there that you should be sharing, I'll get mine one way or another."

"I'm not hiding anything," Chris said. He took a step toward Frank. The man's breath washed over his face. He fought to prevent himself from cringing at the smell of rotten eggs and burnt coffee.

The aggression in Frank's face subsided. He laughed.

Chris stepped back, surprised, but still defensive.

"Glad you're not one of them pansy boys." He held out his hand.

Chris took it, returned the handshake hesitantly, and introduced himself. "You a newbie, too?"

Frank chortled. "Nah. New to B-block. Not to Fulton. After that riot, guards say the warden wants to mix everybody up, break up the gangs and whatnot. Plus, I heard there's a bounty on someone's head here in B-block, but everyone's been tight lipped about the whole thing." He leaned in. Rotten eggs stung Chris's nostrils again. "You wouldn't happen to know who that'd be, would you?"

Chris forced a laugh and shook his head. A sly smile spread across Frank's cracked lips as the round old man rubbed his hands together. Maybe Frank didn't know as much as Kurt.

He wondered if this bounty interested the old man. Maybe he should heed Kurt's advice and pick a god or religion to save him. In any case, he doubted he would be able to sleep with both eyes closed. Might as well take Kurt's advice and pray.

CHAPTER THREE

S NORES LIKE SAW BLADES CHEWING fresh pine bellowed from Frank's cot. The groans of the building and the howls of wind rushing through the ventilation ducts resonated in Chris's cell. Each time another convict's voice was raised in the darkness, his heart fluttered. His eyelids, though heavy, remained wide and open.

Despite the fear that gripped him and the itchiness of his healing wounds, exhaustion enveloped him until he could no longer resist. His fitful sleep conjured up dreams of Veronica. Her pale blue eyes shone against the dark silhouette of her lithe body. Hardly more than a shadow, she danced in silent, graceful arcs across a stage bathed in blue light.

Her body lit up as the moon broke overhead. Silver flashes of long hair fluttered around her face. Then she stopped. Her mouth opened, screaming silently. Chris could see the words form before he heard them.

"Get up. Get up." Her words became masculine and harsh. The stench of halitosis washed over Chris and jarred him awake. Frank's yellow eyes bored into his own as Chris recoiled from his cellmate's breath. "Wake up! Surprise inspection time, buddy."

The clatter of voices filled the block.

"If you was hiding anything in that book of yours, better get rid of it real quick," Frank said.

"Wasn't hiding anything." Then again, he didn't know what might be in it. He jumped to the desk and grabbed Vincent's journal.

"Doesn't look like nothing."

Ignoring Frank, he flipped through the journal. No hidden packets, no small compartment carved into the journal's cover. Just writing. Pages of cursive text filled Vincent's journal. A couple of scribbled drawings, not too dissimilar from the contents of Chris's own journals. Nothing stood out to him as suspicious and, at least, no hidden razors or other contraband fell out from the flipping pages. He hoped the contents of the journal appeared innocuous enough not to evoke suspicion if the guards scrutinized it.

When the guards came to their cell, the small hatch below the barred window in the door slid open. Chris and Frank stuck their wrists through, one at a time, offering them up for temporary binding. The corrections officers ordered them to the back of the cell. Two guards entered as another stood watch on the catwalk outside. They turned over both inmates' mattresses. With wide swipes, one of the guards spilled Chris's journals on the floor. They shone flashlights into the sink and stuck a thin scanning probe into the toilet to spy on the pipes.

"Man, that riot got you guys riled up," Frank said.

One of the officers scowled. "Quiet." He kicked one of the books across the floor. "Looks like we're all clear."

Another guard held up a comm card and tapped on the small screen. "Christopher Morgan, you will need to gather your belongings and come with us." The other corrections officer released the plastic ties around Chris's wrists and handed him a plastic bag.

He gathered up the journals. Among the hardback books and loose-leaf pages, a paper photograph of Veronica curled out from under a notebook. It had been creased in the search. He refolded it and tucked it into one of the sketchbooks in his bag.

The man at the door frowned. "That it?"

Chris nodded.

"Follow me."

"Nice knowing you," Frank said.

The warden drummed his fingers on the desk as he scanned projections of text. He squinted at the words. Rosacea colored the man's sunken cheeks. A plastic fan rotated back and forth over the desk. Chris waited, his hands in his lap, as the warden hummed. After finishing his tune in a crescendo, the warden's eyes shot up. "You're set for release."

"Sir?"

The warden looked Chris up and down. His nose bobbed like a rabbit sniffing the air. "You want to leave this place or not?"

"I do."

"You do what, kid? Leave or not?"

"I do want to leave, sir."

"You aren't the only one." The warden raised a single white eyebrow that lifted like a floating cloud. Each little hair fluttered in the wind of the fan. He leaned across the desk. "There are others who'd pay good money to take your place. I hope you don't take it for granted."

Opening his mouth to speak, Chris thought better of it and stifled the questions seeded in his mind. Instead, he nodded. "Yes, sir."

"Getting out a year early." The warden's eyes narrowed. "But you're still on parole. You do understand that, right? Need to get yourself a job—a real job—or you'll be one of my boys again. Capisce?"

"Yes, I understand, sir. I've got to get myself a job." Repeating the warden's words, Chris felt like a dejected parrot. The thought of regular checkups and random visits by a parole officer, along with the pressure of finding a job, squashed the budding optimism brought on by his release. If he made one bad decision—hell, if they *suspected* he'd made one bad decision—he could end up right back in the same block with the same unknown men that wanted to stick another knife in his side.

"Apparently, you've already got one job offer on the plate. Must be one of those bleeding-heart liberals looking to reform a dumbass ex-con. Whatever the case, if it weren't for him, I wouldn't be signing off on your release. Got it?"

"Yes, sir." Chris was dubious but didn't question the warden. He wanted out. He'd be delivered from the dangers of prison. But then again, whoever wanted him dead might not be contained by these concrete walls. Maybe the list that Kurt had spoken of came from the outside. Maybe he was being tossed from the ten-gallon aquarium into the shark tank.

What could he do? Tell the warden he felt safer here? That he'd like to be Lash's cellmate?

The warden stood up, indicating for Chris to do the same. "Ride's waiting outside. Better hurry before they change their mind."

As he scrounged for ideas of who had come for him, Veronica's dreamy, pale blue eyes flashed in his mind. Hope welled up like an unleashed geyser. Maybe she had come for him. Changed her mind. Forgiven him.

Rationality prevailed, and he dashed his own hopes against the unyielding stones of reality.

Veronica would never come, not after what he had said to her. Shame and regret turned his thoughts toward his parting words with her. She had tried to kiss him one last time, but he had turned away and pushed her aside.

He had been a fool.

When the gates closed behind him, Chris stood alone in the narrow walkway between chain-link fences with barbed-wire tops. He clutched the plastic bag of his belongings in his right hand. The sack held the journals from his cell—both his and Vincent's—and the comm card that the guards had confiscated when he had been committed to the Fulton State Penitentiary. Sunlight fell across him in a warm blanket even as a brisk wind whistled and stung at his face. He absorbed the outdoor air, breathing it in deeper.

Once more, he looked at the prison. The structure itself appeared no more ominous than a misplaced office building, except for that tall fence tracing its perimeter. Past it, across the parking lot where he headed, trees grasped at the gray sky with barren limbs.

He trudged on. A bullet-shaped Lincoln idled between the lane and the parking lot. A deep black tint obscured the interior as the electric motor whirred.

As he approached, the front door opened. "Christopher Morgan, come in."

The person that greeted him wore a slim suit and aviator-style sunglasses. With his slick black hair, he resembled a male model that might adorn any number of advertising images on the news streams and entertainment feeds, if it weren't for the pallor of his skin.

Chris hesitated.

The man neither smiled nor scowled.

A cold wind tugged at the nape of Chris's neck, and he shivered. He envisioned the man in front of him handing over a hit list to a lackey. That lackey would pass the names on to an inmate with all the right connections, and the next day, men would die, bleeding to death on the floor of the cell block where Chris had almost lost his own life. Fresh to the world outside concrete walls and constant surveillance, he might be about to surrender his new freedoms to a man he had never met. "What do you want from me?"

"I want to offer you a job that I'm certain you'll accept."

"How the hell do I know you aren't trying to kill me or something?" He realized the absurdity of the question but stood with arms crossed. He didn't expect this stranger to answer honestly if he intended to have Chris killed. But the man would at least know Chris suspected his motives. Still, he felt like a child about to get in a white panel van to help a sleazy man search for a lost puppy.

"I'll be honest: you're worth far more to me alive than dead. That's why I appealed for your release."

"You pay the warden off or something like that?"

"Something like that." The man waved a hand dismissively. "Nothing for you to be concerned about."

"I am concerned. Some guy pulls a couple strings to get me out of prison and now he tells me he wants to offer me a job. Damned right, there's something odd about that." He kicked at the loose gravel on the asphalt, ready to turn around. Swallowing, he looked back up at the man. "What the hell makes you think I'd be any good for this job, anyway?"

The man exhaled and readjusted his sunglasses. With his thumb and index finger, he played with a silver ring on his right hand. It swiveled around his bone-white finger. "The reason you went to prison is why I want you to take this job."

Chris frowned.

"At least hear me out. I'll give you a ride back to your condo. You don't need to make a decision today, but I want you to consider my offer."

If this guy wanted him dead, he could kill him now. No need to wait until the condo. "What the hell." Taking one last glance at the twenty-five-foot-tall chain-link fences that had contained him for the longest eight months of his life, he ducked into the open door of the Lincoln.

CHAPTER FOUR

THE CAR WHIRRED ONTO ROUTE 29, headed north toward Baltimore. The sound of the Lincoln's rubber tires on the road, though muffled, whispered into the cabin. Black leather covered the enveloping seats and adorned the interior door panels. Blue numbers glowed from the speedometer, accompanied by the light of the projected road map from the control screen.

The man in the suit sat in the driver's seat, but he didn't operate the steering wheel. Instead, he faced Chris as the car drove itself on its preordained path to Chris's Federal Hill condo in Baltimore.

His head resting in his palm and his elbow situated against the window, Chris gazed over the Patuxent River. A dense fog, rising in wisps, obscured the snaking body of water.

"It's nothing that will be out of your range of research experience," the man said.

"How can I possibly accept a job from you if you won't even tell me who you are?"

"Simple. Tell me that you want the job."

The enigmatic businessman, Chris thought. *Full of mystery, lacking in answers.*

"The work would involve cellular delivery of genetic material for medical therapeutics," the man said. "You would be a bioengineer, responsible for research and product development. How does that sound?"

"I'll need a little more time to think about it. That's okay with you, right?"

"Given your unique background, I don't think you'll be able to find a better job."

"My background? You mean the fact that I spent eight months locked up with a bunch of killers and thieves?"

"No," the man said. "I'm talking about the particular charges that led to those eight months. If you had been in prison for assault and battery, your odds of getting another job in the industry would be more favorable. Companies won't touch you with a ten-foot pole since you got caught stealing technology from Ingenomics and perverting it so you could sell illegal genetic enhancements."

Chris scowled. "I didn't just 'pervert' those genes and the delivery vectors. I made them better."

For the first time, the stranger smiled. It was a slow, subtle curl of his lips that may have been mistaken for a slight tremor, but it was a sincere smile. "I know you did. That's why I want you to accept this offer."

"I appreciate the sentiment, but I'll need time to consider all of this."

Fog whipped around the car as they approached Route 40 into Baltimore. He recognized the looming apartment buildings surrounding a strip mall that advertised all-you-can-eat Chinese and sushi at Forever Yum. The restaurant hosted the usual salty and greasy smells along with the aroma of rubber from the neighboring car repair shop. His stomach rumbled at the mere thought of room-temperature California rolls and dried-out lo mein noodles. Might as well be a Michelin-rated restaurant compared to the food he had eaten in prison.

"This isn't the best way to my place," Chris said. "Sure you put in the right destination?"

"I'm not dropping you off yet. We're making a stop for dinner."

"Dinner and busting me out of prison. You trying to get in my pants? I don't swing that way, buddy."

Chris imagined his mysterious benefactor rolling his eyes behind those opaque shades. The man shook his head. "I haven't quite expounded on the full terms of my offer. I want to make them quite clear for your consideration. A short car ride wouldn't do it justice."

"Just so you know, I don't have any money and don't have a job yet, so I hope you're buying." Chris grinned, aware that the man would not reciprocate.

The businessman's lips tightened. "I'm surprised that you've maintained such a sense of humor when you almost died a few days ago. You do realize that there's still a hit out on you, don't you?"

Chris's smile vanished. Memories of the attack in prison flooded his thoughts. Whoever possessed the power to incite such a riot had the same, if not more, power in the streets of Baltimore. His stomach grumbled, and nausea squeezed it. He wasn't sure if he'd be hungry for dinner anymore.

Seated at Old Ellicott Brewery and Grill, Chris probed the chunk of bread on his plate with a knife. He sat across from the pale man in a wood booth, a candle situated on a brass centerpiece between them. A yellow haze cloaked the room as the candle flames flickered and caused shadows to dance across Chris's plate.

The businessman placed his sunglasses in the breast pocket of his suit jacket. His eyes were as calculating as they were cold.

"Are you celebrating something tonight?" the waitress asked. "Promotion? Anniversary, maybe?"

Chris let out a slight but unenthusiastic guffaw. "Freedom."

"Ah, patriotic," the waitress said. She winked. "Good to see that still exists."

When she asked for their drink orders, the businessman requested a glass of ice water with lemon.

Chris gazed at the menu, overwhelmed by the options. Where his choices had been limited to eating or not eating just a day before, he could now choose from over a hundred beers, draft and bottled.

The waitress smiled but tapped her finger across the ordering tablet.

"Uh, what kind of pale ales do you have on tap?" he asked.

"We have a Beaver Dam Blue from—"

"I'll have that."

"Can I have an ID?"

"You flatter me," Chris said. "I'm thirty-five."

"I never know, nowadays. It's 2058, after all. You could be eighty-two or eighteen and still look the same, you know what I mean?"

He nodded. Working in biotech and around other researchers who specialized in so-called anti-aging therapies, he understood her predicament. He fumbled in his pocket, but he had forgotten his old comm card in the Lincoln. In prison, he hadn't needed an ID, and his old habit of carrying the card around had been lost. He needed to rekindle it now that he was back in the real world. "I'm sorry. It's in the car. I can go get it, though." Chris looked at the businessman, whose expression remained steadfast and stern. "Or not. Never mind."

Placing a hand on his shoulder, the waitress leaned in and winked. "Nah, you're okay." Her breath tickled his ear, and he watched her hips sway as she moved on to a couple seated at another booth.

He flipped the pages of the menu. All the words, the dishes, even the select pictures blended together in a mottled stew of choices. He struggled to pick out an entrée. His mind wandered back to prison. Corrections officers told him when to eat, the cafeteria workers slopped on food whether he wanted it or not, and strict schedules prescribed the allotted recreation time and when to shower. Choices were yet another aspect of life outside prison that he would need to relearn.

The businessman sat with his hands clasped on the table. "Get the venison, sides of garlic mashed potatoes and grilled asparagus."

"You know, I still haven't decided if you're going to kill—"

"Are you all ready?" The waitress dropped their drinks on the table. After taking their orders, she floated away.

Leaning across the table, Chris whispered. "I don't know if you are planning on killing me or if you're telling the truth about this job. When do I get to know what the hell is actually going on?"

The gray-suited man's eyes bored straight into Chris's.

"Nothing?"

"I can't tell you more. You're right to think you're still in danger, but I can promise you it isn't from me."

"You keep saying that," Chris said. "Why not explain to me why you want to give me a job?"

"I already told you: your skill in genetic enhancements has me impressed."

"Bullshit."

The couple dining near them quieted. Both turned toward Chris in feigned concern.

"I'm not the only PhD qualified for a job like that," Chris said. "In fact, there are far more researchers out there looking for jobs than there are available positions. I'm sure there are plenty of people more brilliant than me that would do twice as well as I could. Stop playing hard to get and tell me why you want *me*."

The man's lips trembled slightly. He might have been about to smile again, but the flickering candlelight cast shadows that obscured his features. "I'll tell you, Mr. Morgan. You are in a unique position. As one of the conditions of your parole, you will be required to find work that is commensurate with your education and experience, but also within reporting distance to your parole officer in Baltimore. I have just such a job."

Chris opened his mouth to speak but was silenced by a single skinny, pale finger.

"And I know that you will be desperate for such a position. Not only that, but you have made it clear you aren't bound by state or federal law when it comes to your work."

The businessman's eyes glowed in the candlelight like a cat's at dusk. And he pounced.

"If you accept this offer—and I am sure that you will—I will ask you to do things that are illegal. If you don't..." The man raised his shoulders in a gesture of nonchalant apathy. "That's your choice, but I would no longer be obligated to protect your life."

CHAPTER FIVE

CHRIS STRODE UP THE STAIRS to his Fed Hill condo off
of South Charles Street. The condo was located on the
third floor of a building that his landlord claimed used to
be a factory in the early 1900s. A century and half since then
and a cycle of renovations made the building look no different
than the complexes that stood sentinel along the highways and
roads stretching between DC and Baltimore.

The morning sun usually burned off the blanket of fog that
enveloped the neighborhood. Such persistent haze seemed like
a harbinger of his uncertain future.

His comm card held up to the lock, he opened the door to
his condo.

Shaking his head, he rolled his eyes. He needed to stop
reading so much into the world, as though it contained the
same symbolism and foreshadowing as the books he had
subsisted on for almost a year. The fog was no omen.

In his right hand, he carried his boxed-up food from dinner.
He laid the leftovers and the single bag of belongings from
prison on a coffee table. The air in the two-bedroom condo

smelled of mold and neglect. With lights on, the condo still seemed gloomy. A layer of dust covered the hardwood floor.

He sat on the couch. A cloud of dust puffed up. Punching a command into his comm card, he adjusted the window opacity in the room. The windows transitioned from a dark shadow to an invisible barrier that the fog condensed against.

Take the job, do what I say when I say it, or your life is as good as forfeit.

Chris had been shaken and had told the businessman again that he needed time to think it over. Everything that had happened in prison frightened him, but now he worried what freedom might entail for his safety. Even if the threats were empty, even if the man didn't intend to have him killed, Chris was lost. He needed a decent job. Plenty of biotech companies called the area home. Most specialized in tissue engineering, genetic treatments, or a combination of the two. But how many would hire an ex-con who'd stolen company technology to sell on the street?

He had considered his sentencing lucky: two years instead of the maximum forty for his original charges. The police had screwed up the chain of custody with most of the evidence, and they had only convicted him on an antiquated "intent to distribute contraband" charge.

The damage had been done, though. His criminal records showed the original charges. Any potential employer worth his or her salt would be able to scrounge up enough information from the archived news streams by searching out Chris's name in conjunction with Ingenomics and his convictions.

As he stared at the white plastic box of leftovers on the coffee table, his stomach turned over again. Anxiety and nausea overcame him, and he ran into the bathroom. He threw up into the toilet. His arms across the cool porcelain, he gagged again.

When the nausea passed, he turned on the sink to wash out his mouth. The faucet spat stagnant water and sputtered until a clear stream poured into his hands. He splashed the water into his mouth and across his face. With a washcloth and soap, he removed the greasy polish from his skin.

He wanted to talk to somebody, anybody. He wanted to call Veronica, but he worried what she would say to him now, how she would berate him. How it might hurt her.

Calling Rajeev or Phil from Ingenomics would be out of the question. Though he had worked with both and enjoyed their weekly happy hours, neither had been aware of Chris's extracurricular activities until his arrest. Embarrassment prevented him from speaking to them now.

Jordan. Jordan had stood behind him throughout his entrepreneurial undertakings in illegal genetic enhancements. But all contact with him had ceased as soon as Chris was arrested. Besides, Jordan also shared far too much interest in activities that might land Chris back in prison.

He flopped onto the scarlet couch in his living room. Sprawled out, he stared up at the ceiling and wondered what his next move should be. His parole officer had scheduled a meeting about a month from his release, and he needed to demonstrate an active job search. He would first update his resume and then send out cover letters and applications.

But the condo felt too rotten, too uncomfortable. He'd cleaned it the night before entering Fulton, but that hadn't stopped whatever vermin had moved in with the layer of dust that lived there rent free. Finding a job could wait until tomorrow. Besides, the smell of vomit saturated his clothes, and since leaving Fulton, he had felt the prison grime that stuck to his skin like the dust clung to his apartment.

A shower seemed more pressing a concern.

Steam rolled around him, and he closed his eyes in the shower. Despite his return home, Chris retained the eerie sensation that someone watched him. He shivered and shook his head as beads of water smacked against the shower curtain. He needed to get used to a shower that didn't contain twenty other men.

A muffled clang interrupted his thoughts. At least, he thought he'd heard the sound. Paranoia crept deep within him, a learned survival instinct. He turned off the shower faucet and listened for another sound.

"Hello?" His voice sounded more timid than he would have liked, so he tried again. "Hello? Anybody there?"

No response. Shampoo, slightly gelled, bubbled in his hair. He rubbed his head and body with a towel that smelled like the must in the rest of the condo. Once out of the shower, he slid up the boxers that he had dropped on the bathroom floor.

He crept out and into the narrow hallway. Bending into the main bedroom, he turned the lights on.

Nothing moved. Everything looked just as undisturbed as when he had entered the apartment.

Down the hall where he had left the lights on, nothing seemed amiss. His holoscreen remained off with just a minuscule red light that glowed to let him know it received power. His leftovers and prison bag sat on the coffee table in front of the couch.

The door to the second bedroom, his home office and makeshift laboratory, was cracked open, but no lights glowed from within. He crept up to it. Holding his breath, he nudged the door. It creaked open. Light from the hall sifted into its corners.

Something moved in the shadows.

Chris shoved the door open and held up his fists. He flicked on the light with his left hand, his right hand still clenched. White light illuminated the room.

A brown mouse scurried from a corner and squeezed under the closet doors.

His heart still thudded against his rib cage, but he let out a slight guffaw. The guffaw inspired another until he erupted into uncontrollable laughter. His anxiety evaporated as he saw the tipped-over glass sculpture of the *U.S.S. Constellation* he had bought at a gift shop in the Inner Harbor. Little glints of light reflected on the edges of the trinket from its resting place next to a holoscreen module on his desk. He leaned against the door frame as he laughed. With one hand, he kept himself upright and used the other to hold the healing wounds that throbbed on his side.

All laughter ceased when he saw the footprints imprinted in the dust on the carpet.

CHAPTER SIX

CHRIS GAZED AROUND THE ROOM. He disregarded the scared mouse in his closet. The electric central heater, tucked away within a utility closet down the hall, buzzed as it churned warm air into the heating ducts throughout the condo, making him jump. His eyes darted to the doorway of the bathroom. In his pants strewn on the floor, his comm card lay in a pocket.

Besides the thrumming heater, the whoosh of air above him, and his thudding heart, no other sounds haunted the condo. He retrieved the comm card and went back to the second bedroom, where he knelt to examine the footprints. Two distinct patterns appeared in the footprints, and both sets shared dimensions that dwarfed his feet. A thin layer of dust caked the prints. They weren't fresh. Still, his heartbeat didn't obey what his mind told him.

Standing, he wondered if he should call the police. Someone had been in his condo while he'd been at his extended stay in Fulton. Images of the businessman telling a couple anonymous goons to dig up more information on Chris flashed through his mind. Worse, the men that had been in here might be connected to the people who'd tried to kill him. Desperate to drive the burgeoning anxiety from his mind, he dismissed those thoughts. Maybe the police had scrounged around in here. Still, he'd never been notified of a warrant issued for another sweep. Dirty cops looking for dirty answers to keep him in prison?

In that case, it might not help to call the authorities. Hell, there might be something in the office that he had forgotten. Call the police and ask them to search his condo for evidence of a home invasion when they'd never find the culprits, but they might find evidence that could land him back in prison?

Not ideal.

Instead, he snapped pictures. Just in case, he'd file them away as his own personal evidence for this trespassing. The footprints were concentrated around the filing cabinets near his desk and around the workbench now devoid of the home lab equipment that had been confiscated in the initial search and seizure when his operations were uncovered.

Ring marks and dents marred the wooden surface of the worktable. Only the lone MakerSix 3D printer and an old holoscreen sat on it. Awfully generous of the police to leave those here for him, his attorney had said. If they'd known what he had been able to do with the printer, they never would have left it. In fact, there might still be residue from the DNA-based materials he'd used with the printer.

Better not call the police.

For a moment, he smiled to himself, recalling the ingenuity of using DNA as a biomaterial. He had not been a pioneer in this field. Far from it. His work had been inspired by an academic researcher whose work had delved into printed

DNA-based materials as early as 2013 but had gone neglected by the biotech industry.

The device had not been tampered with as far as Chris could tell. The filing cabinets appeared to contain most of the paper copies of his work, legal documents, and patent applications—minus, of course, the documents still in the Baltimore PD evidence room.

He could not figure out what the intruders had searched for. Nothing valuable had gone missing, as demonstrated by the holoscreens in here and his living room. There was no good explanation for why they'd broken in. He sat in his desk chair for half an hour before accepting the fact that he would not solve the mystery that night.

When he did go to bed, he slept fitfully. He tossed and turned, unused to the silence and relative expanse of his bedroom. It unnerved him. Each time the heat turned on in his apartment, his eyes shot open and his pulse raced. In the morning, the dark circles under his eyes had grown no smaller than they had been the night before, but he needed to begin his job search in earnest. He resolved, first, to take care of his apartment. After the apartment had been cleaned from floor to ceiling, the windows clear enough to be a hazard to negligent birds, and all evidence of his intruders eliminated, he found no more excuses.

Days turned into weeks as he applied for a slew of jobs. He didn't expect any immediate responses, but neither Bio: Formics, the local P&G outfit, Baltimore Tissues, Radiant Healthware, or any of the other companies, small or large, had offered anything more than a form rejection message.

He feared the scarlet letter on his applications burned far too bright.

Almost four weeks after his dinner with the businessman, he found himself in the parole office, waiting in a room full of other ex-cons. A few appeared as nervous as him. Others sat with careless postures, their legs sprawled halfway across the cramped room. A mixture of filtered cigarettes and body odor hung in the air.

The holoscreen near the door to the offices flashed his name. An officer motioned for Chris to follow her through the doorway and into her office. She introduced herself as Officer Ramos and told him to have a seat in the plastic chair across from her metal desk. Taking his hand, she stuck a diagnostic device on his fingertip that bit into his skin.

Ramos squinted at the instrument and looked back up. "Looks like you're clean. How about your job search?"

"I'm applying, but it's a little rough out there." Chris got out his comm card. "I made a list of all the companies I've submitted an application to, if you're interested."

She waved her hand dismissively. "I'm only interested in the jobs you get, Mr. Morgan, not your list of rejections."

He left the office more depressed than when he had entered. As he walked along the littered sidewalk to the Metro station, his thoughts strayed back to the businessman. The man had refused to give his name or any means by which he could be contacted. But he had promised that he would return when he felt certain Chris would accept the offer. Chris warranted that such a time might present itself sooner than he had anticipated.

CHAPTER SEVEN

"**H**ERE'S WHERE ALL THE WET labs are," Randy Nee said. "Could be slippery! Better watch your step!" He laughed and wiped a hand across an eye as though he had been brought to tears by his own joke.

Chris offered a smile that he hoped would placate his new manager's self-indulgent humor and followed Randy into the room filled with equipment. A PCR machine buzzed near the door as a projected readout tracked the RNA replication process in real time. Several large flow hoods lined the opposite wall. A couple of basic microscopes sat on benches next to racks of glass slides.

"The fluorescent scopes are in the room off by the incubators." Randy motioned to the closed door. "Looks like someone's using them, so I won't show you them now. Wouldn't want to bleach their samples with any bright light from out here, would we?" He laughed far more than seemed appropriate.

"No, I don't think that'd be nice at all."

Randy slapped Chris's back. "No, no, it wouldn't."

All of the equipment was familiar. In fact, the lab at Respondent Technologies appeared almost half the size of the Ingenomics lab where Chris had designed muscle-restoring genetic enhancements to treat conditions like muscular dystrophy.

The door to the microscope room cracked open. Green light illuminated a small glass slide on the stage of the scope in the otherwise dark room as a researcher in a long white coat slipped out.

"Tracy, come meet your new colleague." Randy waved at the woman.

Tall and thin, Tracy cut an athletic figure even in the white lab coat. Her large hazel eyes caught Chris's and her red lips curled into a disarming smile. She held up a blue-nitrile-gloved hand in a cursory greeting. "Nice to meet you."

He smiled back, feeling like a sheepish boy meeting a movie star. After his stint in prison and being wrapped up in a job search, he hadn't spent much time out. Seeing an attractive woman like Tracy, a sudden wave of shyness hit him. He nodded back. "Uh, I'm Chris."

"Ah, oh, yeah." She brushed back a lock of hair that had come free from her dirty blond ponytail. Realizing what she had done, she ripped off both gloves and cursed.

"Don't want to contaminate your cells, now, do we?" Randy laughed. "Got time to talk about the project?"

Tracy shook her head, and another long strand of hair came loose to swing in front of her face. As she spoke, she fixed her hair back into the ponytail. "I'm in the middle of something right now. Maybe later?" She stretched on a new pair of gloves, grabbed a box of slides, and went back into the microscope room.

"She always knows how to keep herself busy," Randy said. "Give her a problem and she won't leave until she solves it. You'll enjoy working with her."

He wasn't sure yet if he'd enjoy working at Respondent at all. All the same, he had no choice. The businessman, had shown up at his doorstep as promised, shades and all, to offer him the position. He'd said that the interview he had set up served only to satisfy formal hiring requirements. Chris had the job. He only needed to assure his strange benefactor that he would complete whatever task the man had planned.

Chris forced a smile. "Sure thing."

After the lab tour, Randy introduced Chris to Paul Ram and Kristina Liang. Both were Master's-level biomedical engineers, but Randy said that they were just as capable as any of the PhDs he'd run across. Paul cringed at this, while Kristina smiled with a resigned sigh and a roll of her eyes.

Now, Chris sat alone. As he sifted through HR manuals and paperwork on his comm card, a sudden tap on his shoulder caused him to jump. He dropped the comm card, and it clattered onto his desk. A projected page about confidentiality agreements wobbled before settling again.

"You familiar with APC genes?" Tracy hovered over him.

"Uh, no. Should I be?"

"You're going to have to be." She grabbed an empty seat from a nearby desk and pulled it over. The subtle scent of lilacs drifted over him as she plopped into the chair. "It'll be your project. Was supposed to be mine, but I've got a bit too much on my plate. Randy figures this'll be a good way to get you involved in the group."

"So what's APC responsible for?"

"You're going to read all about it. You want me to ruin the suspense?"

"I don't mind. It's not like I'm planning to read the book, anyway. I'd rather just see the movie."

Tracy smiled. "APC is a tumor suppressor. About a hundred and fifty thousand people a year end up with colon cancer because they lack proper APC encoding. Polyps line those people's colons like weeds. Real nasty stuff."

"Sounds like it," Chris said.

"Anyway, we're going to need you to design a delivery system."

"Just a delivery system? I don't need to work on the actual gene or anything?"

"I already took care of that. Randy told me you're good with delivery systems. You need to figure out the best way to deliver these genes to people so they don't get ass cancer."

Taken aback, he sat silent for a moment.

"Not glamorous enough for you, big guy?" She smirked. "Everybody wants to cure cancer, but no one wants to be the ass guy."

"No, no, it's fine. I'll do it."

"Damn right, you will." Tracy playfully punched him in the shoulder. "Bigger and better things once you get it done." She stood up and held out her hand.

Chris stood up and looked straight into her vibrant hazel eyes. The grin remained across her face as she squeezed his hand.

"I'm glad to have another bioengineer on the team. Can't wait to get to work."

"Thanks," he said. "I'm glad to be here."

Tracy walked back to the lab, her hair swaying in concert with her gait. She strode between the other engineers' desks, her head held high. Stopping, she turned back. "You want to get a drink after work? You look like you need to loosen up."

CHAPTER EIGHT

TRACY EYED CHRIS FROM ACROSS the marred table, a glass filled with a stout in her hand. "What's your view on cheating?"

He forced a brief laugh, unsure if humor or seriousness was the proper response. He'd been prepared to answer questions about where he grew up or where he received his PhD or what hobbies he pursued in his free time. Maybe talk about his favorite show on the holo. Before answering, he took a gulp of his pale ale. "Are we talking about hiding notes on your comm card for a college exam or are we talking relationships?"

"I'm talking relationships. We're well out of school. Why would I care about that?" Tracy gave him a sly look as she propped her elbow on the table and settled her chin in her palm.

He grinned. "Are we on a date that I don't know about?" His ability to flirt had decayed since he had jumped right from a long-term relationship with Veronica to utter isolation from the opposite sex in prison. He cringed a little when Tracy's head flew back and she opened her mouth as though aghast. His face grew warm.

"I'm just giving you shit. But you can tell a lot about a person from that question."

"By asking them their views on cheating in a committed relationship? I feel like that's a pretty straightforward question."

"You'd think that. And maybe you and I would be on the same page. But I can always tell when someone's bullshitting me. They'll act extra disgusted, as if it's a sin just to bring screwing around up in front of them." She licked her lips and closed her eyes. "Those will be the same guys that you'll find with your best friend, naked, and they'll say they helped her move or some stupid shit like that. Real bags of crap."

Chris laughed. What he'd thought would be a happy hour filled with small talk had turned into a roller coaster of conversation. "Okay, fair enough. So, what kind of guy do you think I am?"

"I think you're the kind of guy that would be a horrible liar."

"Is that a good or a bad thing?"

"It doesn't matter as long as you don't have to lie, does it?"

Chris finished off the last swig of his ale and set the empty glass down. He flipped through the menu displayed on their table's mini holoscreen. His stomach growled at the depictions of juicy burgers, thick-cut French fries, and beer-battered fish. The foods, all standard bar fare, still seemed like a luxury to him since leaving prison. He hadn't ventured out much and hadn't enjoyed the proper company to eat a good meal with. Now, looking across the table at Tracy's stunning features and her radiant smile, he felt an immense contentment. "Do you want to grab dinner?"

Tracy's lips puckered up and she frowned. The ephemeral wisp of optimism and confidence that had materialized dissipated when he saw her furrowed brow. Had he been too forward? He needed to get a handle on his interactions with women again. It hadn't been as easy as jumping on a bicycle after a couple years spent walking. No, it felt like jumping on a bucking bronc instead.

"The beer's good enough here, but I'm not a big fan of the food. I do know a place down the street, though, that blackens a killer rockfish and has live jazz. Sound good to you?"

"That sounds great."

The blackened rockfish at the Rusted Scupper melted in his mouth with the perfect mix of spice and the cool taste of the mango salsa that came on top of the fish. Smooth jazz filled the large dining room. Tracy's eyes sparkled with the candle that burned between the two of them, and Chris was sorry when they each finished their white-chocolate crème brûlée and the last drops of their bottle of pinot grigio. As the lights dimmed in the restaurant, a singer approached the stage.

Without so much as an introduction, she belted out Etta James's version of "At Last." Shivers went up Chris's spine as a few brave dancers approached the floor in front of the band. The mood in the restaurant shifted from swanky dining to back-alley jazz club.

"This place is great. Reminds me of Chicago," he said. He moved to pay for the check as it appeared across the holodisplay, but Tracy swiped his hand away.

She wagged a finger at him. "My treat."

"No, I insist." He nudged his comm card forward.

Tracy swiped her comm card in front of the holodisplay. "I told you I'd take you out, welcome you to Respondent, and I'm making good on that promise. Don't make me a liar."

Chris held up his hands in a defensive gesture. "Fine, fine." He dropped his hands. "I appreciate it."

They stood up to leave, and he cast a final glance at the dance floor. More couples had filled the space, their bodies swaying and twirling under the low lights.

"Let's go dance," he said. Maybe the bottle of wine had tipped him over the edge and imbued him with liquid confidence. He felt warm inside and could not remove the smile from his face. Tracy appeared ready to protest. "Just one dance."

"I don't dance," she said.

"I'll teach you."

Tracy shot him a dubious look. "You know how to dance?"

He nodded. Of course he did. Veronica had practically forced him to learn. When they had dated, she couldn't take herself seriously as a professional dancer if her partner didn't know a simple four-step swing dance or a straightforward waltz. He had followed her to ballroom dance lessons, and she had hauled him onto dance floors similar to the one here.

Now he dragged someone onto the dance floor. He did so with a confidence he had never felt when Veronica had wrapped her skinny fingers around his wrist and forced him to lead her in a foxtrot.

Once they were on the dance floor, the tempo of the music increased. He eased Tracy into a simple four-step and introduced a couple of swings into their rhythm. At first, her face appeared frozen in fright as she stumbled to follow. Soon, that melted into a beaming smile as she grew accustomed to Chris's lead. As the singer's voice belted out onto the dance floor, Tracy preempted his moves and tried to lead.

"You have to wait for me," he said, spinning her around. "The man's supposed to lead."

"And who the hell made up that rule?" Tracy smirked but let him take the lead again.

Between dances, they rested at the bar and reenergized with rounds of rum and Coke. Sweat dripped down Chris's back and sheened across Tracy's forehead as the lights turned up on the dance floor and applause filled the room. He slipped his hand into hers as they joined the flow of traffic pouring out of the restaurant and into the chilly night air.

Tapping on her comm card, Tracy peered up. "I'm calling a cab. You live nearby?"

"Not really."

"Good. I can call you a cab, too."

Chris couldn't help but feel a glimmer of disappointment. The balloon of optimism holding him up had been popped.

She hugged him when the cabs rolled up. "This was fun. We'll have to do it again." With a final wave, she disappeared into the vehicle.

Maybe working at Respondent wouldn't be so bad. Sure, he would be working on a delivery system for treating colon cancer, wading through literal shit, but maybe...maybe he could start over. Screw whatever that damned businessman wanted. He'd work hard. Yes, he'd make a new name, redeem himself.

Plus, Tracy had promised they could "do it again."

Chris slid his comm card across the lock to his condo. Instead of unlocking the door, the card dropped. He leaned down to retrieve the card and almost fell over. His vision swam, distorted by one too many drinks.

He admitted that the project didn't excite him. Work wouldn't be easier tomorrow, but it would be made more bearable by the lingering sounds of hearty laughter, good conversation, enjoyable dancing, and the subtle hint of lilac ingrained in his memories.

Once inside, he grabbed a glass of water and then flopped onto his couch. Chugging the water, he fiddled with the comm card to turn on the holoscreen. Maybe he'd catch the *Late Show with Sean Cooney*. Again, he dropped the card. It fell on the coffee table next to the bag of his belongings from prison. Some strange feeling had prevented him from moving the bag, as if sorting out its contents would reconfirm those months spent idling away in cell block B-4, those idiotic mistakes that had gotten him in there, those last few hours when he hadn't known if he'd leave the prison alive.

But he had made it out.

He had survived.

With rekindled determination, he set his glass down and dumped the contents of the bag across the table. One of his tumbling sketchbooks knocked the glass off, and water spilled and rolled across the hardwood floor. He ignored it and threw the empty plastic bag at the front door. He'd throw it in the dumpster tomorrow, forget about the prison, and forget about the time wasted.

He grabbed the closest of his journals. At least he had done something worthwhile. Well, maybe not worthwhile, but at least interesting. Something new.

Flipping open to the first page, he admired a hawk that he had drawn. Its eyes, large like a puppy's, rendered it almost cute instead of fierce. Instead of ruffled, detailed plumage, the bird consisted of a smear of blacks and grays from his charcoal set. He turned to the next page, a winking outline of Kate Winslet from a classic movie.

He skipped through forty-five other pages until he reached a portrait of a golden eagle. The eagle's eyes appeared deep, almost three dimensional. Its feathers were lustrous, each barb drawn out. Slight smudges distorted the details since he had never sprayed the charcoal with any protective coat of acrylic spray. Better than the hawk, though.

For the next half hour, he scanned through his sketches and drawings. He might not be ready for a gallery opening, but he'd done something right. Been like—what had Kurt said? Been like Shadow from *American Gods*. He'd learned his trick from prison.

He leaned back on the sofa, and the room seemed to spin. Pulling his hands through his tousled hair, he exhaled and scanned the books on the coffee table again. The cracked leather cover of Vincent's notebook caught his eye.

There was no title, nothing to mark that it had belonged to Vincent. Just the knowledge that it had sat on his cellmate's desk for the eight months that Chris had been there.

He had never asked Vincent what had landed him in prison. But Vincent had told him about a cheating wife and her secret boyfriend. His cellmate had shared in many a conversation about the progress of synthetic organ technology, the corruption in Congress, or a book that both had read. The man could talk for hours, sometimes without so much as a reassuring nod from Chris, about any and every topic. Vincent seemed to know a little about quite a lot, though every conversation tended to turn back toward the problems with genetic enhancements and artificial selection of genes replacing the natural course of things. Still, he had never spent too much time discussing personal matters or his time outside the pen.

Those answers potentially lay in Chris's hands now. All in the journal that Vincent had scribbled in nightly. Sometimes for just a couple of noisy minutes, sometimes well after Chris had fallen asleep. He found he missed falling asleep to the sound of the pen scratching across paper. It reminded him of the times when, as a kid, he had napped on the family room couch while his mother sat next him and wrote in her daily journal. But it wasn't just that strange Freudian comfort that he missed; he missed Vincent.

When Chris had been stabbed, Vincent had disappeared. Why? Hadn't Kurt mentioned that others had died? Or was it just Frank?

His thoughts spun into a frustrating blur. He stuck his fingers into the journal but couldn't muster the courage to open it. No, it wasn't his to read. It had been Vincent's and would always be Vincent's.

CHAPTER NINE

A WRENCHING HEADACHE MUDDLED CHRIS'S THOUGHTS. The sun filtering in through his windows burned his retinas. A hot shower hardly made a dent in the throbbing pain that filled his skull like a persistent jackhammer.

Sure, more cures for cancer existed now than ever before, but there wasn't a pill to treat a hangover. Or maybe there was, and it had been released while he had wasted away in prison. Screw prison.

As he forced down a breakfast of oatmeal, he watched Baltimore 7's morning cast on the holoscreen. The newscasters spoke in practiced voices rich with obnoxious cheeriness. They reported the incoming threat of a cold front. Chris reported a heavy hangover and turned the projection off.

He put his oatmeal bowl down on the coffee table and stared hard at the sketchbooks he had left lying open. A gull soared over an abandoned beach, its wings spread in the wind. A ship sailed up the ominous roll of a rogue wave in a squall. A couple danced in a packed bar from another century where the smoke of cigarettes filled the air. That image evoked mixed memories of time spent with Veronica and, now, Tracy.

Sprawled across the coffee table were all the little worlds he had drawn in blacks and whites, varying shades of gray. But one world remained closed.

Chris picked up Vincent's journal and debated opening it again. He couldn't do it. Not now.

He slid the journal into the leather shoulder bag propped against the couch. Though it remained empty, he took the bag as if he had something to carry. Papers, lab reports, contraband. Not anymore. He would work on delivering genetic drugs for ass cancer patients, and all he lugged around was a dead cellmate's journal that he superstitiously feared opening.

When he'd gone into prison, he'd thought it would harden him. What the hell had happened? Why did opening a former cellie's glorified diary scare him?

"Good morning, doc." Tracy's voice rang out high against Chris's eardrums.

He rubbed his temples. "What the hell did you do to me last night?"

Tracy laughed. "Sorry, didn't know you drank like a little girl." She pulled up a seat next to him and laid her head in her hands, her elbows propped on his desk. "That was fun, but I don't have time to nurse you back to health. We need to get moving."

He waved a hand in acknowledgment but kept his eyes closed. "Fine."

"That kind of means now. We're supposed to finish this delivery system in a month. Claire's orders."

"Claire?"

"VP of research. Man, they hired you on the spot, and you don't even know who you're working for? Maybe you know something I don't."

"Right, right. Sorry, I know that. I'm just a bit…hungover. I don't know how the hell you do it."

Tracy stood up and slapped his back. "Some people are just born with natural greatness."

He met her triumphant expression and stared hard.

"Tell you what: you read up on APC today. You're going to need to know what the hell you're dealing with before you design a delivery system for it, anyway." She shrugged. "It's my gift to you. Also, lab happy hour is every Thursday. That means tonight."

"I don't think I'm up for it."

Tracy grinned. "You don't have a choice. You want to be a part of our group, you have to go."

Before Chris could protest, Tracy retreated to the lab.

Chris waded through the research papers outlining the role of APC in tumor suppression and how familial adenomatous polyposis led to colon cancer. It took him several times to read over the terms before they sank in as he trudged through the haze that had settled in his head. With the help of a constant supply of coffee, his thoughts clicked into place. The more he dug into the papers, the more he figured his old tricks would suit the genetic treatment well. Designing a genetic modification delivery vector out of DNA-based materials would be simple enough.

Simple enough if he could access all his old vector materials and lab notebooks. All of that now lay stowed away in a maximum-security evidence facility, never to see the light of day, much less make its debut as a scientific publication or patent.

God, he had been stupid. He could have patented the technology. It would have required more time, more financial investment, but its application would have been useful in a variety of genetic enhancement or replacement treatments, such as the one he dealt with now.

Now the only person that might even read about his past inventions would be a bored officer reviewing old case files with a burnt coffee in hand from a crappy street-corner autoserve window.

He recalled tidbits of his designs, but they weren't sufficient by themselves. For his first real assignment at Respondent, he wanted to develop a delivery vector that outshone Randy's expectations. He could prove to his boss and himself that he deserved his position at the company. As an added benefit, it might further endear him to Tracy. Couldn't complain about that.

He took out his comm card and projected a blank page onto his desk. Writing and doodling on the blank page, he conveyed his thoughts as they came, racking his pained brain for the answers to the riddle Tracy had provided him. Flashing back to his days before prison, he strained to remember what the exact vector he had used for his muscle enhancements. He tried to recall the inert DNA strands that made up the bulk material, preventing the immune system from recognizing the vector as an invasive foreign body and thus expelling it, rendering it useless. That sequence and the material made from it had been his bread and butter, and now he couldn't remember how the hell he had ever made toast.

Frustrated, he flicked his comm card across his desk and massaged his temples. The pain flared in his head, and he resisted the urge to pound the desk. That wouldn't make a great impression for his second day on the job.

He leaned his forehead on his arm, allowing him a perfect vantage point into the leather shoulder bag near his feet. With the worn brown cover, Vincent's journal stared out. Was it Vincent's writing in the journal that had been the reason his cellmate had died in the riots? Or was it just bad luck?

His sides itched. Though the healing skin patches from the prison infirmary had fallen off just days before he started at Respondent, he could feel their uncomfortable, ghostly presence. It felt as if the wounds were scabbed and healing again.

He gave up on solving the problem with the APC corrective gene delivery system and searched for archived news on the Fulton Prison riots. Several stories showed up in the results. Most seemed lackluster in excitement and detailed the location, time, and outcome of the riot: seven dead, seventeen wounded.

But the articles listed no names. One mentioned that the riot had started when several unnamed inmates had been spontaneously attacked, but the journalist offered no purported causes for the random attacks. No news stream had reported any external connections or justifications for the stabbings, except for one source that ventured the attacks were gang related. Sure, skinheads occupied a couple cells, and enough imprisoned street gang members ran around to cause problems at Fulton, but gang violence wasn't the cancer that so often afflicted other prison systems. Besides, if the gangs had been responsible for the riots, he wanted to know how he had become involved.

Further investigations provided no more leads on possible gang involvement, so he set his sights on Vincent. Maybe he had had an external connection to these groups and had become a target like Chris. Chris needed to figure out if his cellmate's history held the key to finding out who had wanted them dead and why. He snapped his fingers as he struggled to recall Vincent's last name. When he'd first shaken his cellmate's hand, when he'd first introduced himself, hadn't Vincent given him a last name? It started with a *K*. Ko—? Ka—?

"Head still pounding?"

Chris jumped and dropped the comm card. He closed out of the open sites. "Uh, yeah. Still got a bit of a headache."

Tracy offered a sympathetic smile and put her hand on his shoulder. "I must have messed you up. Why don't I make it up to you with lunch?"

Vincent's last name, just beginning to materialize, dissipated back into the recesses of Chris's mind. His thoughts swirled to Tracy's hand still on his shoulder, and he returned her smile. Sharing a meal with her would be recompense enough for a meager headache. "Yeah, sure, fine."

"Promise that it'll help."

He figured he needed more help than Tracy could provide.

CHAPTER TEN

C HRIS SCROUNGED UP THE ENERGY to make it through the lab's happy hour at Cowboys and Poets. Happy hour extended into a dinner filled with greasy cheeseburgers and overly salted fries. After their meal, Paul claimed he had research papers to review at home and Kristina said that she needed to meet up with her brother, who lived in nearby Glen Burnie, to go over his resume.

"It looks like it's clear who the real men are around here," Randy said.

Seated beside him and across from Chris, Tracy elbowed Randy in the side. "Come on. I'm still here."

"My point still stands." Randy laughed and held his hands on his protruding stomach. "But you know what? Tonight, I'll give you my man card. I'm going to check out, too."

As the other three departed, Tracy and Chris sat alone at a table full of empty plates and glasses. Chris had managed to drink his share from the pitchers of lager that Randy had provided for the table, but he couldn't quite muster up the same confidence he had felt the previous night with Tracy. "You want to go dancing?"

"What happened to the little boy complaining about a hangover?" Tracy laughed. "Last night was fun, but I'm not feeling it right now."

"That's fine. You headed home, then?"

"Yeah, I think so." She smiled. "It's still early, though. You want to come over for a drink? It smells a lot better in my apartment than it does here."

When they arrived at her place, she retrieved a bottle of pinot noir from a wine cooler. She poured a glass for each of them and handed one to Chris. Tracy held hers up in toast. "To the newbie."

Chris clinked his glass against hers but couldn't help remembering when Kurt had called him a newbie. At least this time, he worked a real job. And for all he cared, she could call him whatever she wanted. He took a swig. "You have any music?"

"Of course." Tracy tapped on her comm card, and the apartment filled with the steady beat of synthesized instruments.

"Yeah, I'm not sure about this."

Tracy drew her head back. "What's wrong with my music?"

"It's a little hard to dance to, but we can make it work."

"God, you're persistent, aren't you?"

Chris took her hand and pulled her into the center of her living room as they swayed to the rhythm, each of them balancing a glass in one hand. As he drained the final drops of pinot, his face warmed and he felt an uninhibited contentment brought on by the mix of alcohol and his present company. His thoughts turned from Tracy and he wondered what Veronica would think of him now. So many times, she had filled him up on wine and begged him to live a little, to stop acting so rigid. He lived now.

As they swayed, he leaned in toward Tracy. She smiled before she met him halfway. They ceased dancing and Tracy set her glass on the nearby table. She threw both hands around his neck and pulled Chris tighter against her.

The music followed them into the bedroom as Tracy unbuttoned Chris's shirt between kisses and grins. She pushed him onto her bed and dimmed the lights with her comm card. Tossing it away, she crawled over him and pushed his wrists up toward the headboard as her lips met his. The lingering pinot noir possessed an almost sweet edge on Tracy's lips and tongue. Chris closed his eyes.

When Tracy had sprawled out across her bed asleep, her naked skin glowing in the wintry moonlight, Chris didn't want to disturb her when he felt the pressing need for a glass of water. He tiptoed into the kitchen, crashed against her countertop, and searched through the cupboards. His hands knocked into a stack of plates on one of the shelves. The plates teetered, but he caught them before they came crashing down. He peeked back into the bedroom to see that Tracy lay sound asleep, still stretched out across the bed, the moonlight her only cover. Smiling to himself in drunken reverie, he wondered how they would fare together, wondered if they could last or if this was just a one-night stand. He found it hard to believe that she would ever accept him for who he was and what he had been, but he couldn't help hoping that she would.

CHAPTER ELEVEN

ALMOST TWO MONTHS INTO HIS job at Respondent, Chris
had not heard anything from the businessman. He clung
to a distant hope that maybe the stranger no longer needed
him. Maybe he was free from his indentured servitude and
could keep working as a researcher just like the rest of the
scientists and engineers at Respondent. He'd already begun
to blend in with them. He joined in on their Thursday happy
hours, bantering at lunch over Congress's ineffectiveness just
down the road in DC, and going on coffee runs to the QuickFix
autoserve window down the block. He had even developed
a working delivery system for correcting the defective APC
genes. Animal trials would begin in mere weeks.

Tracy sat on the edge of his desk, her familiar smirk almost
reaching her high cheekbones. "Ready for lunch, doc?"

"Sure thing, sunshine." Chris displayed an equally
mischievous grin.

"Stop calling me that." Her eyes narrowed.

"Or what? You going to dump me?"

"Something like that."

When they settled into a beaten-up booth at Silver Linings Diner, the spot where Tracy had first taken Chris to recover from a painful hangover, her face drew up in a grave expression. "I want you to tell me something and I want you to be honest: Why were you in prison?"

His heartbeat quickened and his cheeks flushed. A mix of embarrassment, shame, and shock surged through him. He struggled through potential answers. Maybe he shouldn't tell her everything—maybe he just did something stupid, like drove his car manually while drunk. Except he didn't have a car. What about stealing something? No petty thievery. She was far too smart to believe that.

"I just want you to be honest." She repeated the word with a look meant to endear herself to him, as if she knew what he was thinking.

"I screwed up."

"No shit," she said. "But *how* did you screw up?"

He felt like he might be able to tell her but wanted to bide a bit more time. "Can you at least tell me how you found out?"

"I did a little stalking on the net." She shrugged. "Wanted to make sure you weren't a killer or sex offender, or something, you know. I mean, you weren't—you aren't." She corrected herself. "But I saw you spent time in prison."

"Then you saw what I did."

She shook her head. "No. I've got this weird feeling like it'd be better if you told me. Straight to my face."

He smiled. "Thanks, I guess." He scratched his head and let out a slow exhale. "You promise you aren't going to go around telling everyone?"

"Are you kidding?" Tracy raised an eyebrow and leaned across the table. "I won't. But if they go looking for it, they're going to find it."

"True."

"Just tell me."

Over a Philly cheesesteak sandwich, Chris explained how he'd been snubbed for several promotions from his role as an entry-level research engineer at Ingenomics. He had been eschewed for less-qualified engineers who'd worked their way up the career ladder through dogged brown-nosing. He consistently produced delivery vectors with higher levels of transfection efficiency, yet his superiors hardly seemed to notice his scientific talent. When he had decided that waiting on a raise wouldn't satisfy him, he marketed his own illegal genetic enhancements through a distributor. He had earned enough from his initial batches fabricated in Ingenomics's labs after hours to build a cramped but adequate setup in his condo to manufacture the delivery systems he used for the genes he made while on the clock at work.

"You sold genies on the street?"

He nodded, scowling at the use of "genies" to describe his illicit work. Enhancers, or the people that used black-market enhancements, often referred to the genetic delivery systems as "genies" for short. The word evoked both a short-form name for the enhancements and the enhancers' desire to alter their bodies with one wish. "I can't excuse my, well, inexcusable actions." He shook his head. "Never again. I was stupid and arrogant, and I don't even know what happened to the people that used my enhancements."

Tracy's expression dropped. "Did anyone die?"

Chris shuddered at her words, and his stomach dropped. The thought that he may have killed someone stabbed at his heart, and his mouth went dry as he fought for words. "I have no idea." He swallowed hard. This wasn't the first time he'd faced that question, but he never liked to dwell on it for too long.

"I'd like to think I was good enough to prevent something like that. I mean, the enhancements I sold were similar to a couple FDA–approved treatments, so it's highly unlikely. But, all the same, I'll never know for sure." Guilt swelled in his chest like an aneurysm fit to burst. "I understand if you want to end this thing between us. If you want me to leave Respondent, I will."

"Randy knew about all this when he hired you?"

He hesitated, reminded of the dealings between Randy and the mysterious benefactor that he knew nothing about. When he had accepted the job offer, the strange man had assured him that Randy knew about Chris's past but would keep the matter confidential. "Yes, he knew."

Her expression relaxed. Reaching across the table for his hand, Tracy shook her head. "No, Chris. I would never ask you to do that. I couldn't. We've all screwed up at one point or another. I wanted you to be honest, and you were. Thanks."

Chris opened his mouth, ready to tell her about how he had actually gotten the job at Respondent. Honesty. That's all she wanted.

But he closed his lips tight again. He couldn't do it. At least, not yet. He promised himself he would tell her. Besides, it wasn't as important or nearly as shameful as the reason he'd gone to prison. Right?

"Thanks for your understanding." He squeezed her hand. "What about us?"

She smiled, weak but reassuring. "We'll see how things go. Randy gave you a chance at Respondent and I tend to trust his judgment. I'll need to think about this, but I might give you a chance, too."

"I appreciate it." Chris felt as though the single phrase could not express the gratitude that burgeoned within him, but he could say nothing more for fear of breaking down. He'd spent far too long wondering if life could be normal again, and Tracy had, unbeknownst to her, flattened the levies that barred those emotions from overwhelming him. Now, she seemed too considerate, too forgiving for what he had done. He vowed he wouldn't take her understanding for granted but could not help wondering why she had not already stormed off in disgust.

Tracy offered a limp smile and shrugged. "You seem like a better person now than the one that would do stupid shit like sell illegal enhancements. But don't mess up." She shook her head. For a moment, she turned away and her face twisted, her lips drawn tight and her eyes narrowed.

"Something wrong?"

"I used to run track in college. Ran both the four hundred and eight hundred meter." She exhaled. "So, while we're being honest: I got kicked off the team for doping. I understand what it's like to want the extra advantage, to think you're above everyone else. I always wanted that extra...that extra oomph that I just couldn't seem to get naturally."

"That's nothing compared to what I did." Chris's forehead wrinkled in concern.

"Hey, shut it while you're ahead." Tracy's lips cracked into her familiar, playful smile. "I'm trying to justify this thing between us to myself."

The smell of stale beer permeated Cowboys and Poets. Horseshoes hung on the walls next to framed couplets from Tennyson, ropes and hats were draped next to a sculpture of Poe's raven, and moving holopaintings of stampeding cattle neighbored Walt Whitman's famous *Leaves of Grass* portrait.

Chris's eyes settled on the portrait of Whitman. If any of the tacky decorations in the dive bar blended the themes of cowboys and poets, it was that portrait. Whitman, with his manicured yet rugged beard and a broad-brimmed hat atop his tilting head, surveyed the rest of the bar with a stolid expression that bespoke a quiet confidence.

"Well, you going to join us or you going to ogle Walt?" Randy grabbed Chris's shoulder, and deep laughter exploded from him.

Chris smiled. "I'll take care of the first round."

Tracy squeezed his elbow as she settled into the booth under the portrait with Kristina, Paul, and Randy. "Thanks, doc."

As Chris made his way toward the carved wooden bar that served as the true centerpiece of the establishment, Randy's voice pierced through the noise of laughter and conversations of the other patrons. "I heard Whitman was a dandy. You know what I mean?" His laughs followed Chris through the mix of professionals that had descended on the bar for happy hour after work and others whose happy hours started at 11 a.m. and ended at bar close.

Chris ordered a pitcher of Beaver Dam Blue and took it back to the table. Randy's cheeks, red with laughter, made him appear as though he'd gotten a head start on the drinks.

Several pitchers later, their conversation had turned from work projects to the Baltimore Ravens' chances in the playoffs to criticisms of President Hartson's cybersecurity policies. Kristina, her eyelids half closed, looked at Paul with a lopsided smile. "I think I better take off. Too much of this and I won't make it home alive."

Paul, at the end of the booth, stood in a hurry. "Oh, well, in that case, I'd like to make sure you do indeed get home alive. I mean, we kind of need you on the colon project."

Chris noted the interaction, for the first time realizing that he and Tracy might not be the only couple engaged in an office romance. He shared a look with her and she shrugged back.

"Don't talk about that shitty project again." Randy pointed at Kristina with a wobbling finger and slapped the table with the other. Her empty mug jumped and fell. It rolled across the table until Chris caught it. She mouthed the word "Thanks," and he nodded back.

"Maybe it's time we all call it a night," Chris said.

Randy lifted the half-empty pitcher. The beer sloshed and splashed around. "Let's finish this one off before we go." He leaned forward with squinting eyes and slurred words. "Let no good beer go to waste."

Paul and Kristina declined, apologizing, and left.

"Fine," Tracy said. "But it won't be our fault if you feel like shit tomorrow."

Randy laughed again. "Shit. Colons. You're funny."

Tracy rolled her eyes.

"All right, I'm going to grab a smoke first." Randy tottered out of his seat and out the back door.

Earlier that day when Randy had been far more sober, Chris had presented him with a prototype of the new delivery system for replacing the tumor-suppression genes. The engineered vector system protected by DNA-based material microparticles had achieved nearly seventy-five percent delivery efficiency.

"Shoot for at least ninety-five percent," Randy had said. "An undelivered quarter dosage is just money that we're wasting in production because you can't do it right."

When Chris had brought the news to Tracy, she'd shaken her head and responded with a curt, "Shit." Even if they developed an efficient new system that day, the verification assays for the cell culture tests would take a couple of weeks. He had been given an extension when the first deadline couldn't be met. Now the new target date was just a week away and they would have to push back the animal trials.

Yet Randy would not let them work late into that Thursday night. He'd demanded that they come out for a couple of drinks, and he'd hear no excuses.

"So, you think we're going to get this done on time?"

Tracy shook her head, a tangle of hair falling in front of her eyes. "Hell, no. But I did have a new idea."

"What's that?"

"Modified DNA," Tracy said. "No more plasmid DNA. We can improve the efficiency of our gene delivery with modDNA."

"But that'll take weeks—maybe a couple of months."

Tracy shrugged. "Your delivery system seems flawless to me. It's my part of the project that needs reworking. Plasmid DNA has never been the most reliable method of genetic therapy, and I was just lazy when I started the project."

"There's no world in which I can imagine you being lazy."

They toyed with the idea for a while, exchanging ideas, an electric wave of excitement shared between them. They outlined their plans on their comm cards. It occurred to Chris that that Whitman, still guarding them from his portrait, would likely disapprove of their inability to enjoy each other's company without reverting to conversations regarding work.

"Randy might not be happy about the delay, but this will at least work." She looked up from the comm card. "What do you think, doc?"

Chris's triumphant smile drooped and his face drew up in concern. "Randy's been gone a while. Maybe I should go check on him."

"Yeah, you're probably right," Tracy said, the flush of enthusiasm in her face draining away. "I wouldn't want to find him drowned in a puddle of his own piss outside or something."

He laughed but couldn't prevent himself from entertaining the idea. It might not be too far from reality. He stood up from the table. "I'll go take a look. Want to make sure our tabs are square so they don't think we bailed?"

Tracy raised an eyebrow. "Is this just a ploy to get me to pay for your drinks?"

"Take my comm card." He handed her the card and walked to the back of the bar. The bartender nodded at him as they caught each other's eyes, and Chris picked up his pace. Maybe Randy had passed out outside. The January night held a biting chill that would be liable to leave its mark on anyone foolish enough to underestimate the cold.

Chris pushed open the back door and looked out into the alley. Dumpsters sat against the walls of the alley. Bags of trash, a couple ripped open and left spilled on the ground, sat next to the dumpsters. The weak yellow glow of the light above the door provided only a pitiful guard against the shadows filling the alley. "Randy?"

There was no reply. He stepped out, letting the door close behind him. He turned the handle again, but the door remained closed, locked to the outside. "Dammit." His breath curled up in soft white plumes, and he rubbed his arms against each other to warm his skin.

Low, urgent sounds echoed down the alley, just beyond the neighboring building. Edgar Street could be seen at one end of the alley. Halfway toward Edgar, shadows bathed an alcove. He crept toward it. The voices became less muddled as he approached.

"...vectors now. We need the specimens intact."

He thought he heard Randy's voice, but it sounded more sober than in the bar. "Please, I haven't had a chance. How was I supposed to...?"

"I don't care. Boss don't, either. You've been talking to them, haven't you? Trying to sell us out?"

Chris froze against the wall. There was nowhere to hide from the two gigantic beasts of men facing the alcove. With their backs turned to him, their dark overcoats provided an ominous curtain that hid whomever they threatened.

"I can't. Not now," the hidden person said.

Chris felt certain now that the voice belonged to Randy. He tiptoed closer, his mouth open to say something.

A sickening crack sounded as one of the large men shoved their victim to the ground. "This is your last chance."

Now Chris could see Randy huddled, struggling to his knees beyond the two aggressors' legs.

"He's worthless," one of the men said. "He's already said too much, and it ain't worth our time trying to get anything else from him."

Randy reached up. "Please. Please."

Chris took a slow step backward. He needed to do something, but these men were large. Almost as big as Lash had been. He took another step back.

But he could not leave Randy with these two. He dug into his pocket for his comm card.

The card was gone, missing. Dammit, he had given it to Tracy.

Chris inched away. As he crept back, his shoe crunched on the neck of one of the empty beer bottles littering the alleyway.

Randy caught his gaze before the other two pointed. "There. There." His finger shaking, he pointed at Chris.

The two men looked at each other. Without a word, the one lunged after Chris. The other lashed out at Randy and stabbed the research manager over and over with a silver knife.

Chris turned to run. Randy's screams devolved into bubbling gurgles that chased after him. He sprinted.

A vise-like grip around his arm stopped him cold. The man that had given chase lifted him with one hand around his neck, pinning him against the cold brick wall. Chris swung his arms and legs. Even when he connected with the man, the giant didn't flinch. Nothing seemed to register within his attacker's icy blue eyes. No anger, no pain.

His assailant's hand squeezed tighter around Chris's neck. A violent urge to cough made him gag, his tongue stuck to the top of his throat. He thought he heard the door just down the alley open and close. If only he could scream out. Maybe someone could help him.

Chris wished that Lash was here now.

Lash. *Save me.*

CHAPTER TWELVE

CHRIS'S VISION BLURRED AND HE stopped flailing his arms. This would be it.

The grip around his throat loosened. The powerful hands held him by the shoulders now. Another man had shown up beside the attacker. Lash.

Chris blinked. He struggled to regain a semblance of lucidity. No, it wasn't Lash. He was still in prison.

"That's him," the second man said.

A flash of worry lit up the assailant's blue eyes. He set Chris on the ground but did not let him go. The vise-grip tightened on Chris's shoulder with the same strength that had almost killed him.

The two men looked at each other, seeming to confer without a spoken word. Chris's throat throbbed, already sore and bruising. Ghost pains from the stab wounds in his side flared up, ignited by the attack.

"I think we should take him with us," the second man said, breaking the silence.

A sudden flare of sirens sounded. The echoing screams of the police cars could not have been more than a block away.

Though the attacker still held Chris in place, they paid him no heed.

"Shit. Do you think they can ID us?"

"Boss won't like that."

The door to the alley opened. Two shapes appeared in the gloomy alley light, their shadows stretching across the overflowing dumpster across the way.

One of the voices, startled, called out to them. "Chris?"

The two men sprinted back toward Randy. The research manager lay still and made no sound as the men scoured his pockets. As the sirens grew louder and spinning red and blue lights lit up the brick walls, the attackers dashed away. Despite their size, they vanished from the alley as a police car rolled in from the opposite end.

With their car parked, two officers got out and rushed toward Chris and Randy. One called out on her comm card. "Two suspects, headed south. Males. Both appear to be six feet in height, dark clothing and coats." The other officer knelt down by Randy.

"Chris! Are you okay?" Tracy crouched next to Chris, her long hair loose and tickling his face.

He tried to smile. "I survived a stabbing, remember? I'll be okay."

She didn't laugh. Instead, she pulled him close to her, burying his face in her chest. She said nothing until he asked if she could give him space to breathe. "Of course, of course."

One of the officers. "Sir, we've called emergency medical personnel." She tugged on Chris's collar and examined his neck. "Did they do anything else to you?"

Chris shook his head.

"I know you've just been through a lot, but did you happen to see their faces? Can you describe them to me?"

He described the two men's ominous figures, their dark overcoats and collared shirts. He described his assailant's vivid eyes, his pale skin and rugged, expressionless face. No scars, no tattoos. He had not gotten a good look at the second man—his vision had still been hazed in tears and a fading consciousness—but he detailed the man's dark brown skin and deep brown eyes. The man's nose had been bent, maybe broken before.

"You saw how big they were, right?" Chris said. The footprints in his apartment...maybe they were the right size, but he didn't mention it to the officer. His eyes glazed over.

"Sir, is there something else?"

"Blue eyes on one, brown eyes on the other with a crooked nose," he repeated. "That's all I got."

When she appeared satisfied, she left and joined up with her partner.

Chris shivered, wondering what those men had wanted, why they'd spared his life.

"Take my coat." Tracy draped her jacket around his shoulders.

He cursed at himself for being such an inconsolable, pathetic wreck. It was a miracle he had ever even tried to penetrate any underground markets with his illicit genetic enhancements. He wasn't meant for such things. Couldn't even handle this strange alley mugging.

Tracy helped him stand, his back against the brick wall.

Randy had not moved from where he had been attacked. Blood pooled around his body and a hint of copper hung in the air.

"He's dead," Chris said, indicating Randy's still form.

Tracy nodded.

"I didn't think..." He shook his head. "I should have said something. I should have done something." His stomach churned.

"No, there was nothing you could do."

"I watched this happen."

A couple more patrol cars arrived on the scene, along with an ambulance. One of the paramedics approached and asked Chris to sit down for a quick assessment. He waved the man off as he marched toward the first two officers on the scene. Both talked with the bartender now as the man described how he had been about to take out the trash when he had seen a man choking Chris.

He tapped on the shoulder of the officer that had first run to Randy. "Do you know what happened? Have they caught the guys yet?"

The officer offered up a consolatory smile. "Have you seen a paramedic?"

Beside him, the paramedic stood with arms across his chest. "He won't let me sit him down."

"What's your name, sir?"

"Christopher Morgan." He folded his arms across his chest.

The officer held out a hand. "I'm Officer Dellaporta." When he didn't take it, she continued. "Mr. Morgan, once the paramedics have looked at you and you've sobered up, we'll ask you for a statement. Your descriptions have already been helpful. I'm sorry for what you must be going through right now." She glanced at Tracy. "Why don't you wait with your friend?"

Chris stepped toward the officer. "There are two killers running around out there. They just murdered my friend. Do you have any idea what's going on? Shouldn't you be doing something about this?" The vessels in his neck bulged amid the bruising. "I mean, you just let them run away."

Officer Dellaporta's partner motioned to excuse himself from the bartender. "Sir, please calm down. There are other officers on patrol looking for the suspects right now. Again, I'm sorry, but we're doing what we can."

"Doing what you can? Randy's dead." Chris held up his hands. This time, they shook not out of fear or cold but in frustration. Now he felt certain about the footprints, the men. But the officers wouldn't believe what he knew to be true. Something more than a street robbery had just taken place.

"I'm sorry, sir. Please, once you have calmed down, we'll take a statement about the mugging."

"It wasn't just a mugging," Chris said.

Tracy grabbed Chris's arms and tried to pull him away from the police. "Come on. Let's go. Let them do their job."

He turned to her. "They think it's just a mugging." His face turning red, he spun back to the officers. "I'm telling you, there's something else going on. They threatened Randy, asked him to deliver a specimen." He frowned. "Probably thugs interested in stealing genies from our company. This could be a big case, and you can't let these guys get away."

Officer Dellaporta glared at him, a stern expression across her face. "Mr. Morgan, the victim's comm card is missing and he has no cash on him. We're the officers, and, believe me, this is not uncommon. My condolences, but it appears as though your friend was a victim of an armed robbery gone wrong."

"Of course he doesn't have cash on him. No one carries cash." Chris threw up his hands, exasperated. Dellaporta's partner took another step, his hands on the cuffs attached to his belt.

"Chris." Tracy yanked him away from the officers with surprising strength. Before Chris opened his mouth, she whispered to him. "You don't want to get on their bad side. You're not in a position to be telling the police what they should be doing."

"Randy's dead," Chris said. "And it's my fault."

"Stop saying that. For one, it wasn't your fault. And second, you don't want them"—Tracy gestured to the officers—"to think you had anything to do with it. Especially spouting off things about genetic enhancements."

A cold rage swelled in him, but he knew that she was right. That logic did not assuage his anger. He sighed. "Fine, fine. You're right. But I'm telling you, something about this isn't right. They said I was the one. I was the guy."

Tracy cocked her head. "What are you talking about?"

He looked away. He thought back to their earlier conversation regarding honesty. In the red and blue haze of emergency lights, surrounded by a growing presence of officers and crime scene investigation teams, Chris sighed again and closed his eyes. "You're right. We should get out of here."

CHAPTER THIRTEEN

G UILT SNAKED THROUGH CHRIS'S MIND and tightened around his heart. Each day he showed up to work and Randy's office remained empty, he envisioned the businessman telling the two men to kill Randy. Eliminate anyone who knew of the mysterious benefactor's connection with Chris.

Randy had known about Chris's stint in prison and why he had spent eight months there. But he had never asked Randy about his associations with the mysterious businessman. The man's ties to his mysterious benefactor must have been more complex than he had realized.

As far as he knew, Randy might have been the only person at Respondent who knew anything about the real reason why Chris got a job at the company. Maybe if he had refused the businessman's offer, Randy would still be alive to tell jokes and buy drinks for the team.

He tried to come up with a reason why anyone would want to kill Randy and then leave Chris alive. As he lay in bed wondering these things, he stared at the ceiling and listened to heated air rush through the vents.

"You awake?" Tracy asked.

He nodded.

When he'd signed on at Respondent, had he also signed off on Randy's death warrant? First the prison stabbings, then Randy.

Death followed him now. He needed to find the businessman; he needed answers.

Tracy rubbed his back. "How's your neck?"

"Fine." He took a deep breath. "I'm not sure we should be together anymore."

Eyes wide, she sat up and pulled the sheets around her, her hair draped over her bare shoulders. "What the hell are you talking about?" Her mouth hung open. "I don't understand."

Chris straightened himself up against the headboard. "I just don't think it's safe."

A quick flash of relief seemed to loosen the confused grimace on Tracy's face. "It's not your fault. You need to stop blaming yourself."

He frowned but didn't protest.

"Look, I'll go make coffee. Let's get out and forget about this for today." She slipped out of bed. "And quit saying shit like that."

With one hand, he rubbed the scars on his side. "Sure."

In his closet, Chris grabbed a collared shirt that he knew would help hide the fading bruises around his neck. He rubbed the area, self-conscious about the discolored skin and the constant questions when people saw it. Without so much as a friendly greeting, he'd been asked, "What happened to your neck?" as if it had been everyone's business at work.

The smell of frying bacon lured him into the kitchen. Tracy toiled over the stovetop, and Chris kissed her on the cheek. "Thank you."

They avoided the topic of Randy's death and the second round of interviews with the police that Chris had scheduled for later that day. Instead, their conversation wound toward a comparative listing of pets that they had kept as children. Tracy's list consisted of one golden retriever.

His contained a leopard gecko, turtles, salamanders, garter snake, baby ducks rescued after their mother had been killed by a feral cat, dwarf hamsters, rats, and two dogs. "Not all at once, of course."

She laughed. "Of course, that would just be ridiculous."

"Oh, and I can't forget about the fish. Couple of different tanks throughout the years."

"It's a wonder you didn't become a veterinarian."

"I thought about it."

Chris took another bite of his scrambled eggs. The flavors of the cheese Tracy had sprinkled into the eggs sparked childhood memories of weekend breakfasts. Almost consistently, it would be a plate of scrambled eggs and cinnamon rolls. His mind's eye gazed toward the old house his family had lived in, nestled on a two-acre corner lot purchased from a farmer who'd no longer wanted all that land. He glanced out the window to the street, where cars nudged against each other, bumper to bumper.

"Why don't you have any pets now?" Tracy asked.

"If I'm being honest, I just figured I didn't have time for any."

"No time for even a fish?"

"I just don't want something that depends on me. Don't want the responsibilities."

"What about now? You're back on your feet, fresh start. Why not just get a ten-gallon? Just start off with a couple of mollies or something. You know, a cute little breeding pair of spotted mollies. Make a lot of molly babies."

Chris smiled. "You know a bit more about fish than I thought. Didn't you say you only had the dog?"

"I tend to forget about the fish. They're pretty, but they don't cuddle with you like a dog, you know?"

Reaching across the table, Chris lifted her hand in his. He caressed the top of hers with his thumb. "Why don't we go visit the aquarium today?"

"Sam's Pets on Fourth?"

He chuckled. "No, no. The National Aquarium at the Inner Harbor."

"Sounds perfect." Tracy smiled.

When they left their cab at the Inner Harbor, the Baltimore National Aquarium stood out against the blue-gray waters beyond it. The building appeared like the three white sails of a ship. Its unique architecture fit in with the rest of the skyline along the harbor, sucking in tourists and locals alike.

Hand in hand, Chris and Tracy looked into the tanks to identify each of the inhabitants based on the interactive holodisplays outside the reconstructed habitats. They marveled like children at the luminescence of a moon jellyfish as its strange body contracted and expanded. Peering into a ten-gallon, they remarked on the vibrant colors of the peacock shrimp with its strange, globular eyes.

Following a curling walkway, they took a glass tunnel through a display of blacktip reef sharks and whiptail rays. The sharks circled the reef, gliding through the water, their mouths in a permanent frown. Their tails curled back and forth as they passed under green sea turtles and glowing tangs.

Besides the animals, they were alone.

Chris's thoughts crept back to the night before as shadows of sharks and fish danced around them. A blue glow bathed the tunnel and undulated with the movement of the water's surface.

"If you want to stick around, I think there's something else I should tell you," Chris said.

Tracy looked up and down the tunnel. "Right now? Right here?"

"I feel safer here than I do in my own apartment. There's no one around—or nothing around—that would overhear us. Maybe that comes across as a bit paranoid."

"Maybe." She gripped Chris's hand tighter. "But it makes sense given all the shit that happened last week."

"It's not just that. There's more to it."

As the sharks and rays glided above them, he recounted everything from the attacks in prison to his meeting with his mysterious benefactor. He told her about the job offer and about the ominous favor that the man had asked in return. Tracy listened, nodding but showing no emotion.

"So you think that Randy's murder has something to do with this associate of yours?"

"He's not my associate. I don't have any relationship with the man except for this job."

"And whatever favor he wants from you."

Chris peered back into the tank. "I think I know what that favor might be. The men who attacked Randy asked about a specimen. I'm certain it has something to do with the delivery vectors or the genetic therapies we make." He turned to her.

"I meant it when I said they were probably involved in black-market enhancements."

"But how do you know that any of this connects to that businessman?"

"When the one attacker tried to kill me, the other told him to stop. Said that I was the guy. How else would they have known who I was, unless they heard something from that businessman?" He breathed out and watched a stingray glide through the water. "Why else would they care?"

For a moment, they both stared through the glass walls. Chris imagined all the sounds of fish eating, shrimp clicking and cleaning, bubbles rising to the surface and popping, air and water filters working tirelessly contained behind that clear barrier. The tunnel, in stark contrast, only carried the sound of air whispering through.

"Why don't you just tell the police about all of this?" Tracy asked.

"If I do that, I can see two possibilities: One, I go back to prison and I get attacked again. Or two, the businessman puts out a hit on me or whatever. I die then, too." He clenched his fists.

"So what are you going to do?"

"I've got to find out who the hell that guy is and what he wants. And if I can, I'll get out of all this before anyone else gets killed."

CHAPTER FOURTEEN

ETECTIVE JACKSON SAT ACROSS THE table from Chris with a look of permanent skepticism in his furrowed brow. "Are you sure you didn't recognize the two men that attacked Randall Nee?"

"No, I'd never seen them before that night," Chris said. Agitated, he folded his arms across his chest.

Next to Jackson, Officer Dellaporta sat with an equally skeptical expression. However, she didn't speak with the same accusatory tone that saturated Jackson's questions. "You understand why we're asking you, right? It's natural to assume, based on your history and your statements last Thursday night, that you were familiar with these men."

"I'd never seen them before in my life," Chris said.

Jackson nodded but appeared unconvinced. "Have you heard about them from when you peddled your crap? Maybe a description? A name?"

Frustrated, Chris turned away. The apparent witness interview felt more and more like the interrogation of a person of interest. His parole officer would be following this investigation, too. The thought of any of the officers misinterpreting his statements or his role in Randy's murder sent a shudder down his spine.

"You seem nervous," Dellaporta said. "Is there anything you aren't telling us? If we find out you're hiding something, you'll end up back in Fulton."

"No. I've told you everything I know. I walked outside, the men seemed to be threatening Randy for something. I couldn't hear what they wanted. I got choked, they stopped and ran away. Then you both showed up. That's all there is to it."

Jackson stood up and leaned against the wall of the small room. Beside him was a one-way mirror, which signaled they might have more interest in him than a simple bystander witness to a brutal crime.

Chris straightened. "Can I ask you a question?"

Dellaporta gave a slight nod.

"Is this the first time you've heard about guys like this randomly attacking people? It seems to me that two men their size—you saw them yourselves—would be fairly prominent. I mean, if there's a string of violent muggings like this, I couldn't have been the only one to see those two thugs."

Jackson walked toward the table again. "Truth is, besides intergang crime, most armed robberies and muggings don't end up with someone dead. Most of those crimes involve either a desperate junky or a gang of jacked-up kids looking to beat the shit out of someone."

Frowning, Dellaporta shot Jackson a piercing look and turned back to Chris. "So, what we're saying is that two large, well-dressed men committing armed robbery is pretty damned unusual. Plus, you come babbling to us about illegal genetic enhancements. We search into your background and see the shit you pulled…things seem fishy, Mr. Morgan."

There seemed to be nothing he could say to convince the officers that he wasn't hiding anything. Well, he hid something, but he'd be damned if he told them. If he told them why he thought those thugs had murdered Randy, if he told them about people breaking into his apartment or Lash saving him from a shanking, he would end up either back in prison or, more likely, lying in an empty alley like Randy. "Officers, am I free to go now? I would like to be presentable at my friend's funeral."

Jackson acquiesced and waved for Chris to leave.

As he walked through the door, Dellaporta stopped him, her hand on his shoulder. "Please, Mr. Morgan. We just want you to help us understand what happened. We were ready to write the whole thing off as a poorly executed armed robbery, but you seemed to insinuate something else. If you can help us catch these men, we might be onto something bigger. You can prevent someone else from ending up like your buddy. We'd like to talk to you again."

"Should I bring a lawyer next time?"

Dellaporta shrugged. "Your call."

Scowling, Chris turned and strode out the door.

The late Friday afternoon turned gray over Western Cemetery. Tombstones, many pitted and marred, others shining slabs of granite, rose up from the grass. A nearby stream splashed, overflowing with that morning's rain. Accompanying its gurgling, a couple of ducks called out to each other, their calls piercing the priest's words as the coffin was lowered into the ground.

Tracy pulled Chris close to her. Her eyes were wet, though no tears rolled down her cheek.

The priest spoke a final blessing. The portly man's black cassock billowed in the chilling wind as he made the sign of the cross.

"I can't believe he's gone," Kristina said. Paul hugged her close against his body.

Chris watched the priest walk away from the fresh grave. Guilt surged through him as he replayed Randy's death again. He had felt helpless, useless, as he had watched the thugs threaten and kill his boss.

You might be able to detect and treat cancer or prevent the slow decay of multiple sclerosis. You could buy nanotreatments that would destroy clots and plaques in your arteries, preventing a heart attack or stroke.

But you couldn't buy a medicine to prevent murder.

Tracy grasped Kristina's arm in a reassuring gesture. "Neither can I. But you know he would want us to go have a drink on his behalf."

Paul half smiled. "Yeah, yeah. 'Work hard, play hard.' What do you say, Chris?"

Chris had known these people for a couple of months. They knew practically nothing about him. How could he contribute anything in a conversation about a man he'd let die? "Sounds about right."

As the four departed from the crowd, back toward Paul's car, Chris scanned the other attendees. He could not help but wonder who the woman with the red hair was or how the gangly, tall man knew Randy. Family, friends? He took a glance at another man with sunglasses. The shades stood out on such a dreary day, but several others at the funeral wore sunglasses, ostensibly to mask their crying eyes.

This man, though, obscured his identity. It had been months since Chris had seen him, but he knew the yellow-gray eyes hiding behind those opaque aviators.

He tugged on Tracy's coat sleeve and leaned into her ear. "That's him. With the shades."

She cocked her head. "Who?"

"The man that got me the job. The man that made me make that promise."

Tracy's eyes widened as she stared at the businessman in his trim black overcoat.

The doors to Paul's car unlocked with an audible click as they neared it. Chris held up a hand. "I'm sorry, you guys. I need to go talk to someone real quick." He set off toward the businessman.

The man's Lincoln turned on as he grabbed its door handle. "Wait! Wait!"

Several people, walking to their own cars with somber expressions, eyed Chris suspiciously. He ignored them and broke out into a sprint.

As the man ducked into his car, Chris yanked his shoulder. "What the hell are you doing here?"

Chris thought he could see the man's eyes light up in red anger even behind the opaque sunglasses.

"You have the nerve to ask me? I have known that man far longer than you. The least I could offer is my presence at his funeral."

The man stabbed his finger into Chris's chest. Chris could not confirm it, but he felt the man's eyes exploring his neck. Self-conscious, he tried to obscure the bruises with a hand. "It's your fault that he's dead, isn't it?"

"No, Mr. Morgan. It most certainly isn't." He shook his head. "It most certainly isn't."

Chris stared at the reflection of himself in the man's sunglasses. "I want out of this. I'm not going to do what you want. I don't want anyone else killed."

The man left the car door open but stood up straighter. "You'll do as you've promised or I promise that you'll regret it."

"Fine, send me back to prison. It looks like I'm headed back anyway because of this." Chris motioned toward the tent poled up over Randy's grave, where two men filled the hole with dirt.

Gazing across the graveyard toward where Chris had come from, the man spoke in a calm voice again. "This is no longer just your life at stake, Mr. Morgan. I would regret having to involve someone else. You'll do as I ask or others will be punished on your behalf. Besides, it's already begun, whether you know it or not. You can either get on the train or you can lie down on the tracks." The man pushed Chris back.

Catching himself against a tree, Chris stood back up. "What's started?"

The man stepped into his car and closed the door. Chris slapped the opaque windows of the Lincoln. "What's started?"

The car drove away, gravel spitting up from the tires.

He held up an arm to shield his face. He'd had his chance and ruined it, let the man go. No answers, but more fresh threats.

CHAPTER FIFTEEN

HAVING SHARED A ROUND OF beers with Paul and Kristina, Tracy announced she felt under the weather and no longer in the mood to celebrate Randy's life. Chris and Tracy took a cab back to Chris's condo, where he stretched out on his couch and situated himself up against the plush armrest. He threw his suit jacket onto the coffee table and loosened his tie.

Tracy, still in her black dress, sat at the opposite end of the couch. "Can you tell me what happened now?"

"He wouldn't tell me anything. Just said that it already started."

"What the hell does that mean?"

"I wish I knew."

"Are you sure you don't know this guy from before prison?"

Chris's forehead wrinkled, his face growing hot. "I have no idea who this guy is. You sound like the police interrogating me." Looking away, he willed the heat from his face to dissipate. "I'm sorry. I'm a little on edge."

"I can damn well tell that." Her voice was sharp. "I want you to tell me everything about the police and about what the hell happened after the funeral. I need to know what's going on here. Especially if I'm going to help you."

He inched closer to Tracy and put his hand on hers. "I don't want to get anyone else killed. If you want out, please, I wouldn't blame you."

She withdrew her hand, but her expression softened. "Stop being an asshole. It wasn't your fault and I don't want out."

Chris couldn't help but smile.

Tracy hit him on the shoulder. "Quit it. You're creeping me out." But she allowed him to envelop her in a hug.

"Thanks."

Tracy guessed that if something was going on and Randy had been involved, they might find something out at the lab. Instead of waiting for Monday, they called a cab to head straight to Respondent when the building would be virtually empty.

Chris ducked into the back of the taxi and Tracy followed. Just to be safe, he entered the Cowboys and Poets street address into the cab's destination display. He didn't want an unwarranted late-evening visit to Respondent tied to either of their comm cards. If he could, he preferred to avoid providing any evidence with which Baltimore PD could start to build a case against him in Randy's death.

The gloomy clouds above them broke during the ride. A little trickle of rain erupted into a downpour. The pattering of the rain on the roof and windows of the cab echoed inside the small cabin. After a couple minutes, the cab stopped in front of the bar and prompted them for a payment.

"Do you mind?" Chris asked. "I just don't want any of this tied to me while I'm on parole."

"I get it." Tracy grinned. "I'm your sugar mama."

Chris shook his head but didn't bother to protest. "Ready to get a little wet?" He opened the door into a sheet of rain. Holding Tracy's hand as he went, they darted down the street toward Respondent. They passed a storefronts and restaurants, lit up from the inside and full of patrons, but hardly anyone got in their way on the sidewalk. They splashed through puddles as a stream of brown water rushed along the gutters beside them.

Ahead of them stood the five-story building that housed Respondent. Its iron-trimmed, crested roof directed and concentrated the rain to flow like a waterfall over the sculpted white columns interspersed between wide black windows. As they approached, the main-floor doors parted for them. Puddles of water formed on the marble floor at their feet.

While the exterior of the office appeared elegant and ornate, the interior had been renovated with a more modern, minimalist undercurrent of exposed beams and decorations bathed in stark blacks and whites. A simple, flat desk erupted from the middle of the empty lobby. The weekend security guard must have been out on patrol or slacking. Either way, they did not bother checking in.

They shed their soaked coats in the elevator up to Respondent's research laboratories and offices, which occupied the entire fifth floor of the building, leaving them in the coat closet near the elevator entrance by an empty receptionist desk.

The halls were dimly lit to conserve energy outside of work hours. The plants that lined the walls cast shadows reminiscent of long, grasping fingers on the white-tiled floor.

"What do we do now?" Chris asked Tracy.

Tracy directed them to the labs. "Put on some gloves."

He raised an eyebrow as he put on the gloves. "You got an experiment in mind?"

"We're not doing anything in here. I just don't want an ex-con dropping fingerprints over his murdered boss's office, you got me?"

"Gotcha," he said. "It seems like you're the one that knows how to commit a crime. Why was I the one in prison?"

She scoffed. "Because I'm also the one that knows how to get away with committing a goddamn crime."

He laughed as they exited the lab and passed by the cubicles where their desks sat. Tracy yanked on the doorknob to Randy's office. "It's locked." She knelt down eye level with the lock and tied her hair back. "Good thing we're cheap around here." Using a paperclip she had grabbed from her desk, she fiddled with the lock as she slid her comm card into the space between the door and the doorjamb. With a gratifying click, the door opened.

Everything appeared just as it had the Thursday they had all left for happy hour together. Randy's faded print of Georgia O'Keefe's *Manhattan* hung on the wall. The bottom right border of the print was labeled with the Smithsonian National Art Museum logo. Besides the one odd print, the walls of the office were bare. On Randy's desk, a large node for a holodisplay rested quietly like an oversized black beetle. A single folder on the corner of his desk contained a few papers.

Tracy placed her hands on her hips and scanned the desk and bookcases along the edges of the room. "So, what do you think we're looking for?"

Chris shrugged. "Hell if I know. Anything out of the ordinary is great."

She pointed to *Manhattan*. "That's pretty out of the ordinary."

"You know what I mean." He rolled his eyes.

"Seriously, Randy was an odd dude. You must have picked up on that since you got here. I mean, the guy worked at a technology company but had a thing against technology."

Chris stopped flipping through papers in a folder and cocked his head. "What do you mean?"

As Tracy started scanning the bookshelves, she held up her hand and counted on her fingers. "For one, he never went to the automated coffee shops. Needed to speak to a real barista. Two, he hated holodisplay art." She glanced back at the O'Keefe print. "Case in point. Three, he always printed off results instead of just storing them on our servers." She patted the bookshelves. "That's what all this shit is. He even handwrote in a lab notebook instead of using our computer notebooks. Kind of tedious, if you ask me."

"I didn't know he did that." He slumped into Randy's chair.

Tracy stopped searching through the bookshelves and put a hand on the cold glass window. It extended from floor to ceiling. Rain still poured down, splattering and streaming down the glass pane. "Isn't that one of the cars from the funeral?"

Spinning around in the seat, Chris peered out the window. "The black one?"

"Well, yeah. The Corvette," she said. " I wonder what they're doing here."

"There were a lot of black cars at the funeral. Besides, I didn't see a Corvette."

"Maybe you didn't, but I did. Remember what I told you? My dad obsessed over them. I can name the year, special edition, give you specs on total motor wattage or even horsepower on the old fuel-injection models. You name it."

"Even if it is the same car you saw, and the exact same people in the car, it was Randy's funeral. It makes sense, right?

It's not like we were the only people from Respondent there today."

"Yeah, that makes sense," Tracy said.

"Wait a second."

"You recognize the car now?"

"No," Chris said. "What did you say before about Randy's lab notebook?"

"The paper one?"

Chris nodded. "Yes, yes. Do you know where he kept it?"

She shook her head. "No. He always took it out of the lab—which I think is against standard research policy, right?" Her face lit up in comprehension. "Wait a second, do you think...?"

"Yes." He stood up. "My bet is that if Randy was involved in something, working on something illegal, something he didn't want on the company servers, it'd be in a notebook like that."

"That's so stupid of him," Tracy said. She stared at the O'Keefe print dubiously. "But that might be right."

With renewed fervor, they scoured the bookshelves, looking for notebooks that seemed out of place. They skimmed through research reports and printouts of experiment results. Unfamiliar with the lab's work before he'd started his job, Chris became frustrated with having to ask Tracy over and over if each project was a legitimate effort that had been pursued in the lab or if that might be the one project that Randy had been involved in under the table.

"Why don't you just let me deal with the shelves?" Tracy said.

Chris agreed and flopped back onto Randy's chair. He turned on the holodisplay to see if there might be anything on the computer, but a security prompt asked for Randy's fingerprint. He slammed his fists on the desk. The holodisplay module jumped and the image distorted.

Tracy frowned at him. "Keep it together."

Sighing, Chris searched the desk a second time. He took out the pens, random Respondent marketing materials, and loose-leaf paper. Reaching for a stack of notecards in the back of the deep bottom drawer, he shifted his weight. The chair rolled out from under him. "Shit, shit." He fell forward, his hand punching through the flimsy wooden bottom of the drawer. Through the fracture, he saw a worn red leather cover. "I think I found something."

Tracy stopped her searching and knelt down beside him, peering into the drawer. "Shit. Yeah, you did." She peeled back the broken wood and pulled out a nondescript laboratory notebook.

As Chris gloated over his clumsy find, the elevator down the hall dinged. The grinding of the opening doors carried into the hallway, filling the empty corridors and piercing the drone of rain falling against the roof of the building. Footsteps clacked against the tiled floor and echoed against the walls.

"Shit," Tracy said.

Chris sat frozen in the seat, listening to the footsteps. Muddled voices carried down the corridor, sounding confused, angry.

"I think we need to get out of here," Tracy said. "Grab the notebook and let's go."

Nodding, he crept up from the desk. The voices continued as they fled the office. He pointed at a glaring red exit sign. "We should take the stairs."

He risked a glance down the corridor, but whoever had ridden the elevator up remained beyond his line of vision. The voices had quieted, and the footsteps retreated down a hallway toward the Regulatory division of the research labs.

"Doesn't sound like they're headed our way," he said.

Tracy didn't appear convinced. "Maybe they don't know which way they're supposed to be heading."

The sound of rain on the roof intensified as they tiptoed toward the exit stairwell closest to their lab.

"We don't have our coats." He stopped and grabbed Tracy's hand.

She shook her head. "We're going to have to deal with it."

"Fair enough." He eyed the notebook in Tracy's hands. The voices had gone silent. No footsteps could be heard. These unknown visitors must have been lost in Regulatory. "We should look at the notebook before we leave."

Tracy shot him a skeptical look. "Seriously? We don't have time for that."

"For one, we don't even know if whoever is here is even after us. We could just be paranoid. Might just be someone on FDA duty getting called in on the weekend."

"Sounded like at least a couple angry people to me." Tracy raised an eyebrow.

Chris shrugged. He tried to maintain a look of nonchalance despite the doubt welling up in his mind. "Who knows? In any case, what if whatever Randy wrote about in the notebook is still in the lab?"

"You mean like samples or something? Those specimens the killers mentioned, huh?" Tracy's harsh demeanor melted into something between curiosity and disbelief. "God, yeah, you're right." She flipped open the notebook, scanning it with her forefinger. She read, mouthing the words to herself.

Chris look over her shoulder, nudging them behind a partition in the cubicles that would shield them from any vantage point from the hallways. He peered at the open pages of the notebook. "Holy shit."

Tracy stopped and turned to him. "What's up?"

"This is mine."

"What the hell are you talking about? This notebook is yours?"

"No, the vector." He underlined the description of the DNA-based materials with his finger. "This...this is from when I dealt enhancements."

"What do you mean when you were dealing? Didn't you use these materials for the colon project?"

"I did, yes. But this is different. This—I struggled to remember this. They confiscated all my enhancement documents. I thought the police had locked it all away in evidence somewhere."

"Whatever this is, these materials appear to be a pretty damned good delivery system, if Randy's results in here are real."

For a moment, Chris swelled with pride. He smiled at Tracy. "Hell, yes. They're great."

"That's fantastic, but it would be better if we could find actual samples."

Tracy flipped through the pages, scanning the words. Watching her progression through the notebook, Chris stood beside her, his eyes darting between the notebook and the hallway. If they could just find a canister number and location for something that might be suspended in liquid nitrogen, or a drawer number for the walk-in four-degree cooler, they might find something worth pursuing. Something that would give them a clue as to what the businessman wanted from Respondent. Something to use as a bargaining chip.

"This is odd," Tracy said.

"What is it?"

Tracy pointed to a series of letters and numbers in a nonsensical list. "This appears to be the same numbering system we used to use on the old negative-eighty-degree freezer."

"Okay. So when you say 'old,' does that mean it's not around anymore?"

She shook her head. Chris could see the disappointment in her eyes. "I'm afraid not. When we moved all the samples and reagents to the new freezer that's in the lab now, we changed to a different labeling system."

"Shit."

"Yeah, shit."

For a moment, neither said a word. Chris listened for the sound of footsteps or voices down the hall. No sounds greeted his ears.

"These numbers seem familiar to me." She squinted and traced her upper lip with her tongue, her brow creased in lines of thought. "They're definitely mine."

Chris cocked his head and joined her again, peering into the lab notebook. "Are you sure?"

"I kind of have a thing for threes."

"What do you mean?"

Tracy shrugged, a reddish hue coloring her cheeks. "Can't explain it. But I always kept my samples in 'three,' 'six,' or 'nine' canisters in the shelves of the old freezer."

"Great," he said. "But you're going to have to tell me why that's interesting."

"Because I stored my experiments in these locations. Extra viral vectors, results from synthesis." She scanned the list with her finger. "Not all of them, but a few of them."

"What are all the experiments from?"

"There's an old hemophilia one, CFTR gene delivery for cystic fibrosis, bladder cancer—all projects that ended a few years ago."

"Those canisters that aren't yours—do you recognize them?"

Tracy shook her head. "I bet they're all Paul's. He was the only other one in research around the time we worked on those projects."

"Strange," Chris said, looking down at the book. "The date on that page is from just a couple months ago."

With a grin, Tracy picked the notebook up. "You know what he was doing, don't you?" Before Chris could answer, she continued. "He was storing these samples—whatever they are—in all the old lab projects."

"Why would he do that?"

"Come on, you have to be smarter than that." She opened the lab door and motioned for him to follow. "We never use those old samples, but we're supposed to save them in case we get an FDA audit or something."

"And if we did get an audit, Randy would be the first to hear about it."

"Exactly."

Tracy booted up a database on the holodisplay to match the old projects with their new destinations in the freezer. As she searched for each project and wrote the locations on a sheet of paper she'd ripped from Randy's notebook, Chris stuck a chair in the door of the lab to keep it open. He didn't want anyone to sneak up on them unheard.

"Okay, why don't you start looking for the samples?" Tracy handed Chris the sheet of paper. "I'm going to finish locating everything in here, but at least you can put them together."

"Sure thing," he said. "I'm thinking I should put them in a freezer box for now."

"You might be right. We might want to get them out of here, huh?"

"Just in case our friends down in Regulatory are searching for the same thing we're looking for."

"So now you don't think they're on FDA duty now, huh?"

"Gotta be a little paranoid, don't I?"

Tracy smirked and went back to scrolling through the locations. "It's a pretty big division down there, but if they're looking for Randy's stash, they won't be too much longer. If we're real lucky, they'll head over to Production first."

Nodding, he picked up a small white plastic box a cubic foot in volume. He checked the battery charge and turned it on. He opened the large gray door to the negative-eighty-degree freezer. An inner wall of stainless steel drawers welcomed him. Each led to separate compartments within the shelves. He shivered at the cold escaping the freezer and located the first compartment on the list. A box lay inside, labeled "CFTR" with a date from almost three years ago. He opened the box and searched through a variety of tiny plastic vials in a rack. Each vial contained just a milliliter of frozen liquid. Suspended in each droplet were aliquots of genetic material packed into delivery vectors.

Chris brushed away the frost that had built up on each vial to unveil the labels. He squinted to ensure Tracy's handwriting decorated each label and that it matched the project each sample should have been associated with. Sure enough, the final sample in the small box was unlabeled. He held it up, eyeing it in the dim blue light that emanated from Tracy's holodisplay.

Without proper analysis of the contents, he couldn't be sure of what it contained. He placed the vial in a small metal rack within the freezer box.

The next set of vials revealed another unlabeled sample, as did the third and fourth locations on the list. Four found projects later, Chris had gathered another four unlabeled samples. Their suspicions must have been correct.

"All right, I think I have the rest. How are you doing?" Tracy walked over and peeked into the freezer box. "Fingers frozen yet?"

"A little numb," he said, "but I'm about halfway through the first list."

"Awesome. I can get started on the second list, and we'll have this done in no time."

As she opened another drawer, a shrieking alarm went off.

CHAPTER SIXTEEN

"WHAT THE HELL IS THAT?" Tracy reeled back. "Oh, dammit. It's the freezer. We left it open too long. Dammit, dammit."

Chris slammed it shut. The alarm fell silent. As the adrenaline in him surged, his heart thumped against his ribs.

"We need to get out of here," he said.

"No shit."

The lock clicked as he shut the lab door. He grabbed the freezer box with the samples they had retrieved, and Tracy picked up the lab notebook that she had left open near the lab's holodisplay. They raced toward the other end of the lab, where another exit door led to the closest stairwell and elevators. Chris pushed through the door, and they emptied out into the dark hallway.

Tracy stopped and tugged on his arm. "I forgot the lists with all the other samples."

"Too late." He grabbed her hand and sprinted down the hall, leading her away from the lab. The elevators would be unreliable and would alert whoever else was there to their location, so he opened the door to the stairwell. As Tracy ran past him with the notebook tucked under her arm, he saw a light spill from the lab's exit door window down the hall. "We've got to get the hell out of here."

Their footsteps rang against the stairwell's walls as they ran. His motions felt restricted in his funeral suit. He wished he had left it at home and exchanged it for a pair of jeans and a T-shirt. As Tracy bounded down the stairs, he marveled at her pace in her black heels. At least he didn't have to deal with those.

Instead of going into the lobby, they took the back exit from the stairwell that led onto West Fayette Street. Torrents of rain greeted them as they ran along the sidewalk. Chris's thoughts turned toward the coats they had left in the closet. He made a mental note to retrieve the coat on Monday but couldn't help wondering if returning to work would even be a viable option.

While parked cars lined the one-way street, few vehicles hummed along the road. A block away from Respondent, the office buildings gave way to neighborhoods of restored and renovated townhouses. Shops and bars interspersed the townhouses, reminiscent of an early 1900s neighborhood.

They jogged in the freezing rain. Chris's shirt clung to his skin, growing transparent as water soaked through. Water beaded up on Tracy's bare arms, along with a rash of goose bumps. Still, she led the pair onward as Chris lagged. A stitch formed in his side as he fought to keep up with her and a metallic taste manifested on his tongue. He struggled to breathe.

"We should duck in somewhere," Tracy said. She pointed at a bar. Above its entrance hung a wooden fox face painted blue with crimson letters bearing a fitting name, the Frozen Fox.

When they entered the bar, a blast of warm air rushed past them. Chris shivered. The hairs on his arms stood up amid goose bumps. Tracy's teeth chattered as a couple of grizzled men in their late thirties eyed them suspiciously.

They chose a wooden booth near the back. The smell of deep-fried food permeated the bar from the kitchen door near them. Chris placed the freezer box with the samples next to him. Tracy ordered a coffee spiked with Bailey's to warm up, while he chose the Beaver Dam Blue. Dark silhouettes moved beyond the clouded glass of the front windows. He wondered if the black Corvette Tracy had seen cast any of those amorphous shadows. Even if it did pass, there was no guarantee that the car contained their pursuers. In fact, maybe their so-called pursuers were only a couple of security guards on their weekend rounds.

Chris sighed. "Do you think we're crazy? Are we overreacting?"

"I'm not sure, but I'm not about to take any chances."

Chris placed his hand on the notebook that lay in between them on the sticky table. "Maybe we should take another look." His other hand had not left the small, white box that sat in the seat next to him.

"Let's at least wait until we get out of here," Tracy said. "You know, just in case."

"All right. Take off after we finish these up?" He motioned to their drinks.

"So soon? Can we at least dry off a bit first? Then I'll call a cab."

Raising his shoulders, he offered a weak smile. "Fine. I guess we could use a drink or two."

"Don't act like it's such a terrible thing to be having a drink with me."

"It's not so bad, I guess." Chris rolled his eyes playfully and leaned across the table. "I'm not going to lie, though. I'm dying to find out what else is in Randy's secret little book."

"Can't forget about our little frozen friends, too." Her eyes shot to the box at his side. "I have a feeling those fellows are hiding something even more interesting."

By the time they made it back to Tracy's apartment on West Lexington, the rain clouds had departed. A few bright stars punctuated the otherwise murky sky. Chris gazed up at the moon.

In prison, he never saw much of the open sky, day or night. Before that, the streetlights and the glow from the thriving mass of buildings that choked downtown Baltimore obscured all but the most brilliant burning balls of gas. Staring out the window of the fifteenth-story apartment, he recalled camping out on the beach with Veronica, just hours away from Baltimore, and observing the starry sky over Assateague National Seashore. Even in Illinois, he had lived far enough outside the city, between fields of corn and soybean, to lie in the grass next to his brother and sister while their father pointed out the constellations. He missed the stars.

Tracy wrapped her arms around him and kissed his neck. Her lips crept up his jaw to his lips, and she pulled back with a grin. "Call me crazy, but I love the smell of good beer on your breath."

Chris chuckled and swung her around in front of him. The cutting aroma of coffee still hung on her breath. Without taking their lips or arms off each other, they made their way to Tracy's bedroom.

Her breath, heavy and warm, tickled Chris's ears. His mind raced to the portable freezer box that sat on the granite bar in her kitchen, but that ephemeral thought evaporated just as quickly as it had arisen. She slipped off her dress, then tore off Chris's shirt as she dragged him onto the bed. He threw himself into her and lost himself in her, like the stars lost their glimmer in the lights of Baltimore City.

Darkness still pervaded Tracy's apartment, broken by the light glowing above her kitchen table. She scoured Randy's notebook and made her own notes on a yellow-papered legal pad. "It looks like there are even more samples we missed." She pointed to another list in the notebook. Her eyes seemed alight with energy, wide and gleaming.

Chris held his head in his hand. His eyelids drooped and felt heavy as he listened. He sipped his third cup of coffee, waiting for the caffeine to do something, anything to alleviate the fatigue that clouded his mind.

"Man, I'm glad you found this today. This answers a lot of questions."

Making a huffing noise in reply, he cocked his eye to get a better view of her notes. The scribbles appeared illegible to him, but the multiple exclamation points and question marks jumped from the page.

He should be the one tracking down the businessman. But that late at night, he could not match her unbridled enthusiasm.

Tracy stopped writing. She held her breath, and the old analog clock above her kitchen table clicked off the seconds of her silence. "There's a list of names." She laughed. "Holy shit, there's a list of names." Her giddy smile vanished. "Holy shit." She looked up at him with eyes wide. "Your name is on this list."

"What the hell?" Shaking his head, he rubbed his eyes. "There's no way those names mean anything. Randy couldn't be that dumb."

"I don't know. He did a pretty shitty job of securing the samples and this." She shook the notebook at him. "Look, there's a question mark next to a couple of these." She slid the notebook across the table, swiveling it around for him to see.

With a gulp, Chris widened his eyes as he grabbed the notebook, pulling it closer. As he scanned the list, two names drew his immediate interest. His heart sank and his palms grew clammy. He opened his mouth to say something but lost the words before they reached his tongue.

Tracy leaned across the table. "What is it? Do you know somebody else on this list?"

Chris's headed bobbed. "Yes. I think so. A name or two."

"Who?" Her voice rang sharp, edgy.

He pointed to one of the first names. "Jordan Thompson. He was a friend. Kind of helped me with distribution."

A sour look spread over Tracy's face. "So, he's a dealer?"

"A little bit higher up than that, I'd say." Chris pushed aside his coffee. He no longer needed the caffeine boost.

"You haven't talked to this guy since—"

"I haven't heard from Jordan since well before I went to prison."

For a moment, Tracy's eyes seemed glazed over in thought. Chris waited with his own thoughts as company. Dread built up in him like a boiler set to explode. He didn't want to end up back in prison and he didn't want to end up murdered. With no idea of who wanted him dead and hardly a clue what the businessman wanted from him, his thoughts roiled in increasing confusion. And if Jordan was somehow involved or being targeted like him, he wondered where he could turn for escape. The pressure rose as he waited for her response, and he sank into his seat.

"You don't want to go to the police, right?" Tracy's look of disgust had been replaced with one of concern.

"I can't. You think the police would care for an outlandish conspiracy story from a crackpot, convicted illegal genie manufacturer? I have no credibility and no evidence. They already think I know something about Randy's murder. If they're to believe me at all, I need to figure out what the hell is in those samples and how they're linked to Randy's death. For all they know, we could've fabricated the whole lab notebook with a handwriting analysis app on our comm cards."

He massaged his temples. "And who would believe me about a mysterious, pale man who wears sunglasses all the time? I would need to tell the police I agreed to a verbal contract with the guy that meant I would oblige any request, legal or otherwise."

Tracy shook her head, and a brief glimmer of something like relief flashed in her eyes. She pointed at the list in Randy's notebook. "All right. If you're so sure about this, why don't we talk to your friend here and see what he knows?"

"Yeah, sure," he said. "That might not be such a bad idea. In fact, maybe we could bring the samples with us."

"Why?"

"Jordan has access to a nice lab."

"Do I even want to know?"

Chris smiled. "Better that you don't."

"I'm not sure if I trust this associate—"

"Former associate."

"Whatever," she said. "I'm not sure if I trust this Jordan with what may be the only hard evidence we have to figure out this whole damned mess."

"I understand, but we can't take these back to Respondent. I don't want to be caught there with whatever is in these things."

"I'm in agreement on that."

In the end, Chris proposed leaving the bulk of the samples in the portable freezer box at Tracy's apartment. They would take just a couple of the vials to Jordan for analysis.

Through the glass panel doors of the small balcony attached to her kitchen, a hint of rust orange broke over the horizon of the Chesapeake Bay. Chris's comm card displayed 7:08 a.m. in green, blocky numbers.

"It'll be another day, soon enough," she said.

"It's already another day."

"Do you want to talk to Jordan? See if we can meet up with him?"

"Not right now," Chris said. "Jordan was never known to seize the day at the break of dawn. Most of his business is at night. He's probably just gone to bed, and we aren't going to get any favors out of him by getting on his bad side."

A disappointed frown replaced Tracy's hopeful expression. "Fine. I guess we may as well take a quick nap before we bug your friend."

After maximizing the opacity of the electronic windows in the bedroom, Tracy slipped out of her robe and into the bed. Chris joined her under the covers, and she wrapped an arm around his chest. A smile spread across her face as she nestled into the space between his neck and shoulder.

While her skin pressed against his, his thoughts turned toward the second name that he had recognized on Randy's list. He had been thankful Tracy hadn't pressed him for further details on the names, distracted by the prospect of invoking Jordan Thompson's potential help in resolving matters.

But Chris could not shake his worry. Having no idea of what the list could mean, he feared for the lives of those whose names Randy had haphazardly written. It had been months, bordering on years, since he had seen her face, but everything came rushing back in a blizzard of unforgiving memories. The curve of her cheekbones and her toothy grin. Watching her dance as a guest artist when the Moscow Ballet had hosted their annual touring performance of *The Nutcracker* in Baltimore. The studio in her apartment full of paintings she claimed he had inspired, all in vibrant colors, shapes alive and practically throbbing on the canvases.

Now, thanks to him, her life might be in more danger than she could know. He would need to see Veronica, if she could bear him, and warn her, try to save her from the businessman and his associates.

CHAPTER SEVENTEEN

W HEN CHRIS AWOKE, HE REACHED over the side of the bed to his nightstand. His hand fumbled around in empty space for his comm card before he remembered that he was in Tracy's apartment. He reoriented himself to the bare-brick walls and the hardwood floors masked in shadows.

Disoriented by the darkness, he was filled with a sudden worry. What time was it? He sat up in the bed, blinking and rubbing his eyes. "Dammit." He jumped out of the bed and his feet landed on the floor. He cursed as he pulled on the crumpled pants that he had left at the foot of the bed.

Awakened by Chris's lumbering, Tracy yawned. Her voice sounded dreamy and distant. "What are you doing?"

"We slept through the whole day." Crawling on the floor now, Chris searched under the bed for his socks.

Tracy's eyes grew wide. "Son of a bitch. Did you call Jordan already?"

"No, no." He hopped around on one foot, slipping on a sock.

"Calm down. You said he was a night owl anyway."

"Yeah, but who knows what the hell he's up to."

Tracy slunk out of bed, stretching as she did. She picked up her comm card from atop the headboard. "It's six. I mean, it's a Saturday evening, but he can't be too far gone yet."

"Trust me, you don't know this guy."

Notes written in Tracy's slanted handwriting littered the surface of the kitchen table. Moving a couple of the papers aside, Chris found his comm card. He searched through his old contacts list to seek out Jordan Thompson but found no match. He had never bothered to save Jordan's contact information to the comm card. In fact, he'd never called his old friend from his actual card.

For business purposes, he had used tracker cards. The prepaid data that came with the cards also meant that he could pick one up from the local CVS, call his illicit business associates, and throw the card away without any permanent communication records attached to his name. The only agency with copies of his communications might be the NSA. And they were too busy allegedly seeking out cyberterrorists to rout out any trite synthetic gene enhancement dealer wannabes. It wouldn't be worth their time trying to ID him or the people he called on the tracker cards. He racked his brain, trying to remember the manual contact number for Jordan. It had been almost two years since he'd called his friend's so-called business line. Self-assured by his independent wealth and the illegal safeguards he could afford with it, Jordan could not be bothered by such inconveniences as constantly buying and throwing away tracker cards. Chris tapped in the first numbers that came to mind.

A gruff, low voice answered. "Who is this?"

Chris hung up. It wasn't Jordan. His second, third, and fourth attempts did not work either. When he cursed, Tracy poked her head out from the bedroom. "What's up? Can't get a hold of him?"

He shook his head. "Can't remember how to connect with him."

"Some friend, huh?" She vanished back into her bedroom.

"I think we're just going to need to drop by his place."

Tracy entered the conjoined living room and kitchen area of the apartment, slipping on a brown leather jacket. "You think that's a good idea?"

"It's the only option we have." Chris frowned. "Man, I wish I had a coat right now."

Tracy laughed again. "I'm afraid what I have to offer won't cut it." Her lips drew tight. "Do you think he'll be happy if we just drop by his place unannounced? Kingpin drug dealers, as you describe him, don't seem like the kind of folk that like surprise visitors."

"He's not a crazy drug lord. Stop saying that."

She held up her hands in a defensive gesture. "All right, all right. You need a cup of coffee, Mr. Attitude?"

"No, no." Chris buttoned up his shirt. It still smelled of an unappetizing mixture of rainwater and sweat from the day before. "I could go for a clean shirt, though." He straightened out the shirt sleeves and exhaled. "Jordan was a decent friend of mine from Northwestern. Ended up out here in Baltimore, too. So it's not like he's just a shady, underground overlord."

Moving over to the portable freezer box on her counter, he pulled out a couple of the samples that they had selected to bring to Jordan. "We aren't going to be able to transport these for long. Without any idea of what might be in them, we can't just throw them in our pockets, you know?"

Tracy shrugged. "What do you think we should do, then? I still don't think it's a good idea to take the whole thing. I'm not risking it, no matter how much you vouch for this guy."

"Fair enough." He grabbed a cup from her cupboard.

Filling it with ice from the icemaker on the refrigerator door, Chris turned back to Tracy. "Do you have any foil for the top of this?"

"Sure," Tracy said. "You know, I've got a cooler that we can take, too. It doesn't get as cold as this guy." She patted the negative-eighty-degree portable freezer. "But it'll help."

"Yeah, yeah. That'd be good."

While Tracy dug through her closet, Chris deposited the two plastic vials in the red plastic cup filled with ice.

"Here it is." Tracy deposited the cooler on the counter. "Found it under a couple lawn chairs in the storage closet. Don't know how long it's been since I've used any of that."

He smiled. "Maybe when this is all over, we can go on a picnic."

"A little cold for that, don't you think?"

Chris looked back out at the window. Instead of yesterday's freezing rain, a light snow floated down. Snowflakes glimmered as they caught rays of light beaming from streetlights.

"Are we going to get going, or you just going to daydream?" Tracy pinched Chris's arm playfully. "Come to think of it, what happens if Jordan isn't around?"

"There are a couple people we can try to track down, if we need to."

"That's fine and all, but what about the samples? You think that's wise to risk letting them thaw? I'm worried whatever's in them will denature if we don't get them to a decent freezer, and I'm not talking about your run-of-the-mill icebox."

"You're right. That wouldn't be great. I mean, we've got others, but I'd hate to lose these." A sudden realization coursed through him like a shock of electricity. "Shoot. I don't know why I didn't think of this earlier, but I've got a freezer in my apartment."

She shot him a skeptical look. "Yeah, that's pretty much standard with a refrigerator."

"No, no. I mean, I've got a minus eighty." He pointed to the portable freezer. "Just like this one."

"Why did you—" Tracy stopped, her glare replaced by a look of comprehension. "Oh. Right. I suppose we should just pick that up."

"Yeah, one of the things the police let me keep."

A brief flutter of relief shone a light through the fog of worries in his mind. At least he could solve this problem. He needed to think more, needed to stop being so tunnel visioned. If he kept his options open, he might just be able to get out of his deal with the businessman. He just might make it through all of this.

Chris grabbed Tracy's hand as they waited for the elevator. He wasn't the only one in danger here. He still needed to figure out why the list contained Jordan Thompson's name. Veronica's, too.

Snow fell outside the cab as they passed an array of shop fronts and restaurants in Federal Hill. Though most shared a homogenous red-brick exterior, each awning and windowsill along the streets displayed its own unique combination of colors.

A few pedestrians marveled at the snow. They held their gloved hands out to catch the flakes. It seemed as though winter had arrived in earnest.

As they passed Frederick's Seafood with its black-and-purple sign glaring into the night, Tracy tugged his arm. "That's the car." She looked behind their cab at a car following them with its headlights off.

"What do you mean?"

"It's the Corvette we saw at Respondent. The same one from Randy's funeral."

Everything seemed like a distant memory. So hard to believe that it had been just yesterday. He squinted at the vehicle, but its curves seemed to blend into the night like a passing shadow. "Are you sure?"

"Goddammit, yes I'm sure!"

"Do you think they're following us?"

"Hell, yes."

If she was right, if she wasn't just being paranoid, it would not be in their favor for these stalkers to know what they had planned. "Okay. If they're following us, they already know who I am. Don't you think?"

Tracy shrugged. "I'm not sure."

"They suspect something. Someone suspects something, anyway."

"Maybe we should head straight to Jordan's. We can try to lose them on the way. No need to lead them to back to your place." Tracy grabbed his arm. Her grip felt unexpectedly strong.

"I'm already in danger, and if they're following me, they probably already know where I live. Besides, they want me, not you."

"But—"

Chris held up a hand to silence her. "They probably don't even know about you, and they aren't going to want to follow an empty cab around the city."

She appeared uncertain. Her lip quivered, but she nodded. "I guess so."

"Can I have your comm card?"

Her hand shaking, Tracy reached into her inner coat pocket to retrieve the card. She handed it to him. "What are you planning on doing?"

Instead of answering, Chris tapped an address onto her card. "Take the cab around the block a couple of times and then head to this address when they stop following you."

"Following *me*? What are you planning on doing?"

"I'm going to get these guys off your tail." He opened the door as the cab slowed to a stop at a red light.

"Sir, please pay before departing the cab." The voice rang out from the automated pay system glowing blue in the middle console, and he held his comm card up to the display.

Chris didn't take his eyes off of Tracy. "Hand me one of the samples."

She said nothing, a confused frown drawing lines across her forehead.

"It'd be better if we split them up. Just in case."

She reached into the cooler, withdrew one of the vials, and handed it to him. He stashed it in one of his pants pockets.

"Don't leave," she said.

"They'll come after me. You'll be fine." Chris pushed the door open wider, and the chill of the winter air filled the cabin.

"I'm not so sure about this." A sudden look of worry crossed her face "If they catch you—"

The blustery wind that assaulted his ears drowned out Tracy's voice as he shut the cab's door and sprinted down the street, running back toward the black Corvette. In the reflection of a café's windows, he could see the light turn green behind him. His heart sank as the cab took off and the Corvette followed.

For an instant, he wondered if they were just being paranoid. He stopped and watched the car make it halfway down the next block before it shuddered to a stop. In the middle of the four-lane street, the car took a sharp U-turn, almost crashing into a red Honda going the opposite direction. The Corvette came barreling toward Chris.

He stood, his mouth agape and his feet frozen in place. Panic screamed at him to run. As soon as he could, he took a left in a connecting alley flanked by a green dumpster and two brown plastic recycling containers.

As he ran down the alley, he saw Randy's body in an alcove. Feathery down, soaked red, puffed out from the tears and rips in the man's marshmallow coat, his body shadowed by a pool of syrupy blood.

Chris shook his head to rid himself of the painful memory, and the vision gave way to a homeless man huddled in rags. As he neared the exit of the alley, he heard footsteps bouncing off the brick walls behind him. He didn't turn around lest he lose speed and his pursuer catch him. He ran across the next street, dodging a white car.

The screeching of rubber on asphalt signaled the arrival of the black Corvette from around the corner.

At least one pursuer chased him on foot. Chris dodged onto a narrow one-way street. Parked cars lined both sides, and he leaned up against a small Fiat as another car drove past. It grazed him with its mirror.

With no other vehicles racing toward him, he ran. His legs ached as he took the slight incline. As he inhaled, sharp pains stabbed his lungs. He fought an urgent desire to cough as the back of his throat succumbed to the cold air. While he ran, his thoughts flitted briefly back to his time in prison. He wished he had spent more time running during recreation.

He grimaced as his muscles strained.

Headlights lit up the street from behind him. He could see his shadow looming far ahead of him. The Corvette raced down the street in the wrong direction. He ignored his cramping legs and ran faster toward where the road ended in a T-intersection. Without looking either way down the cross street, he sprinted to the bottom of Federal Hill Park, its massive shape appearing before him like a giant in the night. He rushed up the cement stairs. Once, twice, he lost his footing and grasped the metal railings to right himself.

The Corvette could not follow him here. It would have to circle the park, driving laps around the hill, watching for his exit.

But the stairs were no obstacle for the faceless pursuer still on foot.

"Stop, stop!"

He could hear the man call for him in a gruff voice. But it sounded more distant as he reached the crest of the hill. He ran through the middle of the park, past the display of cast-iron cannons from centuries ago. As he reached the other side of the park, he risked a glance behind him. Streetlights framed the silhouette of his pursuer and the coat that whipped in the wind behind him.

Chris turned again at the edge of the park, where the hill sloped dramatically downward. The stark brick-faced wall of the American Visionary Art Museum stood in front of him. His pursuer drew nearer.

With a running start, Chris jumped at the edge of the hill and slid down the slope on his side, his feet pointed toward the black wall. Wind whipped at him and he gritted his teeth.

He slid, aided by the slick grass coated with a layer of frost and fresh, wet snow, along with the steep grade of the hill.

When he reached the bottom, he stumbled forward, moving his feet as fast as he could to retain his momentum. Across Key Highway lay the waterfront. To his left, north of the park and beyond the curve of the road, he would find those same taunting black waves of the Chesapeake. Southward, there were few places that would allow him a place to hide from the Corvette if it happened upon him.

Behind him came the heavy grunts of his pursuer as he slid down the hill. Chris needed to get the man off his trail. A small crowd gathered around the exit of the Visionary Art Museum. If he could become anonymous in the crowd, he might stand a chance at disappearing.

Of course, he could not easily blend in with the trickles of people milling about the museum. Most gathered in groups of two to four, not amicable to a sweat-soaked and shivering stranger in their midst. Everyone else laughed and talked, bundled in coats, scarves wrapped around their necks, and hats atop their heads.

The man stood up now, just a short throw away. Chris debated calling the police or waving down a bystander. But that, too, would come with a price. They might ask too many questions. He could make up a story about the pursuer, a mugging, an attempted robbery. But it would be too suspicious given his recent police interviews. If they caught his pursuer, whatever story the man came up with would, in all likelihood, not corroborate his. If the man vanished at the sound of sirens, Chris would be no better than a boy crying wolf.

Then there was also the matter of the plastic vial tucked away in his pocket. Given his parole, the police might be inclined—and allowed—to search his person for illegal genetic contraband. He still didn't know what the vial held. If the police found it, it might land him back in prison.

He couldn't throw a crucial piece of the puzzle away, either. As he struggled to resolve these options, his hunter grew closer.

Throwing logic to the icy Baltimore wind, Chris ran toward the museum entrance.

CHAPTER EIGHTEEN

C HRIS RAN ACROSS THE GRASS toward the sidewalk and slowed his pace as he approached the curving brick building that contained the American Visionary Art Museum. He strode through the entrance, feeling eyes on his back from the crowd outside. A small beep signified that his comm card had been charged for the entrance fee. Ahead of him, a staircase wound upward, enclosed in glass. Paintings hung from the ceiling, suspended in the air. With the bright lights shining inside the building, he was blind to the night outside the windows.

He rushed past the form of a woman constructed out of plaster and encased in bottle caps. Large wings made of goose feathers sprouted from the woman's shoulders and, instead of legs, a serpentine tail wrapped around a pitchfork pointed at any that dared pass her on their way to the third-floor exhibits.

A startled cry rose up from the entrance of the museum. From the overlook on the third-floor landing, Chris could see a tall man with broad shoulders barreling past others exiting through the main doors. He could make out the man's blue eyes and swept-back blond hair.

His heart dropped as he recognized his pursuer. He rubbed the sore bruises on his neck. Intense pain seemed to flare as though the blue-eyed man's fingers wrapped around his neck once more. The spook squinted as he surveyed the lobby and scanned the floors.

Just as the man's gaze approached the railings of the third floor, Chris ducked behind a fairy dollhouse built from tree trunks.

Moving through another hallway, Chris rushed toward the skywalk that connected the indoor museum exhibit with the larger warehouse next door.

In his head, he thanked Veronica for introducing him to the place. He remembered scoffing at a couple of the stranger displays, such as the large wooden door with soiled plastic dolls nailed to it and dripping red paint. The macabre piece of art seemed much too horrific to be taken seriously, but Veronica had scolded him for not acknowledging the intent of the artist who had constructed the piece. Not to mention, the artist had been a prisoner. But he had no time to try to understand the piece any better now, and Veronica was not there to guide him. He relied upon the memories of their visits together to plan his escape.

A few people still meandered through the exhibits, in no particular rush to depart the museum before its closing time in twenty minutes.

Chris pushed past them into a room filled with sculptures constructed of pulsating neon lights. Vibrant blues, reds, and greens lit up the room in turns. The lights made a show of a man running from an avalanche, starting from the entrance of the room and ending beyond the next hallway. He rushed alongside the running figure to the exit. There, he could run to the new fourth floor, where holodisplays depicting the various stages of Hell lined the wall, or follow a skywalk made of glass toward the warehouse.

Going up offered two exits: leaving from where he had come in or going down a staircase that led to the main entrance. If he went that way and his pursuer followed, there would be little chance for Chris to evade him.

He ran across the skywalk. It was lit up with lines of multicolored LED displays. Below him, three stories down, his running shadow swept over the ground. He sprinted to the large warehouse. Another hulking shadow formed on the sidewalk below. The blue-eyed man pounded across the skywalk.

A lonely holodisplay announced that the warehouse of kinetic art had already closed for the evening. Chris jumped over the metal chain blocking the entrance. He plunged into the darkness of the two-story building and sprinted across the catwalk. Try as he might, he couldn't quiet his clanging footsteps. He hurried down a spiral staircase. On the ground floor, his footsteps grew quieter.

His pursuer's pounding feet pierced the quiet. Chris hid behind an enormous poodle built around an ancient Volkswagen Beetle. Outside both the north and south exits of the building, he could catch a cab.

Still, he couldn't risk the thirty seconds it might take to run from the interior of the old warehouse to the exit and then to the cab. The man chasing him appeared too formidable. He didn't want to guess what his fate might be if his pursuer caught up in those few seconds.

Chris needed a better way out. For now, he ducked behind the poodle's front paw and caught his breath.

The man slowed and sauntered down the stairs. His head swiveled back and forth.

"Christopher Morgan. I'm not going to hurt you. Please, just come out. It'll save all of us a lot of trouble."

Chris struggled to prevent himself from wheezing. Once again, he wished he had taken advantage of months of recreation in the prison. If he could just run and be able to take a breath without feeling like he gasped for the last molecules of oxygen that existed in the world, he would have felt much more comfortable, more self-assured.

"Come on out. I just want to talk. I know what you must be thinking right now, and I want to assure you that we're on your side."

The man's shoes squeaked as he pivoted in place in the middle of the floor. His silhouette seemed to blend in with that of a hybrid steam-engine train/biplane built around an ancient gasoline-powered truck.

"Mr. Morgan, we can help you."

Chris pressed himself tighter against the poodle's leg. He looked toward the closest exit near him. The south exit. Between his current position and the exit, another sculpture hung from the back of a truck. A person, sedentary and fat, constructed from various footballs, soccer balls and baseballs, sat on a couch made from hockey sticks, baseball bats, and goal posts. Crouching, he inched his way toward it.

"Stop this, Mr. Morgan."

He froze in the shadows, certain the man had seen him. But the man swiveled around again, looking toward the north exit.

Chris backed up, his eyes glued on the man, and used his hands to guide him until he could feel the cool, varnished wood of the exhibit. He grabbed at it, feeling for a loose piece somewhere, anywhere.

He cursed inwardly. These artists might have been better craftsmen than he realized. He backed around the oversized couch made of sports equipment. Streetlights filtered in through the southern doors, lighting up the perfect runway for his exit.

As he moved toward the double doors, an inhuman yodel filled the room. The glass case near him lit up, displaying a miniature wooden man with hands cupped over his mouth yodeling on a mountaintop, his torso bobbing back and forth. Chris grimaced, wishing he had remembered the annoying display that he had so often complained to Veronica about. While children seemed to love running back and forth in front of the display to spark the yodeling man's ugly howls, he would cringe each time the voice cried out. Now, a meager cringe seemed an insufficient reaction to the yodeling.

He gasped, pressed himself against the wooden couch again, and froze. As much as he wished to run, his muscles would not move. The man's footsteps grew closer.

"Come on. Let's make this easier. I want to get you out of whatever deal, whatever bribe or blackmail is hanging over your head. You have to trust me."

Holding his breath, he explored the wooden sofa sculpture again. He just needed one loose object, one passable hockey stick. With his right hand, he groped around until he discovered the handle of a baseball bat that gave when he applied a little pressure. The bat creaked loose. He ripped it from the seams of the couch. A couple of metal nails clattered across the cement floor, but he no longer cared.

Stepping out from behind sculpture, he took a wild swing at the man's head. The bat connected with a solid thwack, but not with the man's skull.

"Just come with us. This can be so much easier." The man held the business end of the wooden bat in his left hand and lowered it as Chris gritted his teeth and strained his arms. "Forget about the other night. I didn't know who you were." The man held the bat as Chris tried to pull it from the his grip.

"What the hell do you want?"

The man seemed almost perplexed. "You know what we want."

The chain at the end of the skywalk clanged above them. Both Chris and the man turned up toward the sudden sound.

"Hey, we're closing for the night." A woman's voice called out from atop the catwalk. She reached her hand out, and the lights in the warehouse buzzed on. "You're going to need to—"

The tall man and Chris froze, each holding opposite ends of the bat. Chris let go of it and jumped to the side. The blue-eyed man stumbled forward, tumbling over his own weight.

Chris sprinted through the south exit and ran toward the street, flagging down a taxi. The first cab drove by, its occupant giving him a strange look. The second stopped, and he jumped into it, welcoming both the warm air and the locked doors. He input an address and commanded the cab to take off as his pursuer slammed his fists against the window.

The man ran behind the cab, but the car outpaced him. Chris settled into the crackling leather seat and moved back toward the holodisplay to change his destination. It would be a mistake to go home to retrieve a coat and the portable freezer. That would be the first place the black Corvette would try to find him. Instead, he headed straight to Jordan's.

CHAPTER NINETEEN

WHEN THE CAB ARRIVED AT 427 North Charles Street, gray fog and the haze of falling snow silhouetted the sculpted spires of the building. Harsh winds tugged at Chris. He wrapped his arms tighter around himself, shivering as he approached the building.

Under the small outcropping near the entrance, he scanned the nearby street. There was no sign of his pursuers or Tracy anywhere, and any trace that might have existed had been covered by a blanket of snow. He tried calling her once more, the shrill ring drowned by the wind against his naked red ears. She did not answer.

Chris touched the display screen at the building's entrance, selecting a button labeled "J. Thompson." He bobbed up and down on his feet, trying to conjure just a bit more warmth in his numbing limbs. While he waited, his eyes darted between the snow-covered streets and the pinhole for the video feed that routed his image to Jordan's penthouse apartment.

"Come up." The voice didn't sound like his old friend's. It seemed rougher and more aggressive than Jordan's normally buoyant greetings. He wondered if someone else had gotten to his friend first. He might be delivering himself straight into the hands of his pursuers.

In the lobby of the building, a contingent of Grecian columns stretched like ivory fingers from the marble floor to the reliefs carved into the ceiling. Everything from the lush tropical plants adorning the artificial creek to the enormous holodisplays of rotating Greek pottery was just as gaudy and magnificent as Chris had remembered.

He rubbed his arms together as the elevator hummed and rode upward. Though a current of warm air washed over him, his arms shook and his teeth chattered. The elevator pinged and announced that he had reached the Penthouse level. As the doors slid open, he took a nervous step forward into the atrium with its wide glass ceiling and a spurting fountain that changed colors, competing with the building's lobby for gaudiness.

Without warning, a large man stepped in front the elevator's entrance and held Chris against the cool stone wall.

"Is this the guy?"

"That's him," a familiar voice said. "Chris, good to see you."

The sentry released him.

Dressed in a suit and almost a head taller than him, Jordan Thompson stood with outstretched arms. The man grinned with a smile to rival the Cheshire Cat's and almond-brown eyes that matched his smooth skin. Chris approached but shirked his friend's embrace.

"What gives?" He glared at Jordan.

"Sorry, my man. Can't be too careful." A look of concern spread over Jordan's face as he studied Chris's neck. "What the hell? Did that just happen?"

Chris pulled his collar up over the bruises. "No, no. Those are from a few days ago."

"Oh, good. I mean, bad for you, but I'm glad Greg didn't do it."

Greg, his muscled arms crossed over his bulging chest, let out a low grunt of acknowledgment. "I'm gentler than that, Jordan. You should know."

Jordan laughed and gave Greg a dismissive gesture. "You're supposed to be watching out for us, not telling jokes."

Chris frowned, glancing between Jordan and Greg, but decided that this route of conversation would not be conducive to figuring out what the hell Randy's samples contained and why a suited thug had chased him down. His stomach tightened in knots as he remembered someone else had been pursued. "Is Tracy here?"

"She's in my office right now."

"What's she doing?"

Jordan shrugged. "Beats me. But she made herself right at home after interrogating me."

"Sounds about right."

Jordan led Chris through the archway into his expansive living area. A wide sitting area contained suede couches. Chris's eyes lingered over the fire crackling in a fireplace. A massive preserved tree trunk served as a coffee table. Next to the sitting area, a polished mahogany bar jutted over a hardwood floor. He recalled several parties Jordan had hosted there. Most of the time, Jordan had mixed and served drinks from behind the bar. He'd smiled as his patrons sipped and chugged each of his concoctions.

"This way." Jordan motioned to the French doors near the bar. Beyond the glass panes, Tracy pored over something on Jordan's desk. Her hair, tied up, swung as she scanned back and forth. Chris knocked on the window, and she whipped her head around. When she saw him, her eyes widened and she ran to the door.

She wrapped her arms around Chris and squeezed him tight. "God, I'm glad you made it."

"Yeah, me, too."

She kissed him on the cheek. "Are you okay?"

"I'm fine." He frowned. "Why didn't you answer my calls? I was worried about you."

Tracy held out her comm card. It blinked red. "Sorry, it's down. The shitty little thing hasn't been working since the cab ride. Firmware problems, I think."

"What about his?" Chris nodded toward Jordan.

Turning away, Tracy's cheeks adopted a red hue. "I don't have your ID memorized." She turned back to him with a raised eyebrow and accusatory stare. "You got mine memorized?"

Chris exhaled. "Fair enough." Still, he couldn't shake the idea that she might have tried harder to get in contact with him while nestled in Jordan's apartment. He tried to dismiss the idea, reminding himself he had told her to come here, to stay put and wait for him.

Jordan clapped his hand on Chris's shoulder. "So, Tracy says you've got something for me."

"You haven't told him what's going on yet?"

Tracy shook her head.

"She told me she was your girlfriend, showed a couple of holos of the two of you on her comm card to prove it, and said you might be in danger. Something about people chasing you."

"Jordan, you've gotten a little lax on security," Chris said. "I, an old friend, get the royal treatment when I come in, and you let a stranger into your home no problem. And into your office, no less." He waved a hand, indicating the shelves full of hardcover books that lined the office. It was more library than workplace.

"A beautiful woman comes walking up to my door and I turn her away?" Jordan shook his head. "I thought you knew me better than that." He motioned to the sitting area with the wraparound couch. "Why don't we have story time? Coffee, anyone?"

"Please," Chris said, already settling into the couch and pulling Tracy down next to him. Even if he had not wanted a hot drink, he knew it would be no use refusing Jordan. The man would not accept a refusal of any kind. Jordan had never hired any employees to relieve him of his cooking or drink making. He relished his time in the industrial-sized kitchen. His meals were often things of artistic beauty, and Chris found himself wishing he possessed half as much talent in any of his own undertakings.

Tracy began to shake her head no, but Chris shot her a look to encourage her to accept Jordan's hospitality. "Uh, yes, that sounds great. Thanks."

When Jordan set the mugs of coffee down, Chris told him everything, starting from his final days in prison and continuing all the way until the last moments of his chase through the Visionary Art Museum. Then he explained that he and Tracy wanted to find out what those samples contained, but they feared that analyzing the vials in their own laboratory would be an invitation for scrutiny. They didn't want to attract the suspicions of their coworkers or any other researcher that might stumble upon results that might be associated with illegal genetic enhancements.

He exhaled at the end of his story and offered a pathetic smile to Jordan. "Will you help us?"

Jordan smiled apologetically. For a moment, the man said nothing. His brown eyes gleamed in the soft light of the sitting room. Shadows played across his face as the fire swayed and crackled from the brick fireplace. "I'm not sure that's such a good idea, my man. After you went to prison, I figured it would be a good time for me to get out of the business, too. I don't want to get back in."

"I have a lot of questions, and nobody's been able to give me any answers," Chris said. "Hell, people have tried to kill me multiple times in the past couple months. I don't know what's going on, and I just want to clear this up, clear my name so I can move on. That's all I want."

Looking out the window that led to his rooftop garden, Jordan would not meet Chris's gaze. "I don't know. I want to help, but I don't have any equipment here."

"That's fine. That's more than fine. I don't have anything in my condo now, either. We can bring the samples to your lab."

Jordan sipped from his mug. "My lab hasn't produced genetic enhancements for humans in over a year now."

Before Chris went to prison, Jordan's shell of a company had advertised its research as a step toward producing a suite of new tools for improving the health and meat yield of livestock. They'd secured a few government grants, but that was not where the company had produced its income.

After hours, the lab's undocumented employees kept busy producing genetic enhancements for things like strength (Chris's own specialty) and improved eyesight—even enhancements thought to reduce the need for sleep. The enhancements had not been scientifically proven other than by a ramshackle collection of shoddy papers published in countries with little oversight in scientific literature. Still, who would report that their illegally obtained genetic enhancements didn't perform as advertised? Even better, with Chris's help in improved delivery vectors made from DNA-based materials, evidence of stereotypical illegal enhancements like viral vectors or metal-based nanoparticles did not present in Jordan's products.

"The lab's abandoned? Even better. We can do the analysis ourselves."

Tracy's head bobbed up and down. "We'd be glad to."

Jordan laughed and put his mug back down on a coaster. "No, no. Like I said, we haven't produced anything for humans. We're into horse racing now."

Chris's mouth dropped. "You mean you're doing enhancements for animals? For real?"

"I am. And since equine athletics have not caught up to the same standards of organized human sports regarding such improvements, business has been quite lucrative."

Chris chuckled. "I bet you've put a lot of stud horses out of business."

"I do feel pity for the studs. I have to admit: I admire true athleticism over these cheats but not enough to refuse making a couple bucks off those same cheats."

Tracy leaned forward across the table. Her brow furrowed and her eyes seemed alight. "You don't think athletes that take advantage of enhancements work hard? Maybe they've got to get them just to be on an equal playing field."

Jordan appeared surprised but held up his hands in a defensive gesture. "Fair argument."

"Regardless, we do need to figure something out," Chris said. "Any information we can gather would be helpful. I promise that we can be discreet about it."

Exhaling, Jordan appeared ready to refuse again.

"You do realize that you're probably in just as deep shit as we are," Tracy said. "Your name came up on a list of Randy's. And I think that anybody with their name on that list is in danger."

"That's what I have Greg for," he said. "Besides, where do you get off on such an absurd idea?"

"Because five of the eleven people on that list are already dead." She narrowed her eyes, speaking slowly for emphasis.

Only the crackling of the fire could be heard as the three sat around the couch, absorbing everything that had been revealed in that short time. The snow flurried against the skylights over their sitting area.

Chris shivered again, and Jordan looked sympathetically at him. "You don't look so good, my man."

"Don't feel so good, either," Chris said.

Tracy put the back of her hand against his head. "You feel a bit warm, too. I think you've got a fever or something."

"Just a headache, I think."

"I'll make you a deal," Jordan said. "You go and take a warm shower, borrow my clothes, and I'll talk to Tracy here. We'll see if we can't work something out."

"Thanks," Chris said. He could feel his face draining. "That'd be great. I appreciate it."

"No problem. You know where everything is, right?"

He nodded. "As long as you haven't changed your place up like you did your business, I'll be fine."

"Same place you're used to waking up at with a hangover," Jordan said.

Thanking Jordan again, Chris went back to one of the guest bedrooms. He closed the door behind him and unbuttoned his shirt. Throwing it down on the ground, he gazed around at the queen bed clad in a puffy comforter, where he'd woken up several afternoons with a pounding headache and patchy memories.

Chris closed his eyes as the showerhead hissed to life. As the water washed over him, his head pounded, but not with the throbbing ache of a night drowned and forgotten in alcohol. Rather, stress and anxiety hit him like storm tides on a rock wall. He clenched his eyelids tighter. Even as he closed them, flashes of red and black exploded in his vision. Maybe Jordan and Tracy were right. Maybe he was getting sick, exposed to the cold so long without protection. It made sense.

But the knots in his stomach and the nagging worry in his mind were not solely physical reactions to a virus attacking him in a moment of vulnerability. A weakened immune system was not the reason his face had paled and he found it hard to breathe.

Veronica might have been found lying in a pool of her own blood, stabbed like Randy. He would never see her dance again, never see her paintings. Never apologize to her.

He tried to rationalize that she was no longer in his life, should no longer be so important to him. She was no different than anybody else on that list that he didn't know. His thoughts flickered to Tracy, sitting on the couch talking to Jordan. Two different people from different times colliding in a situation beyond any he had ever expected to face.

When he turned the faucet off, he opened his eyes and stood up straighter. He would need to move forward. He couldn't dwell in the past if he wanted to change his future.

CHAPTER TWENTY

BRUSHING HIS FINGERS THROUGH HIS still-wet hair, Chris joined Tracy and Jordan in the sitting room again. He sat down on the couch in the spot nearest the fireplace and let the smoky warmth dry his hair.

Tracy turned. "Did you know Jordan's writing a novel?"

"Oh, yeah. He's always talked about being a writer." Chris dismissed the statement with a wave.

"Ah, but now I'm actually writing," Jordan said. "I'm more than just fancy talk. I've put my pen to paper, as they say."

Fascination lit up Tracy's eyes. Ceaseless energy seemed to emanate from her, infecting Jordan. But Chris could not bring himself to share in their excitement. The shower had cleaned away the grime and sweat from the evening's events, but it had not washed away the thoughts and worries that had compounded since Randy's death.

"Tell you what, my man, why don't you keep low and stay at my place for a day or so? We can catch up," Jordan said. He motioned to the bar, his voice smooth and calm.

"I appreciate it, but I don't know if that's such a good idea."

"Come on," Tracy said. "It might be good for us to clear our heads. Besides, if those two meatheads are staked out somewhere, I'd rather deal with them in the daylight than tonight again."

"I don't want to waste any more time," Chris said. "Maybe you can hide out here while I go back to Respondent."

"Hell, no," Tracy said. "It would be stupid for you to go right back to Respondent with the samples." She grabbed his hand, squeezing it. "We need time to think about things. Jordan offered to talk it all over with us."

He exhaled. "Fine. We'll stay."

"Fantastic. I'll go make mojitos." Jordan stood up and walked toward the bar. He patted Chris's back on the way. "You might not realize it now, but this is exactly what you need."

As Jordan went to the kitchen, Tracy drew closer to Chris on the couch. She traced her hand along his jawline. Her fingers caught on his stubble. "You feel any better?"

"I think so."

She draped an arm around him, enveloping him in a one-armed hug. Chris felt as if his ribs cracked.

"I'm glad you're okay," she said. "I was pretty damn worried."

"Me, too." But he didn't feel okay. His thoughts swirled in a cloud of doubt and worry. "Could you tell me who else died on that list?"

With a somber slowness, Tracy nodded. "Sure, I made notes next to each of their names." She handed him the paper ripped from the notebook with the names.

Taking a deep breath, Chris skipped over all the names until he got to Veronica Powell. Next to her name, no mark, no note indicated that she had died. Or at least, she had not been found dead yet. "You're sure that these are the only people found dead so far?"

Tracy shrugged. "I mean, I can't give you a hundred-percent guarantee. But those are the only ones I could find anything on." Little creases formed along her brow as her eyes narrowed. "Didn't you recognize another name on the list? You never told me which one."

"No, no."

"You definitely did."

"No, I mean, I was wrong. It was just the one. Just Jordan." He glanced at the bar, and Jordan winked at him as he crushed fresh mint leaves.

"Hey, Greg," Jordan called out into the front hallway. "Why don't you join us? I've made enough for four."

Greg lumbered into the room and plopped down on a chair in the opposite corner of the sitting room. He nodded a greeting and then looked toward Jordan. "You want me to stay the night, too?"

"I think it might be a good idea," Jordan said. He brought over four skinny drinks. Flecks of green mint leaves floated among ice cubes suspended in the glasses. He handed them out. "Cheers to staying alive."

Chris's glass clinked against Jordan's, but he didn't return the man's smile.

"So, what's the deal with the samples?" Chris asked. "If I'm staying here for the night, is there any way we can at least take a look at them tomorrow? I'll do whatever's necessary to keep it all under wraps, too. No one has to know we even used your lab."

"Here's what I've decided: I'll have Greg bring them to the lab and we'll give them a once-over ourselves."

"Tracy and I would be happy to do it. No need for you to get involved."

"You've already gotten me involved." Jordan shook his head. "Besides, I don't think it's a good idea for you to show up at my place of business. A guy with a record like yours shouldn't just be dropping in on a place with a reputation like mine, you follow?"

Chris begrudgingly agreed.

The night wound down with more drinks and conversation. Snow covered the skylights. The flowerpots and benches on the rooftop garden were only white protrusions on a bleak landscape. As Chris settled into bed with Tracy and his body succumbed to exhaustion, he found his mind racing for the second night in a row with thoughts of Veronica. He needed to warn her, to tell her to get way. And he'd already waited one day. It could already be too late.

Her breathing slow and steady, Tracy turned and her body pressed against Chris. She seemed to be smiling in her sleep. He winced as she gripped his side, caught in a dream, her fingers grabbing at the white scars below his ribs.

CHAPTER TWENTY-ONE

VERONICA'S EYES SHONE A VIVID blue as she brushed back the long dark hair that had fallen in front of her heart-shaped face. She wore a loose-fitting shirt that flowed over the sculpted curves of her muscular yet petite body shaped by a lifetime spent performing in dance companies and highly technical workshops and classes. Several rings, a few gaudy, one simple, decorated her fingers. "Come on. If this is just a ploy to get me back, it's not going to work." She poked his arm playfully and then folded her arms over her chest. "I'm coming here as a favor to you, because you begged me."

Chris could tell she had not bothered to put on any makeup. Still, he found it difficult to maintain eye contact, distracted by thoughts of his own inadequacies and a self-conscious nagging that kept him wondering how unhealthy and scrawny he must appear sitting across from a woman as vibrant as her.

The feeling was not new.

When they had been together, she had told him early on that a LyfeGen Sustain had been implanted within her. The artificial organ, crafted for individuals based on their DNA, cost more than most—including Chris—could afford. On an artist's budget, Veronica couldn't pay for it, either. Instead, the implantation procedure had been a gift from her parents when she'd graduated from the University of Iowa with dual bachelor's degrees in studio arts and dance.

"No, I'm with someone else now," Chris said. "You don't have anything to worry about. I mean, you do, but it's not me you have to worry about."

Chris thought now, as he had before, what it would mean that she might grow old with skin free of wrinkles and eyes full of sparkle as he decayed in front of her. He would deal with the natural afflictions as they came; glaucoma, cancers, arthritis, and other diseases would have to be treated reactively. Veronica, instead, was blessed with an artificial organ that enhanced her body's natural healing capabilities, with cells specialized to identify and react to afflictions too nascent for even a trained physician to identify. She would age gracefully, beautifully, as he shriveled and became sick in front of her.

Taking a sip of her mimosa, Veronica cocked her head. Her hair caught a beam of sunlight and glowed. "Oh? Someone else?" She gave him a doubtful look.

"That's not important right now."

"Well, I suppose I could keep any affair between us secret. This could be interesting." She smirked.

"What? No!"

Veronica laughed. "I'm just kidding. Have you lost your sense of humor?"

She poked at her blue crab eggs Benedict. Every time they'd brunched at The Point at Fell's, she would insist on the same dish and drink the same mimosa. Despite her endeavors in all manners and styles of dance and the artworks she created that ranged from simple portraits on canvas to complicated holosculptures projected from a holodisplay, she never strayed from her Sunday tradition. It was sacred to her.

In front of Chris sat a steak meant to be medium rare but sufficiently cooked to well done, with fried eggs more brown than white. He pulled a hand through his hair, donning a serious expression. "I think your life's in danger. Please. Just go visit your parents in Illinois for a while."

Again, Veronica chuckled. "You always said that when you got involved in your side businesses." She never referred to his illegal genetic dealings as anything more than a side business. Even after she knew he had been convicted and gone to prison, she refused to say the words aloud, as though an evil spirit would curse her if she acknowledged what he had done.

"I know," he said. He sighed. "You know that's why I couldn't stay with you, right? I couldn't put you at risk like that."

"But you couldn't quit your little business, either."

His cheeks turned red. He couldn't look her in the eye. "I was an idiot."

"What about her?"

"Who?" Chris turned back to her.

Veronica's eyes seemed almost pleading, sad. He wondered how she could always show such sympathy for people she hardly knew. He supposed that untapped connection with anyone and everyone had enabled her to express the brutal power of emotion in her art.

"Your new girl. If what you're telling me is all true, then don't you worry about her?"

He reached across the table and grabbed her hand. "I'm not joking around. At least five of the people on that list are already dead. You're on that list."

"I'm sorry, but I never got involved in any of your business. I don't have anything to fear."

"Goddammit, Veronica. I'm trying to help you."

Again, she smiled. But her smile appeared morose. "Chris, I can't deal with your games anymore." She drew her hand back from his.

He closed his eyes and sighed. Veronica's soft fingers grasped his again. A surge of warmth spread through him.

"If you're this concerned, I'll leave as soon as our show is over next Saturday. This is the last weekend we're performing at the Lyric stage."

Opening his eyes, Chris let out a slow breath. "You promise?"

"Sure. I promise."

"And if you see anything, or anything weird happens, you promise you'll leave right away?"

"I'll be fine. I will."

"If anyone strange tries to do anything to you, so much as talk to you, just let me know."

"Okay, okay. I will. I promise."

"I'm serious, Veronica. Can I at least walk you home?"

She appeared skeptical.

"No funny business. I swear." He held up his hands. "It would make me feel better."

While Chris walked along the sidewalk with Veronica, kicking up freshly laid salt with every step, his mind churned with excuses for Tracy and Jordan. He had barely managed to get out the door, telling them he just needed to be alone with his thoughts. Tracy had almost exploded on him, her face red with a mixture of anger and worry. Fortunately, Jordan had held his hand out and explained how Chris had always needed his solitude from time to time.

He had promised he would be back soon and that he would stay well away from both Tracy's and his apartments so as not to draw the attention of last night's pursuers. Still, an unread message on his comm card from Tracy blinked in red lights.

He slid the message open. "How long will you be?" He shoved the comm card back into his pocket before Veronica saw it.

Veronica skirted around his incarceration by asking if he had read any decent books or taken up any new hobbies since they parted ways. For a time, they discussed a couple of classic books written by turn-of-the-century author Jeffrey Eugenides. Chris recalled that Eugenides had visited the University of Iowa several times during his writing career—of course, well before she had attended the university. He wondered how great it would have been to have talked to the author that he and Veronica had read voraciously. Their conversation lit up in remembered jokes they'd shared, and his urgent worries seemed to retreat from his mind.

As they drew nearer to Veronica's apartment, he felt an instinctual urge to hold her hand.

She pressed a hand against the small of his back. "Do you want to come up for a bit? It'd be good to catch up for a while."

CHAPTER TWENTY-TWO

T HE SUNLIGHT PERMEATING THE CLOUDS over the Chesapeake emitted a dull gray glow over Baltimore. Flecks of sunlight glinted off the piles of snow along the streets not yet soiled by pedestrians, plows, or passing cars. Chris kicked at a dirty gray puff of snow as he left Veronica's apartment. He prepared new excuses for his tardiness when he returned to Jordan's lofty penthouse.

His khaki pants, borrowed from Jordan, stuck to the back of his ankles with the wetness they'd soaked up from the ground. He kept stepping on the cuffs with his heels. While he'd never considered himself short, he couldn't help but feel vertically insufficient wearing Jordan's clothing.

As he walked along Pratt Street back toward the Inner Harbor, he hailed a cab on his comm card. He looked down at the display as he trudged along and tripped, ripping the seams on the cuff of the khakis in the process. "Ah, hell." A cab rolled up, and he lowered himself into the back seat. Even Jordan's shirt, trim and svelte on Jordan's frame, made Chris appear as if he had borrowed clothes from his older brother's wardrobe. He entered in Jordan's address.

Before confirming the destination, he cleared the screen and retyped the address of his own condo back on Fed Hill. The cab passed by people wrapped in long dark coats and scarves, hats, and gloves. He felt thankful that at least today he could swim in the warmth of one of Jordan's coats, but he longed to wear one of his own. Besides, he meant to go to work on Monday despite all that had happened in an attempt to appear ignorant of what had transpired over the long weekend. He couldn't show up wearing such ill-fitting clothes and expect people not to at least make a joke about them. And he didn't look forward to the jesting, much less questioning, from any of his coworkers.

Memories of his early-evening chase through the Visionary Art Museum persuaded him to change the destination to a location one block away from his condominium complex. At least he would have the opportunity to survey the area for any idling Corvettes.

The cab stopped on the corner of East Ostend and Light Street at the Cornerstone Bakery and Coffeehouse. Chris debated stopping in for a hot coffee to go but figured that he'd already taken sufficient time for Tracy and Jordan to question his tardiness. He took his comm card from his pocket, surprised that neither of them had called to inquire regarding his whereabouts after Tracy's initial message. With hands in his coat pockets, he trudged along the salt- and puddle-covered sidewalk toward his building. He saw no sign of the Corvette on the street. Of course, the men might not be in a Corvette now, wise to Chris's knowledge of their chosen mode of transport.

Still, he made his way toward his building and ducked into the side entrance on East Ostend. He lunged up the stairs to his floor. There, the hallway was empty except for a couple of plastic plants standing sentry next to the elevator doors.

He crept toward his own door and pressed his ear to the cool metal. He heard no noises, no breathing, and no voices from within. Gripping the door handle, he held up his comm card. The lock clicked open, and he stepped in. No one rushed to subdue him. No one yelled his name. Everything in the apartment appeared just as he had left it, at least from the doorway.

Tiptoeing through the hallway, he peeked into his bedroom and the office just to be sure. He peered out his bedroom window over South Charles Street but saw no suspicious onlookers or black Corvettes.

When no one showed themselves, he packed a duffel bag with an extra change of clothes for the rest of the day and for work on Monday. From a dresser drawer, he pulled a set of Tracy's clothes that she left at his apartment for when she spent the night. He slipped out of Jordan's clothes, folded them up, and put on a pair of jeans and sweater from his own closet. A wave of comfort washed over him, with his own clean clothes fitting as they should. No dragging pants cuffs, no hands swallowed by shirt sleeves.

In his office, he picked through the closet. He found the stainless steel portable freezer packed in a box of cords and other electronic knickknacks.

Continuing to search through the box, he found the electric charging station for the freezer. He pushed aside the collared shirts, pressed pants, and underwear in the duffel to make room for the device. As he stood up, the brown leather of Vincent's notebook on his desk caught his eyes.

The notebook lay closed, where he had left it weeks, almost months, ago. He couldn't bear to open the thing, and he had stopped trudging around with the journal stowed in his leather bag. The memories of the attack returned. While he spoke about his prison experiences with Tracy, albeit infrequently, his words often came out as if he relayed distant dreams or scenes from a movie he had seen as a child. The scars on his side reminded him of his near-death experience each time he rubbed body wash over himself in the shower. But still, those scars could have been from anything if his imagination and denial proved strong enough.

The notebook, though, reminded him of someone he was supposed to have died with. He could not snoop through its contents lest he evoke a deep-seated emotion that he had struggled to suppress those meager months he had been reporting to his parole officer.

Now, a strange urge to bring the book with him manifested itself within him as he left the office. The nagging voice in him grew louder, demanding he take the notebook. Slipping it into his duffel, he left the condo, directing his thoughts back to Tracy, away from prison and Vincent and the notebook. He hoped bringing a fresh set of her clothes would be an adequate peace offering or at least an effective distraction when he returned later than expected.

When Chris arrived at Jordan's place, the elevator opened up to an empty loft. No one greeted him in the atrium. He called out for Tracy, Jordan, and Greg but heard no response. No one rustled about in the bedrooms or in the kitchen. No one sat on the plush white couches or served drinks from the bar. His pulse raced. He checked his comm card again, but he found no missed messages or calls.

He placed a call to Tracy and waited for her to answer. A muffled buzzing piqued his interest. He walked toward the sound, which was coming from Jordan's office. As he pushed open the French doors a voice answered the card. "Hello?"

Tracy turned around in the leather chair at Jordan's desk, the comm card in her hand. "Hey, that didn't take long."

"Really?" Wrinkles formed along Chris's brow in a skeptical expression.

Looking at the time on her comm card, her eyes widened. "Oh, I guess not. Must have lost track of time."

"Where are Jordan and Greg?"

"They left for the lab a while ago. The more we talked about everything that happened, the more I think I piqued Jordan's interest. I told him about the weird guy at Randy's funeral that you call the businessman. Jordan asked me what the shithead looked like, I told him, and then he got curious about this business. Are you sure you didn't know that man from before? You know, when you worked with Jordan."

He let out an exasperated sigh. "I'm positive. I never saw the guy until the day they let me out of prison. Does Jordan know him?"

"Don't know. He said he didn't, but he changed when I described what the guy looked like. I think if he doesn't know the guy, he has an idea about what that guy represents."

"What does he represent?"

"If I knew, I'd tell you. Either way, it seems like Jordan wants to know what the son of a bitch had to do with Randy's death. Or, more accurately, Randy's hidden samples."

Chris dragged a wooden chair from a corner of the office and placed it next to Tracy. He sat down and scanned the documents she had projected from Jordan's computer onto the desk. "What's going on here?"

With rushed, excited words, Tracy explained that she had investigated the names on their list further. The five that had died particularly interested her. While he had been gone, she had uncovered a wealth of information.

"See, I got interested in this bastard here." Tracy gestured on the computer to bring up a holoprojection of a man with cropped black hair and a short goatee. "Gordon Katz. I found his obituary easy enough, but I couldn't find out why he died. No police reports and nothing in any of the Baltimore crime blotters suggested a suspect or arrest that might be responsible for Katz's death. Nothing. Weird, right?"

"I guess. But what if he died of natural causes?"

"Sure, sure. I considered that. Then I found three more of the guys' obituaries, but no cause of death. Nada." She made a cutting gesture to emphasize the point. "All right, all right. Maybe something is fishy, or maybe all these guys died of natural causes, right?"

Tracy continued before he could answer. "Well, this guy, this bastard right here." She brought up another floating head on the holodisplay. This time, a bald man with baby smooth skin and a prominent Roman nose appeared over the desk. "Ugly asshole. Anyway, this guy died in a stabbing. Want to know what's even more screwed up?"

Chris nodded.

"He knew Randy. Or at least, he did a long time ago. Both of them worked, I think in research, at Myogenetics before Randy left for his current—er, former—position at Respondent."

"Okay, so you're going to have to explain to me what all this means."

Tracy's eyes widened with an excited, almost rabid look. "I don't know. I have no idea." She leaned closer. "But there is no way this is just a coincidence. News streams say he got stabbed just two days before Randy. Both worked in genetic research.

And we both know Randy's been dabbling in extracurricular shit on the side. There is just no way this means nothing."

"Fair enough. You're still going to have to explain the significance of the other four guys and what it means that you couldn't find out about the causes of their deaths."

"You know I can be a bit stubborn, right? A bit tunnel visioned, if you will?"

He chuckled and nodded. "No, no. I've never thought that."

Tracy nudged him in the side and gave him a quick peck on the lips. Despite the innocuous intentions of the prodding, he recoiled at her touch. Maybe she was stronger than she thought or maybe his sides remained weak. He wondered when he'd get over someone getting near his rib cage, playfully or not, and whether or not the pain was real or just a fragment of a memory left embedded in his mind by the prison stabbings.

"I appreciate your white lies, but let's not bullshit around. Anyway, I just caught myself staring at Jordan's bookshelves, wondering what the hell was going on. And I didn't get it. Couldn't figure it out. Then it struck me." She prodded his side again and he winced. "The stabbings, Chris. You told me about the riots and how others died. How your roommate—"

"Cellmate."

"Same damn thing. Anyway, here's what's important," she said. "All four of the other guys—their deaths match up with the date of the riot."

"Are you sure?"

"Sure as shit." Tracy smiled triumphantly.

"Can you show me the other guys?"

She called up a projection. "Terrence Hart." Another. "Brady Allen."

When she brought up the last image, a pit formed in his stomach. He reminded himself to breathe. There before him shone a face he had gotten to know well over the eight months in Fulton. He recognized the small scar on the lip, the bright green eyes that always seemed to glow with an uncanny and often unwarranted cheerfulness. "Vincent," Chris said.

Raising an eyebrow, Tracy shook her head. "No. The guy's name is Jeremy Kar."

"No way. That's Vincent."

"You sure?"

Chris nodded.

With a couple quick commands, Tracy performed a quick search. "Holy shit. You're right. Full name: Jeremy Vincent Kar." She stared hard. "Are you sure you don't know anything else about this guy?"

"Of course, I know plenty of other things. But I don't know what's relevant. He told me he went to prison for murdering his wife and her lover."

Her eyes narrowed until only the smallest portions of her pupils were visible. "That's it? Never said anything weird, nothing about this businessman of yours? Nothing about Randy?"

"No. Nothing. I swear, Tracy. Why does it always feel like you're interrogating me?"

"I'm not interrogating, just trying to see if you might've forgotten anything."

Chris disagreed but didn't bother voicing his protest. "I had no idea. Was he actually in prison for murder?"

"Apparently so." The excitement in Tracy's eyes seemed to fade. "Sure, enough. Killed his wife and a Raymond Borsch. Borsch was the alleged lover." Tracy's eyes were lost in stories projected on the desk that Chris could not quite make out. He scooted his chair nearer to her. As he did, she jumped back from the articles, waving her finger at the projected words.

"Look! Shit. Shit. Your buddy Vincent got a PhD in molecular engineering from Hopkins."

"All right. Where'd he work?"

"Consultant at Tallicor. Not so close a connection."

"Maybe he worked for Tallicor, but he consulted at biotech companies." His tone made his statement sound more like a question, but Tracy's eyes lit up again.

"You might be right. That would make sense. Please, tell me you know something else about this guy that we can use. Now I want know what the hell is going on."

"Believe me, I do, too." Exhaustion, emotional and physical, dropped over him in a hazy shroud. He leaned back in his chair and sighed. "I just want this all to be over."

Tracy grabbed Chris's wrists. "I know that I can't possibly know what you are going through. I do know this, though: if all of this is not just a big coincidence, if that businessman of yours makes good on his threat, it's not just a matter of you going back to prison. It's a matter of your life. And if you want to pretend you aren't being selfish, you've got to think about the other people on that list. There are three other women and three other men that are still out there, Jordan included, that might not even know their lives are in danger."

In his mind's eye, Veronica's blue eyes flashed and danced. Her fingers interlaced with his in a warm, soft grip. "I'm not just thinking about myself anymore." He put his hand on Tracy's. "Maybe I should just give it up and go to the police. If I give them this list and Randy's notebook, they'll have to believe me. Hell, we could even turn over the other samples to them."

Tracy recoiled. "No, no, you can't do that."

"What do you mean? It's the right thing to do."

"No. It's not. If they think you're part of this, you'll be thrown back in prison. And if the Baltimore PD doesn't think so, you can sure as shit bet that your parole officer will when you lose your job because all this comes out at Respondent."

"Hell, at this point, maybe I'd be better off if I just ended up back in prison."

Tracy waved her hands in a panic. "No, no. Come on. I don't want you to go back. I want you to be here." She held both his hands in hers and massaged them with her thumbs. "With me." Her cheeks flushed red. "I know it sounds stupid, but I'm worried that going to the police will just backfire. Besides, the businessman friend of yours told you things would just get worse if you went to the police, didn't he? The only way going to the police is going to help us is if we can find out more. If we give them the entire puzzle, put it together into the pretty little picture they want, they won't have to do any work. They'll have to take your word for it."

Chris half smiled at her and closed his eyes. He waited a moment, breathing slowly.

"Come on. Don't be an ass."

Opening his eyes again, he embraced Tracy in a tight hug. He gave her a quick peck on the lips and looked straight into her eyes. "I don't think I can do that. Every step forward we think we're taking just puts you in danger." His thoughts whirled to an apartment on Fell's Point filled with canvases, a few adorned in lush oil paints, others half finished. "I can't go on this fool's errand and get anyone else hurt."

"Dammit, Chris." Tracy stood up. "Don't be so goddamn stubborn. I'm already in this with you. I'm not going to give up on finding this businessman and putting a stop to all this."

"You want to find him now? How deep do you think we need to go before we can turn this guy in? Is it worth risking both our lives?"

She paced back and forth behind the desk. Chris watched her, his hands clasped in his lap.

When Tracy sat on the edge of the desk, she looked away. She wiped the side of her face, and Chris thought he saw a lone tear budding at the edge of her glistening eye.

"I have to go to the police. It's the best thing I can do."

Eyes reddened, cheeks flushed, Tracy turned to him. A venomous grimace spread across her face. "It's not. It's really not. But, if that's what you want, we'll go to my apartment now. We'll get the damned notebook, the samples, and we'll give the PD everything we have."

"It's what I think is best for me. For everyone." He tried to grab her hand but she pulled it away. "I don't want you to risk your life for me. I couldn't live with it if I lost you." She let him take her hand this time. "We have to at least try to get the police on our side now, and I think we have enough evidence to make a worthwhile effort."

"Fine," Tracy said, closing her eyes. "But I'll be pissed if you let them throw you back in prison."

Chris smiled. "Well, if I tell the PD that, I'm sure they'll see our side of things."

CHAPTER TWENTY-THREE

S ILENCE DOMINATED THE CAB RIDE to Tracy's apartment, broken by the occasional muffled squeals of the tires or a jolting bump as the cab hit one of the many potholes that pockmarked Baltimore's streets. Each time the car jostled in response to the shoddy roads, Chris winced. He gazed out the window nearest him, while Tracy stared out her window.

While the air still bit with a cold wind, the sun pierced the gray clouds. Treacherous icy patches melted into puddles of water, and the sunlight warmed his skin. People milled about on sidewalks toward clothes boutiques and coffee shops, bags in tow. Laughing, chatting, everyone seemed in a better mood than the one that pervaded their taxi. His eyes, it seemed, unconsciously sought out couples walking side by side, hand in hand, and he scoffed aloud. Everyone else probably fought about stupid things like whose turn it was to do the dishes or who left the toilet seat up. The arguments that characterized his relationships possessed an unhealthy habit of revolving around illegal genetic enhancement conspiracies.

"What?" Tracy turned to him, her narrowed eyes expressing a sour sentiment.

"Nothing." Chris shook his head.

"What?"

"Really, nothing."

She sighed and turned back out the window, her chin resting in her hand.

Blocks away from her apartment, a pressing thought made Chris straighten up. He stared at the back of Tracy's head for a moment before speaking. "Maybe this is stupid, but do you think it's possible those guys might show up at your place?"

A brief glimmer of something—hope, happiness, maybe—shone in her eyes before she frowned. "The Corvette guys, you mean? Shit, I don't know. I didn't think that they caught a glimpse of me or even know who I am, but you might be right." She pushed her palm into her forehead. "Oh, God. They probably saw me with you that night they killed Randy. Dammit. They could be at my place."

He shrugged. "Could be. I didn't see them at my place today."

"I suppose we should put a hold on your plan for now, huh?"

Chris input a new destination in the taxi's display. The cab passed by the main entrance to Tracy's apartment and took a left to circle around the blocky gray building.

"Wait. Where are we going?" Tracy asked.

"We'll just make a lap around the block to make sure we don't see the Corvette."

"What if they aren't in a Corvette now? They could be in any one of those other cars, more inconspicuous now."

"That's right," he said. "They could be in every single car in the whole goddamned city, and we'd never know. The least we can do is look for the car we recognize. If it's not here, we'll just hope they didn't switch cars. And if they did get a new car, it's not like we can just hide in Jordan's apartment for the rest of our lives and worry that every single passing car is going to start chasing us."

Tracy slumped back into her seat.

"Besides, we'll take the stairwell entrance on Vine Street," Chris said. "Stay out of eyesight of Lexington."

"Fine."

They exited the cab, Chris following Tracy, and took the stairs up to her floor. As they walked toward her apartment, another door opened. A woman wearing exercise clothes waved. "Hey, I don't mean to be a bother, but can I talk to you real quick?"

"We're kind of in a hurry." Tracy walked past to her own door.

The woman followed. "An awful lot of noise came from your apartment last night. I didn't want to call the police or anything—I mean, you've been a good neighbor and all. But it might be nice to give us a heads up if you're planning a big party."

"But I wasn't here last night." Tracy furrowed her brow. "Are you sure it came from my apartment?"

"I guess it might not have been, but I could've sworn it did," her neighbor said.

Chris's pulse quickened as he stepped toward Tracy's apartment door.

"Well, thanks for telling me." Tracy waved as the woman continued back down the hallway toward the elevator. "What the hell do you think that's about? You think those assholes got into my place?" Her expression turned hopeful. "Hell, maybe they left something behind that might help us find 'em."

He shrugged. Tracy's lips drew tight as she approached her apartment. His pulse throbbed louder in his ears as she slowly turned the door handle. Chris thrust out an arm in front of her. "Wait. Let me do it."

She raised an eyebrow but let him pass in front of her. He inched the door open, but no one jumped out. He couldn't hear any sounds from within besides the whooshing flow of heated air through vents in the ceiling and floor.

Hesitating a moment, he turned back to her. "I don't see anyone or anything, yet." He pushed the door the rest of the way open and froze. Again, his pulse quickened and his eyes opened wide as he took in the scene before them. He stepped into the room, taking care to avoid the fallen lamp in his path. Little glass shards sparkled on the hardwood floor like glinting snowflakes. Drawers in the kitchen were haphazardly open, most with spilled contents spread across the tiled kitchen floor.

The coat closet gaped wide open, with coats and shoes tossed about in front of it as if a bomb had exploded from within. Tracy went into the apartment, picking up her coats and placing them in a pile to clear a walkway. The sofa in the living room area lay on its back, the cushions torn and fabric across the bottom of the couch slashed. Tracy kicked at the loose stuffing. "What in the hell?"

"Where are the samples?"

Tracy's head snapped up. "Holy shit, I can't believe I forgot. We left them on the counter, right?"

Chris glanced at the granite countertop. A couple of broken glasses, scattered silverware, and boxes of dry noodles, ripped and spilling penne and vermicelli pasta, lay where they had left the silver freezer box with the rest of the samples. "They took it. All we've got left are the two vials we sent with Jordan." He shook his head. "I'm not even sure if the one I took will be ruined or not. I should've just left it with you."

"No, we needed to be safe," Tracy said. She stepped over a chair that had been tossed aside. The kitchen table, too, had been flipped upside down. "What the hell is this?" Her face flushed red. "They must have seen the samples right away. They got what they wanted. Why'd they need to fuck the whole place up?"

Chris, jaw set and eyes darting wildly, peered into the bedroom. He threw open the closet doors and checked the bathroom, looking behind the door and peeling back the shower curtain. He found no sign that anyone remained in the small apartment.

Satisfied, he stepped back out into the kitchen area. He cursed at himself, wondering how he could have been so careless, what he had done to lead them back to Tracy, to where she lived. How fortunate that she and Jordan had convinced him to stay at Jordan's place the night before. Had they stayed here, had Tracy been alone…Chris could not bear to imagine being responsible for her abduction or death. He surveyed the scene again and used a dish towel to collect the broken glass on the countertop into a pile. "It wasn't just about the samples. It's more than that."

Righting one of the kitchen chairs, Tracy sat down in it. "They know that I'm in this with you. That damned businessman wants me to stay out."

"Exactly. They're sending a message."

Tracy's narrowed eyes and tight grimace gave way to a mischievous grin. "They took Randy's notebook, too."

"And that makes you happy?"

She stood up. "That means you aren't going to be able to go to the police now, are you? We've got almost nothing except for a couple crumpled papers and the vials that Jordan has."

Chris kicked at the glass shards on the ground. "Dammit." Then his eyes wandered out the window. "We do have a notebook, though. I should've mentioned this before."

"What are you talking about?"

"Vincent, or Jeremy Kar as you know him. He kept a journal when we were cellmates. Maybe there's something in there that can help us."

Tracy stepped toward him, slapping him on the shoulder. "Why the hell didn't you say anything about that before? I can't believe that. I mean, it's probably a long shot, but we don't have anything to lose by looking. Do we need to drop by your place to pick it up?"

Rubbing his shoulder, Chris smiled. "Nope. It's back at Jordan's."

"God, I hope there is something in there to connect all this together. If we get a hold of that businessman's little neck..." Tracy trailed off, wringing her hands together, her eyes aflame in a fierce, distant gaze.

"If we get a hold of him, we'll turn him in to the police and make him face the consequences—legally—of what he's done." His thoughts turned to Veronica. He hoped the businessman had done nothing else in the hours since he'd seen her. "We'll make sure he pays."

CHAPTER TWENTY-FOUR

THE SUN SET OVER THE Chesapeake, and Jordan's apartment glowed in a fury of orange and red hues. Waves of amber light floated in through the windows around his home, giving the penthouse a peaceful ambiance.

Chris basked in the glow of the warm colors and stretched his arms above his head, yawning. "Should we bother going in to work tomorrow?"

"Yeah, I think we should," Tracy said. "You're probably right that these people will be watching out for us, but we can't risk acting too suspicious, either." She held up her index finger. "Plus, we'd be risking our jobs just not showing up like that."

"I worry we'd be risking our lives by going."

"I don't know. I don't think that this guy is willing to blow his cover by attacking us in the middle of a work day in a busy downtown business district—don't you agree?"

"I just don't want them to follow us back to Jordan's." He traced his tongue around the inside of his lips. "Then, again, they didn't worry about trashing your place quietly."

The merry-go-round of anxiety circled in his mind as his worries flitted from his concern for Tracy, Jordan, and

Veronica to his curiosity about the businessman's motives, Randy's involvement in this complex scenario, and why it all had started with a series of deaths in a prison miles from here.

Jordan sat down on the couch. He passed out glasses of merlot. Inhaling from his, he swirled the wine and sipped it. "I'd rather you two stay safe in this building, where we've got, if you'll excuse me for saying so, much more robust security than either of your places." He raised his glass to the wide windows that let in the last rays of the sun. "Plus, we've got Greg."

Greg nodded and smiled from an armchair that matched the L-shaped couch where Chris, Tracy, and Jordan sat. He was absorbed in a novel projecting from his comm card.

"How's it looking so far?" Jordan asked.

Tracy frowned and shot a look at Chris.

"Your third draft is certainly better than the first. I'm still a bit confused by Mandy's motives after killing her husband, but I'm hoping that'll be a bit clearer when we get to the point where Adam turns the whole company around."

"I hope so too," Jordan said.

Chris smiled but anxiously tapped on the bottom of his wine glass. "Are you going to tell us what you found now? We have something we'd like to look at sooner rather than later." When Tracy and Chris had arrived back at Jordan's apartment, prepared to delve into Vincent's notebook for possible clues, Jordan had persuaded them to have a seat to discuss his day's findings at the lab first.

"Ah, I love a good bit of suspense." His lips parted as his teeth shone in a wide grin. "It's been a long while since I did any benchwork myself. I've been far more comfortable on the business side of things, if you will. But I relished the opportunity to get back to my roots. I'll admit I considered getting back into the development side of things with my equine genetic enhancement projects." He took another slow, antagonizing sip of wine. "But Greg reminded me I've placed far too many irons in the fire. If I'm to be serious about running a company, I can't stretch myself too thin."

Tracy let out an audible sigh. "That's true. That's all true, Jordan. I don't mean to be rude, but what the hell did you find out today?"

Jordan chortled. "You're right. I'm being inconsiderate."

"People's lives are in danger, Jordan. Please, I appreciate everything you've done for us but like Tracy asked, what did you find?"

Another long sip. The remainder of Jordan's wine vanished as he pulled the glass from his lips. "Well, my friend, I'm afraid I haven't been able to answer the questions you asked me to find out."

"What's that supposed to mean?" Tracy's eyes narrowed and she leaned forward over the edge of her seat. Her wine glass sat neglected on the aged and preserved tree trunk that served as a coffee table.

"Quite simply, it means that there was nothing to be found."

Chris's jaw dropped. "In both samples? Were they ruined?"

"No, no." Jordan shook his hand, waving away Chris's concerns. "We found delivery vectors in your samples. Fully intact, as you had designed them."

"I don't follow," Tracy said. "Talk straight, please."

"The delivery vectors were made of your printed DNA material. Small nanocapsules, similar to the designs we made when we were in the business together. A work of beauty. Elegant and ingenious, I always thought.

"Anyway, those were easy enough to characterize with a healthy dose of transmission electron microscopy and a couple of follow-up DNA content analyses. They seemed to comprise elements of those early capsules you designed, along with those of the colon cancer project you described to me; though, as far as we could tell, the delivery vectors didn't contain anything."

"No," Chris said. "That doesn't make any sense. Why would Randy have bothered keeping samples of empty vectors?"

"There was one difference," Jordan said. "Instead of targeting epithelial colon cells, they targeted molecules for neuron cells. That much I did find."

"What do you think they're supposed to do?" Chris asked.

"Maybe my own predications are colored by our previous experiences, but it seems Randy—or whoever he worked for—wanted to deliver genetic enhancements to the nervous system."

"Well, yes, I understand that." Chris frowned.

"Remember how your strength enhancements focused on skeletal myocytes? They produced nice increases in muscle cell size and strength, but that's not the sole way to produce strength gains, though everyone in the enhancement business focuses on those methods."

Tracy nodded, putting down the glass after her first sip of wine. "No, you're right. Most initial strength gains during training are a result of more or less getting your nervous system to do a better job of recruiting muscle fibers and cells."

"Precisely," Jordan said. "Now, if I must guess, I think that this businessman of yours wants to combine your work with DNA-based vectors with your old experience in loading those vectors with genetic strength enhancements. Could you imagine the gains someone might achieve by targeting both the nervous system and skeletal muscles simultaneously?"

Chris nodded. "I still don't understand why I'm involved in this at all, though. You've got to remember that we faced pretty fierce competition."

"I couldn't forget." Jordan settled back into the couch and crossed one leg over the other. "But I always knew you were talented. Someone else must have picked up on that, too."

"Come on. I'm no super genius. There are plenty of others in genetic enhancements, both legal and illegal, that have better products. I just made the delivery vectors better." Chris tossed up his hands in defeat. "Now it looks like our friend Randy found no issue replicating my delivery vectors. This businessman guy doesn't even need me."

"He's right, Jordan," Tracy said. "There's got to be something else here. Are you sure you didn't find anything else in those samples? You checked both vials, right?"

"I'm positive. One thing's for certain, though. These people know what they're doing on a scientific level. And if everything you've told me is true, I think you might be in over your head chasing these ghosts around."

"Ghosts?" Chris shook his head. "This isn't a Bigfoot chase. This is real. People's lives are at stake here. Your life might be at stake."

"I'll admit that I was frightened when Tracy first explained everything to me. This isn't the first time anyone's threatened my life, directly or not. You should know that as well as anyone. Could it be that your friend Randy tried to analyze these samples himself? Maybe he became involved in this business. Maybe he wanted to track down this businessman friend of yours."

Tracy's forehead wrinkled as she appeared to contemplate Jordan's statements. "That still doesn't make sense with the prison attacks or clear up anything about the list we found in Randy's notebook."

"I'm only thinking aloud." Jordan examined his empty wine glass, rolling the stem between his fingers. "In truth, I'm more in the dark about any of this than you are. Either way, I think you ought to let things cool for a week or two. Then I suggest you forget about all of this. Sometimes it's better to act as though nothing has happened if you want to move on. The more you know, the more reasons these people will find for eliminating you. You're both becoming a growing risk to their business or whatever it is they're doing. Death is an inevitable cost of running an organization like theirs." He let out a slow breath. "Or like ours was."

Chris massaged his temples. He felt the budding of a headache. "I never killed anyone. Hell, you know I wouldn't be in favor of that."

Standing up, Jordan walked to the edge of the room and peered out the window. Night swallowed Baltimore. Lights from apartment windows, streetlights, and the headlights and taillights of cars passing along the streets shone like stars, reflecting on the windows. Above the city, clouds obscured the real stars. "You may not have killed anyone. But when people encroached on our business, do you think we won out purely by the quality of our product? I tried to keep you out of it, but that side of the business is inescapable."

"What are you saying?"

Jordan swiveled back around to face Tracy and Chris. He closed his eyes and lowered his head. "I deeply regret it. When we sold enhancements, I employed a couple of men to do the dirty work much like your businessman does now. A necessary evil to ensure payments were made and competition remained scarce. Something that's not necessary in horse racing." He looked up at them and offered a weak smile.

The throbbing pain in Chris's head intensified. His stomach flipped and he gagged, stifling an intense urge to vomit.

"You need to find a way out of this," Jordan said. "Trying to follow the lion back to his den is not the way to do that."

Chris rested his elbows on the tree-trunk coffee table and put his head in his hands as he willed his stomach to settle. The onset of the headache was just another painful coincidence. Too many coincidences, too many questions. He massaged his temples.

"I'm sorry. I know that's a lot to take in."

Tracy stood up. "You know something else, don't you?" Her raised voice resonated in Chris's ears and felt like knives sticking into his brain. "There's something you're hiding. About the samples."

Jordan shook his head. "No."

"You know this businessman," she said. "That's it. That's why you took me in when I showed up at your doorstep. When I mentioned Chris made a deal with this guy, you knew who I was talking about. Who is he? Where is he?"

"I am telling you what's best for you," Jordan said. "This man that you describe is dangerous. His organization is dangerous." He pointed at Chris. "Getting arrested, spending time in jail, protective custody, and then prison probably saved your life. I didn't know why people were being killed, but too many people in the alternative genetic enhancement business died. Falling into the Chesapeake, muggings gone bad, hiking accidents in Patapsco Valley, for God's sake. The police never cared to follow up on those cases, of course. All I know is that when people on the streets started dying, I got myself out of the business. Later on, I heard descriptions of this guy, pale and scrawny but always wearing a suit and shades, running the big new genie business in town. I don't think anyone knows what he calls himself or his group, but it didn't matter. I'm glad I got out when I did. Now, dealing with horses, no one bothers me. I don't know what they're up to anymore, either, and that suits me just fine."

Jordan took a deep breath and continued. "I'm still alive today because of that decision. I've done you a favor, I've analyzed your samples, but I have to at least advise you not to go down this rabbit hole. If you want to stay alive, you need to get the hell out of Baltimore and give this up or be prepared to face the consequences."

"I can't. My parole," Chris said. His words came out like a pathetic whimper. "I'll be arrested as soon as they think I'm fleeing their supervision."

"Then I suggest you do what this mystery man says, stop pestering him, and end your business with him as soon as possible. It's in your best interest." Jordan's eyes glanced from Chris to Tracy. "Yours, too."

"If the police aren't involved, do you think you should just give up on this?" Tracy asked Chris. "If this businessman is so dangerous, why should we trust that doing him any kind of favor will mean that we're safe?"

"I don't know." Chris tried to reason through his pounding head. "What right do I have to try to stop a guy from running an illegal gene enhancement operation?"

Her eyes narrowed, Tracy spoke in a cold voice. "You said it yourself. People's lives are at risk."

"So are ours."

"This isn't just about us anymore. Do you think it's going to be that easy to just tell the man you'll do as he says, that we'll just go back to living like we did before we stole those samples? Before they chased you down? Before they wrecked my apartment? Even if you say it's over, it won't be over. Not by a long shot." With those words still echoing in Chris's skull, Tracy stomped out of the sitting area and down the hall toward the guest bedroom.

His hands on his face, Chris peered through his fingers at Jordan. "What the hell am I supposed to do? You think I can just go back to life as normal?"

Jordan shrugged. "I wish you could. I want you to." He leaned forward and put a hand on Chris's knee. "I don't want to see you hurt. I know I didn't keep in contact with you once you got arrested, and that's on me. I thought it best to put distance between us, lest we both go down."

"I understand."

"I left you out to dry as soon as the PD came knocking. It wasn't right, my man. I want to make it up to you. I want you to think about this. I don't approve of you and that hot-tempered girl trying to bring down a genetic enhancement ring all by yourselves. I don't think you can win."

Chris leaned back on the couch.

Sitting down beside him, Jordan sighed and shook his head. "Still, I'm not going to let you do this alone. You've got my resources at your disposal, so long as we can maintain a certain level of inconspicuousness. Even though I don't agree with finding this businessman, if you need anything, I'll do my best to be there for you. Please, think this through."

Chris patted Jordan's shoulder. "I appreciate it. I do. For now, could I just get a couple of aspirins?"

CHAPTER TWENTY-FIVE

T HE STEAM AND HEAT ENCIRCLED Chris, numbing the throbbing in his head. As a child, he'd experienced almost daily headaches. Children's pain relievers could never quell the intense pain. His headaches rendered him bedridden on their worst days. Any amount of light would pierce his eyes like a thousand tiny daggers digging into his brain.

He'd found respite in the shower's embrace. Each drop of water contributed to a beautiful sonata of relief. The humid air expanded and cleared his sinuses, letting him breathe fresh, new air, and enjoined the constricted vessels beneath his skull to dilate, bringing with it the promise of fresh oxygen. No amount of medicine suited for children's pain relief could produce the same effect.

Now he sought to rid himself again of the pain in his head. His neurologist could never explain the root of his migraines, resorting to ancient myths of associations with a minor congenital heart defect that consisted of a tiny hole in his atrial septum. The hole allowed the mixing of oxygenated and deoxygenated blood but was not large enough to warrant percutaneous intervention. Because of this, the neurologist had referenced a few studies that claimed an association between an existing septal defect and migraines.

The defect still existed. Without any kind of intervention, it had not magically plugged itself. Yet he had outgrown the migraines for the most part. Now they struck him at times like when he'd been convicted and sentenced to prison or when he'd left Veronica or when he'd found out his mother had died of treatable liver cancer because she'd refused nanotreatments, chemotherapy, and irradiation in favor of homeopathic remedies. His headaches hit him in times of extreme stress.

Stepping out of the shower, he tousled his hair with a towel. Steam obscured the mirror, and only a vague pinkish shape stared back at him from the fog. The last remnants of his headache seemed to undulate like sirens from an ambulance racing into the distance. Slight, weak waves of this distant pain broke against his skull.

Maybe this was what it would feel like to keep moving forward, to keep confusing himself as he sought more answers. More headaches, physical and otherwise.

He opened the door, and a rush of cool air fought to beat back the escaping plumes of humidity from the bathroom. Tracy sat on the bed, her legs crossed and her shoulders scrunched, as she studied a leather notebook. Vincent's notebook.

"If Jordan won't help us, we'll have to do this on our own." Tracy glared, though she didn't look up at Chris.

The towel wrapped around his waist, he sat beside her. "He said he would help. He doesn't want us to get hurt, but he'll help us."

She exhaled. "Sure, I guess that's nice. But I still don't trust him."

"You don't trust him?" Chris folded his arms across his bare chest. "After he put us up here? After he risked his neck analyzing the samples?"

Tracy put the notebook down in her lap. "It's not that I don't think he has good intentions. It's just that we should keep anything else we find out, anything else we do, between ourselves. If we tell Jordan and the police interrogate him—or worse, the businessman does something to him—it'd be best if they know less about what we are up to."

"It's not like we know anything anyway."

With an accusatory frown, she pursed her lips. "Seriously?" Her frown gave way to a triumphant smile.

"I don't understand you. One minute, you're pissed and stomping off, and the next you have that goofy grin spread across your face."

She pointed at Vincent's notebook. "It's because I found something."

The letters *A*, *U*, *C*, and *G* lined the page. "What the hell is this?"

Sticking her finger between the pages to hold her place, Tracy flipped through the other pages in the notebook. A smattering of doodles and words erupted across the pages. She stopped again at the entry littered with the random letters. "Every page but this one just seems normal."

"All right, so you think Vincent went through a crazy spell?"

"Far from it," Tracy said, the smirk spreading across her face again. She cocked a dubious eyebrow at Chris's blank expression. "You don't follow? Need me to walk you through your elementary biology again?"

His eyes widened as he mouthed an "Oh." He shook his head. "I can't believe I almost missed that. Holy shit."

"'Holy shit' is right. Looks like RNA, doesn't it?"

Chris nodded. "Does this translate to anything? It seems too short for any useful protein."

"It does seem to translate to something," she said, "but I don't think it's a protein."

"What do you mean?"

"Well, I already checked it against our protein databases to see if it matched anything, but I came up with nothing. I think it's a message."

Tracy's infectious smile spread to his face. He squinted at the letters. "So, we just need to translate each three-letter codon into an amino acid."

She nodded. "I already knocked out the first few codons: arginine, glutamic acid, and asparagine. Then, he left a little space." She squinted at the paper. "I think it's a space, anyway. There are spaces that appear a little larger between the codons." She pointed at another three-letter codon. "See, here? This is a stop codon. I'm guessing it's at the end of the sentence because there's another space here."

Chris studied the page. "I think you're right."

They translated each codon into an amino acid, then identified each amino acid with its corresponding single-letter code. When they had completed the page-long code, both of them stared at the jumbled letters.

"Ren kavfman has material in chris morgan, terrence hart, rrady allen, gqrdqn katz. If dead ask them."

Scanning the letters with his fingers, he mouthed the letters aloud. "This can't be right."

"Yes, I'm certain it is," Tracy said. "And those Qs in the code? Obviously, they're actually Os, since there is no amino acid that translates to an O. And, I think we both know where we've seen a few of those names before."

"Randy's list."

"Right. At least, most of the names are from Randy's list. But there's one that I don't recognize: Ren Kavfman."

"Who do you think Ren Kavfman is?"

She scoffed. "I don't think it's a Ren Kavfman, for starters. If I need to guess, it looks like Vincent subbed in an *R* in Brady Allen, since there are no single-letter codes for any amino acid that corresponds to *B*. So Ben sounds like a much more believable first name, doesn't it?"

Chris rolled his eyes. "I suppose you're right. But, Kavfman?"

"Maybe Kaufman, with a *U*?"

He nodded. "Sounds better than Ren Kavfman. There's no Ben Kaufman on Randy's list."

"No. There isn't," Tracy said. "But what makes me shit my pants is that last sentence."

He cringed, both at her choice of words and at the phrase that she highlighted with her index finger. "'If dead, ask them?' It sounds like Vincent knew more than he ever let on. But if this was a cryptic warning, this is pretty lousy code."

"Yeah, you've got that right." Tracy sighed. "I bet he banked on the fact that your average prison guard—or prisoner, for that matter—would not have a frigging clue what the hell all those *A*s, *U*s, *G*s, and *C*s meant. But he'd be smart enough to know that if anything did happen to him, if he did get murdered, county forensics would be able to decode that."

"He wanted whoever killed him, or whoever might be responsible, to get caught," he said. "He suspected something, didn't he? I mean, he knew all these names, for God's sake."

"It seems to me like your roommate was guilty of more than just killing his wife and her lover, huh?"

"Not my roommate. Cellmate."

Tracy scoffed. "Is there a difference?"

Chris rolled his eyes and turned back to the message as they had translated it: "Ben Kaufman has material in Chris Morgan, Terrence Hart, Brady Allen, Gordon Katz. If dead, ask them."

He reasoned that the list of names here at least accounted for most of the names in Randy's notebook. But he had never talked to Terrence or Brady or Gordon. He had no idea how they were connected with him.

Not only did Ben Kaufman appear nowhere on Randy's list, but enough Ben Kaufmans existed online to prevent them from identifying any particular suspect. They tried to filter their results with terms related to genetic enhancements, drug delivery, and any other biotech jargon they could conjure, but just as many questions remained. None of the Ben Kaufmans they found appeared to be their suspect. On the other hand, if their Ben Kaufman was related to the businessman, Chris doubted the man would be foolish enough to list himself in any public directory.

Tracy fell back against the bed, her arms spread across the gray comforter. "Who the hell are you, Ben Kaufman?"

He let his body drop beside her. "I want to know what Vincent meant by the part about the 'material is inside' me and those other guys."

With her index finger, she prodded his chest. "You have hidden superpowers. Kryptonite."

"Come on." Chris swatted her hand away. He turned on his side. "Besides, kryptonite makes Superman weak, not strong."

Tracy raised an eyebrow. "Does it matter?" Then, her expression froze. Her eyes wandered away from him and seemed to stare at something far past the walls of the bedroom. "What if this Ben Kaufman is your businessman?"

He raised himself up on an elbow. "How do you figure that?"

"It might explain his interest in you. Let's just operate under the assumption that 'material in' you could just be a mistake. Maybe, it should be 'material on' you."

"I don't buy it. Vincent used *Q*s as *O*s."

"Doesn't mean he didn't make a slight mistake." She sat up on the edge of the bed again. "This issue's trivial, anyway. What we can ascertain, I think, is that Ben Kaufman has an interest in you, Terrence, Brady, and Gordon. Since the other three are dead, all he has left is you. Don't you think it's odd that you get released from prison early, right after getting stabbed, and that businessman—let's just call him Ben, now—shows up to offer you a job?"

Chris shrugged. "Of course, I've always found it odd."

"I think you've got something he wants. Or know something that he wants to know."

With a disbelieving laugh, he shook his head. "I wish I knew what that was. I'd give it to him if it meant all this craziness would stop."

Tracy dismissed him with a wave of her hand. "I think he's trying to protect you until he's ready for something."

"The guy who threatens to hurt anyone I have an association with is trying to protect me?"

"Absolutely. I think he wouldn't care about hurting anyone else, but any threat against you is just hot air. He wants you scared so you'll do what he says."

"Then how do you explain the guys chasing me down?"

"Maybe they didn't chase you down to hurt you."

"That's ridiculous. I mean, the guy said he wasn't going to hurt me, but why else would he chase me?"

"They probably wanted to protect you from me."

Chris's eyes widened as he stared at Tracy. Her lips drew tight and her eyes appeared cold. Then she grinned.

"Okay," she said. "Maybe not from me, but they might have thought something or someone threatened your life. That blue-eyed guy almost killed you, but he let you go."

His hand shot up to his bruised neck, and he massaged it. "Yeah, if I recall correctly, the other guy with him said something about me being the one."

"The one." She grinned again. "See, you're the One destined to save the world." Her voice lifted in a majestic, throaty tone. "You have the kryptonite."

He frowned. "Please, let's just focus on figuring out who Ben Kaufman is."

"You are being such a sour puss." Tracy slapped Chris on the shoulder.

He winced but forced a weak smile to subdue her humor. "I guess I just have a hard time finding all this funny when I saw a coworker murdered and the guy responsible is threatening to kill everybody I know."

Tracy's smile faded. "Sorry." She placed a hand on his leg, giving him a quick squeeze. "I've got a strong hunch that Ben wants something from you and he's trying to protect you."

"Didn't do such a good job of that if he let all the other guys die on his watch." Chris furrowed his brow and shook his head. "In fact, those buffoons of his killed Randy."

"Yes, but his name was not in Vincent's little code like yours. Ben doesn't have materials on or in Randy, whatever that means. Maybe Randy was after you and they took him out for your benefit."

"That doesn't make a hell of a lot of sense."

"No shit. None of it does. I'm just trying to offer suggestions here." Tracy crossed her arms across her chest. "What have you thought of so far?"

Chris exhaled, closing his eyes. The throbbing in his head returned. He brushed his hair back and shivered. He got off the bed and knelt down next to the duffel bag with the clothing he had retrieved from his apartment. Digging around, he found a pair of boxers. He pulled them on and then grabbed a white t-shirt.

The white scars along his sides, a few long, several jagged, stuck out against his olive complexion. Accompanying the dull pain in his head, fragmented memories of that day in the prison rushed back to him. He recalled the blur of arms reaching out at him, the pricks and tears, the wet, warm blood.

Then, just as quickly as his attackers had fallen on him, they had been tackled and lifted from him by his ostensible protector. Lash.

Lash's hulking muscles, his blood vessels dilated and bulging, his eyes bloodshot. Beads of sweat rolling over his dark skin. For all the man's aggressiveness, there was a gentleness in Lash's eyes as the action subsided, as the guards beat back the riot.

No, not just a gentleness, but a sorrow. Lash did not feel any sympathy for him. In fact, he recalled Lash barking at him to stay still. Nothing but rote duty showed in the way he'd treated Chris.

"Oh God."

Tracy froze while tying her hair back behind her head. "What?"

"Lash protected me. Not because he gave a shit about me, but because he needed to. He was supposed to. And the look on his face after the riot ended...he looked like he could cry."

He looked at himself in the mirror again. "He didn't give a shit about me." He turned to Tracy. "Maybe you're right. Maybe this Ben, or whoever, wanted to protect me. Maybe he tried to protect those others too. And Lash—I bet there were others—had been conscripted to protect us in the prison. Lash failed, though. You could see it in his face. I was the only one left after that riot. And he knew it. Oh, God. Yes. He knew it. If Ben threatened me, I bet he threatened Lash."

He plopped onto the edge of the bed, tracing his fingers over the stubble on his chin and cheeks. A shiver coursed down his spine and through his arms.

"What's Lash's real name?"

"What?" Chris's head shot around to face her.

"What's his real name? I want to see if you're right."

"How?"

Tracy raised an eyebrow but said nothing.

Holding one hand up in a protective gesture, he scratched at his head. He hadn't even known Vincent's real name; how could he remember the name of a man he hardly knew? Then he recalled one man who *had* known Lash from outside prison. The man had taunted Lash, called him out, blackmailed Lash in front of other prisoners. He had yelled from the safety of his own cell.

During recreation, Lash had silenced the man. But it wasn't that man that had spoken Lash's name. A couple of security guards had broken up the fight. One had announced Lash's name loudly, telling Lash to come with him immediately. "I think it was Eli, or Elijah, Bierma."

"Unique enough." Tracy input the name on her comm card. Her mouth fell open. Chris imagined he could hear her heart stop beating. "When did the riot happen?"

"October twenty-second."

"Three dead in a fire that police suspect may have been a result of arson. Marianne, Beatrice, and Calvin Bierma. Survived by their husband and father, Elijah Bierma, incarcerated in Fulton State Prison. October twenty-third." Her eyes left the comm card projection and caught Chris's. "This can't be a coincidence."

"No. No, it can't be." He grasped at his throbbing temples as his blood pulsed in his ears.

CHAPTER TWENTY-SIX

L OST DEEP IN SLEEP, TRACY rolled to face him. Even in the darkness, her lips curled ever so slightly in a satisfied little smile. Chris draped an arm over her shoulder, hugging her warm body against his. He stared into the shadows cast by the dresser nearest the window, where the soft glow of streetlights plunged through the windows. No matter how hard he pressed his eyelids closed, he could not fall asleep.

His thoughts drifted to the past. In high school, he had tried out for *Spring Awakening* and *Into the Woods*. He'd been first in line for *The Crucible*, too. But try as he might, he'd never scored a single part. Instead, the drama instructor would put him on set construction duty. Mrs. Sage had told him he wouldn't ever amount to much of an actor. Tomorrow, he would need to forget her damning words. As the reality of his situation with Ben Kaufman—if that's who the businessman really was—sank in, he realized that he would need to feign innocence the farther he delved into Kaufman's illegal genetic enhancement exploits and the surrounding deaths.

Those thoughts swirled in his mind, blending into dreams until morning came with the glare of light on his face. The heat on his skin felt as if the window were a magnifying glass and he an unfortunate ant, victim of a giant, malevolent child.

Tracy slumbered on next to him. They were close enough to Respondent that they didn't need to rush from Jordan's place, so he left her to make himself a cup of coffee. He trudged into the kitchen, where the aroma and gurgle of brewing coffee provided him a small respite from the heaviness in his sagging eyelids.

"Morning, my man." Jordan, freshly shaved and wearing a crisp button-down shirt, smiled. "Tracy do that to you?"

Chris rubbed the faded bruises on his neck and yawned. "What?"

The coffeemaker sputtered to a stop.

"Just a joke." Jordan sighed. "You look awful. Coffee?"

Chris nodded and Jordan poured the hot liquid into one of three empty mugs he had placed on that counter.

"You still use an old coffeepot like that?"

Jordan smiled. "I know it seems antiquated, but I find it better suited to serving guests. With a single-prep maker, it's every man for himself, and that doesn't seem to me well suited for a welcoming atmosphere."

Chris lifted himself onto a wooden stool at the breakfast bar in Jordan's kitchen. The black granite bar offset the clean white floors and crimson cabinetry.

After pouring a mug for himself, Jordan leaned on the edge of the breakfast bar. "Did you and Tracy give any more thought to what I said last night?"

"We did. I think we're going to just take this thing a little further."

Jordan appeared disappointed, but his mouth curled into a wry grin. "Is it the both of you that want to find out who this businessman of yours is, or is it just her?" He traced the rim of the mug with his index finger. "She has an insatiable appetite for solving mysteries, doesn't she?"

Chris smiled. He admired Tracy's intellectual curiosity and her dogged fervor when pursuing answers to seemingly insurmountable problems, whether it was finding the proper genetic coding sequence for a colon cancer treatment or unraveling the mystery behind Kaufman. "Definitely. But I also think she's right. She's always stubborn when she's right. I figure I get a hold of this man and tell him it's now or never. I'll give him what he wants before he hurts anyone else."

Jordan cocked his head. "You don't know why Randy died. You don't know why any of those people died. How can you be sure he won't kill you even if you do follow through on his request?"

"I can't," Chris said. He inhaled the steam that rose from his warm mug. "But it's the best I can do. The police aren't in a position to believe me, anyway, if I don't have any evidence. They'll think I'm just throwing them on a wild goose chase to prevent them from bringing me in for Randy's murder."

"Which you think will make them suspect you all the more."

"Right."

With no further acknowledgment of his decision, Jordan pressed his mug to his lips and closed his eyes.

"Why are you up so early, anyway? I never would've believed you were up at this hour if I didn't see you myself."

"For my guests, of course."

"I know you always play a good host, but I never saw you up at this hour unless you had stayed up the whole night. What's the story?"

"You've caught me." Jordan held up his hands. "I've made it a daily habit to rise early and fulfill my writing requirements for the day. One thousand words, no matter how long it takes me, must be written before I do anything else. I do take my novel writing seriously, you know." He took another long drink from his coffee. "And I don't mean to be rude, but you've interrupted my daily ritual." He smiled.

"By all means, get to your writing. Don't let me stop you."

"Then that I will do. I bid you adieu." Jordan bowed, flourishing his hands as he removed an invisible hat.

"You're ridiculous. Don't let anyone tell you otherwise."

Jordan smiled as he opened the door to his study and nodded back to Chris. He disappeared into the office, and the French doors began to close behind him.

"Ah, wait a second."

A door swung back open and Jordan poked his head back out.

"Does the name Ben or Benjamin Kaufman mean anything to you?"

Jordan frowned. "I'm not sure that it does."

Chris recalled his conversation with Tracy last night. She had said she didn't want to involve Jordan in their pursuit of the businessman and his identity. He covered a yawn with his hand and continued on anyway. "Does our deal from last night still stand?"

Jordan nodded.

"In that case, could I ask you a huge favor? Is there any way you might find out if any Benjamin Kaufman had been involved with illegal drugs or gene production or enhancements or anything like that?"

"That's a rather broad net."

Chris pictured Tracy's face flashing red in his mind. He trusted Jordan, though. He needed the man's help. "I know, I know. I'm sorry, but we found the name connected to mine, among others from that list Tracy told you about when she first came here."

"Mmhmm. I'll see if Greg can scrounge anything up on this Benjamin Kaufman of yours. Do you suspect he's connected to your mysterious businessman?"

"Maybe." He shrugged. "But who knows anymore?"

Taking separate cabs as an extra measure of safety from any suspicious coworkers or secretive stalkers in black Corvettes, Chris arrived at work almost ten minutes after Tracy. He walked through the lobby and up to the elevator without sparking any special considerations from the two security guards stationed in the lobby. None of his fellow elevator passengers greeted him with anything more than a cursory smile. Still, he could not quell the electricity coursing through his nerves.

His fingers trembled, so he clenched his fists. He made his way past the usual desks until he reached his.

A hand patted him on the shoulder and he jumped.

"Whoa, sorry. Didn't mean to scare you," Paul said. "You okay? You don't look so hot."

"Just exhausted. What's up?"

"Claire came by for you earlier."

"Claire? Why?"

"She said she wanted to talk to you when you got in today. Didn't tell me anything else."

"Okay. Thanks." In truth, he dreaded the news. Apprehension filled him. His armpits already responded with a nervous sweat. He trudged back down the hall to the entrance of the floor and took a right toward the office of the vice president of research in the executive suite.

He greeted the receptionist, Scott, outside the suite.

"Claire wanted to see me," Chris said.

"She's in meetings for the rest of the morning." When Chris didn't respond immediately, Scott gave him a look of condescension. "You know, to figure things out now that Randy's gone."

Chris frowned at the nonchalance of the receptionist's euphemistic acknowledgment of Randy's murder. "When can I meet with her?"

Using a hand gesture, Scott brought up Claire's schedule on his holoscreen and pointed at a time visible only to him. "Looks like she can see you after lunch, one p.m."

"Thanks."

"And please don't be late. She's busy today."

"Yes, still dealing with Randy's untimely retirement, I'm sure." Chris rolled his eyes. "I'll be back at one."

As he made his way under the intense glow of the overhead LEDs, he felt a buzz in his pocket. He pulled out his comm card and pressed it to his ear without checking to see who called. "Hello?"

"Someone called me looking for you today." It was Veronica.

He stopped in the middle of the hallway and continued in a more hushed voice than before. "Who called for me? What did they want?"

"I'm not sure." Her tone seemed calm, collected. "He didn't leave a name, and he called from a secured link. When I told him you weren't here and we were no longer together, he just ended the call."

Chris leaned back against the wall, pressing a palm against his forehead. "God. Okay. Did he threaten you or anything?"

"No, nothing like that. Guy didn't sound mean or anything." The line went silent for a moment. "I don't think it's a big deal. I shouldn't have even bothered you with this."

"I think maybe I should come over to talk about things. Just in case."

Paul gave Chris a concerned look as he passed him on his way down the hallway. When Paul stopped, Chris dismissed him with a wave.

"I know you think you're protecting me, but are you sure there isn't something more? I enjoyed Sunday, but I'm not sure I'm ready for a relationship with you again." The smile on her face, her unwillingness to understand the danger, was apparent in her voice alone.

He clenched a fist. "No, it's not about that." A lab technician from Regulatory glanced at him as she walked by. "Listen, I think you need to leave. Get packed up and I'll drop by at lunch. We should talk again and I'll make sure you get out of Baltimore."

"I've got dress rehearsal at seven."

"Please. At least hear me out at lunch."

"All right, fine. Christopher Morgan, you've always been a demanding man, haven't you?"

"I'll see you at twelve." He ended the call and arched his back against the wall. Maybe it was just an innocent call, an old friend, a client, or someone who didn't realize that he and Veronica had ended their relationship more than a year ago. He wanted to believe that the call was innocuous but knew that was untrue.

Back in the lab, he pulled on a pair of disposable gloves and buttoned up his white lab coat. He checked a couple of real-time monitoring systems connected to their experimental groups in the cell culture incubators. Amid all the turmoil in his life, these little tissue samples, snug in their cylindrical bioreactors, responded positively to the genetic replacement therapy system he had designed with Tracy. All signs pointed to high levels of transfection efficiency. The newly incorporated genes had performed well: levels of adenomatous polyposis coli, the protein encoded by the gene that they delivered to these samples, remained at a healthy concentration. The colorectal cells in the cultures no longer proliferated uncontrollably—no more cancerous cells.

"Why so glum?" Kristina stopped pipetting protein concentrates into small plastic centrifuge tubes. "Your data look great. Thinking about Randy again?" She placed a blue-gloved hand on his shoulder and looked up into his eyes as he turned away from the projection screen.

"Just distracted."

Kristina smiled weakly. "It's okay. We all miss him. I know it sounds corny, but you know Randy would want us to keep moving forward."

"You're right." He forced a grin. "It does sound corny. Now would be about the time Randy would make a boorish joke about you saying that, too."

Where Kristina's smile had been a slight curl before, she beamed now. "God, yes. I'll miss his pathetic sense of humor." She turned to a projection display on the lab workbench behind her. A flurry of blue lights danced across the display. "I know you didn't know him for too long, but he seemed to like you."

"What do you mean?"

"He just seemed excited when you came to work for us. Randy always talked a lot, but when he was excited, he could go on for days. You couldn't get a word in edgewise. So, when he said he was hiring this new PhD by the name of Christopher Morgan, he talked you up for eight hours a day." Kristina grinned.

Chris forced a laugh. "Stop flattering me. My cheeks are going all red." He scanned through another projection screen of graphs flashing green.

Turning back to the display in front of her, she continued. "The only times I've ever seen him that excited and chattering was when we got a new grant or new product approval or, I guess, when we terminated a couple of projects due to a lack of funding. He got awfully chatty when he fired one of the old lab techs for stealing syringes from the lab, too."

"Come again?"

She paused her manipulations of the figures in the projection display. "Oh, there was a lab tech that—"

"No, sorry. I mean, about Randy."

Her gaze lifted toward the ceiling. Her voice seemed almost dreamy. "Oh, he was just so positive, I think. Always wanted to appear optimistic. When things went really well or really poorly, he'd just get so excited."

"Like when he talked me up."

"Yeah, like that." Kristina paused. "Hmm. Maybe it secretly frightened him that you came to work for us, and he was acting overly optimistic instead." She laughed. "I'm just joking, of course."

Chris forced another laugh through his lips but grimaced behind her back.

Kristina closed out of the holoscreen and took off her gloves. She flung them into a waste container. "I think he realized how good your work was. Pardon another corny cliché, but I think he knew your research would be great for the company and save a few lives."

At his desk, Chris scrolled through research papers, skimming the documents. His mind raced as his eyes glazed over.

Maybe someone had tailed him to Veronica's. Or someone had tipped Kaufman off about their previous relationship. Why, though?

"I think I might grab lunch with Kristina and Paul today. You want to join us?" Tracy leaned against the edge of his desk. "You seem like you could use a little air."

"No, thanks. Besides, I've got a one o'clock with Claire that I don't want to be late for."

"What's the meeting for?"

He shrugged. "We'll find out."

His comm card buzzed, vibrating in his pocket. He slipped the card out. When he saw the ID of the incoming caller, his pulse quickened and he shoved the card back into his pocket.

"You can answer that," Tracy said, indicating the comm card with a slight nod.

"No, that's fine. I've got work to do."

Tracy folded her arms across her chest, the muscles in her arm tightening. "No one is expecting any of us to come back and cure cancer the Monday after Randy's funeral." She leaned in closer. "You don't need to work yourself to death."

"Sometimes I think it'd be better if I did. Wouldn't have gotten myself tangled up in all of this, huh?"

"Doubtful. You seem to be a magnet for bad luck." She leaned in. "Don't forget to pick up your coat at the end of the day."

Chris's comm card buzzed in his pocket again. He waited for Tracy to disappear behind the partitions beyond his desk and return to her own. The buzzing stopped before he felt it safe enough to retrieve his card.

Another missed call from Veronica.

He glanced around the room, looking for a place with privacy. He stood up and made for the hallway to the elevators at a quick pace.

An arm reached out and grasped his wrist. "Are you going to the cafeteria?" Tracy looked at him with a confused expression. In his haste, he had neglected to remember that his most direct pathway to the elevators brought him right by her desk.

"I think you're right. I need to get myself out of this place for a bit, so I'm going to go grab lunch out."

"Where? I'll come with."

"No," Chris said. He realized he'd been a bit too short with her. "I mean, I need space. Just want to clear my head. I hope you understand." He did his best to appear both pleading and apologetic.

"Fine." She pouted and Chris could not help but feel guilty about his plans. "I get it. You want alone time." She used her fingers to indicate quotation marks around the words.

He flashed a brief smile back. "Thanks." He marched down the hallway and waited for the next elevator, tapping out an anxious staccato rhythm on the floor with his foot.

When he stepped out onto the sidewalks white with salt, he called Veronica. He paced around in a circle, waiting for her to pick up. The call went to her message box, so he called again. No answer. Her most recent call had been at 11:36 and the comm card showed 11:45 now.

He hailed a cab. A yellow vehicle pulled up almost immediately. He got in and made a quick calculation. If he was lucky, he could make it to her apartment, make sure that she was okay, and return just before 1:00. His comm card buzzed with a message hinting that Jordan had come up with a couple thoughts related to yesterday's discoveries. He'd thought of something while writing that morning. Chris pocketed the comm card, unable to entertain these other thoughts while his anxiety regarding Veronica boiled over. Jordan would have to wait.

Chris watched the red dot on the projection display map as it wound through the city streets, growing closer to his destination. Inwardly, he cursed himself for not pushing harder for Veronica to leave the city yesterday. He knew she should have. Her name belonged to a list, and half the people on it had already died. "Shit, shit, shit." He remembered the first time he had seen her flashy blue eyes on stage, the grace with which she could float through the air. Her arms extending and drawing closer to her body as she spun. The audience clapping. His heart racing, the smile wide across his face.

With a lurching force, he was thrown forward. He slammed into the empty seat in front of him. Pain coursed through his neck as if he had wrenched his muscles, and his right arm throbbed. When he tried to straighten himself up, he buckled as an excruciating bolt of pain shot up his right arm. He crumpled back and groaned. This time, he used his left arm to hold his body weight with much more success. A red light glowed on the projection display of the cab as he struggled to comprehend what had just happened.

Traffic had come to a halt. Out the windshield, the front of the cab gave way to a crumpled mess of torn metal. Three other cars were scrunched and tangled in front of his taxi. A single red vehicle, destroyed beyond recognition, looked as if it had smashed into the sides of the row of three cars. His cab had stopped just feet away from being speared with the other three tangled cars.

Holding his right arm, he stepped out of the cab. Pain crept up his shoulder and into his neck. A crowd had already gathered around the smoking mess. Sirens wailed in the distance from several directions around them.

"Hey, man. Are you okay?" A teenager, sweatshirt hood obscuring his face, approached him.

Chris nodded, dizzy. "What the hell happened?"

"Dunno, man. That red car over there seemed to just pile drive these other ones. You think the computer went whack?"

He shrugged. Pain coursed through his right shoulder and up his neck, and he cringed. "That seems unlikely." Too many coincidences.

"Maybe the driver got high, man. You think? Decided he could drive better than a piece of software." The boy's face cracked into a smile. "I know my buddy tried to do that once. Big old idiot, I tell you. I bet that's what happened. Gotta be it, you know?"

Clenching his jaw against the pain, Chris trudged off. He looked at his comm card and glanced around him. Cars still stood motionless. Until the police arrived, traffic wouldn't even begin to snail down the broad street. He called Veronica. Still no answer. He accelerated into a jog, each loping step sending pain up his right shoulder through his neck. The ambulance and police sirens grew louder, piercing the din of muddled voices around the scene of the accident. He pushed through onlookers and checked his comm card to see where the nearest place he might be able to pick up another cab would be. He needed to make it north two blocks to where the obtrusive wreck had not snarled traffic. He cursed the driver of that red car. Realizing the man might be dead, a brief moment of sympathy arose in him. Of course, the delay might mean worse for Veronica.

By the time Chris hailed another cab and walked his injured self to Veronica's, it was almost 12:40. There would be no way he could make it back to his meeting with Claire on time. He did his best to leap up the steps to her apartment building and called her again. Once more, there was no answer.

He raced up the winding staircase to the fourth floor of the building and jogged down the hallway toward her apartment. The agony built, spreading from his arm and neck down his right side. He fought to catch his breath as he willed the dizziness to fade back from his head.

When he reached her apartment, he knocked wildly on the door. "Veronica! Veronica!" He pressed his ear against the cold metal door. It struck him that just days ago, he had pressed an ear against a door, waiting with bated breath in hopes that there would be no footsteps, no breathing from the other side.

Now he hoped that he would hear her light footsteps. She would come dancing to the door, wondering what all the fuss was about. He heard nothing.

He stepped back, ready to resume his furious knocking in hopes that the outcome would be different. As he cocked back his left arm, his eyes darted to the door handle. Scratches marred the edge of the door and the wooden doorframe around it near the lock. While not ornate by any means, her door had been in more pristine condition yesterday.

Still huffing, he wrapped his fingers around the handle and twisted. A click indicated the door was unlocked. He inched the door open, eyes wide and pulse pounding in his ears. When he opened it up all the way, he called out her name and stared down the short hall leading to her living area and studio, marked by large, naked wooden beams.

Those beams framed the macabre scene before him. His vision swam again and the pain in his arm flared. He wanted to yell, to scream out, but felt too weak to even utter a sound. He collapsed in the doorway, his body weight slamming the door against the wall with a thud almost as violent as the sound his body made as it crashed against the hardwood floor.

CHAPTER TWENTY-SEVEN

C HRIS BLINKED AND PROPPED HIMSELF up against the door
frame. He winced and howled in pain as he leaned on his
right arm. Using his left hand, he probed his shoulder,
clenching his jaw, desperate for the pain to ebb. He thought
about heading to the Johns Hopkins Medical Center just down
the road to get his shoulder checked out before remembering
where he was.

Out in the hallway, there were no open apartment doors.
No one had rushed to either help him or hurt him. He limped
into Veronica's apartment and closed the door behind him,
locking it. In an attempt to filter the pervasive metallic scent,
he bunched up his shirt over his nose. He gagged. Bending
over for a moment, he steadied his breathing to ensure that his
breakfast didn't revisit him.

He inched down the hallway. A trail of crimson, fresh
and wet, led to the open living area that Veronica used as a
studio. Against his gut feeling, he hoped it was spilled paint,
splattered and drying. Every nerve in him tensed as he peered
into the studio room.

She was in front of him, on a stool against the exposed brick wall.

"Veronica!" Chris rushed to her. He ignored the fire burning along his shoulder and neck. "Veronica! I'm here!"

She did not respond. Her eyes were bruised shut and her mouth gagged. Hair, matted with blood, stuck to the sides of her face, clinging to a long line cut from her forehead down to her mouth. Blood dripped down from her lips and her nostrils. Her arms were wrenched behind her with her shoulders dislocated. Her wrists, tied together, were knotted in a nylon rope suspended over one of the exposed beams.

In a panic, Chris searched for a knife to cut the rope, scattering paintbrushes, tubes of oil paints, cloths soiled with spatters and smears of color. He found a small shaping knife in her toolbox of supplies and sawed through the rope, gritting his teeth all the while. When the rope snapped apart, Veronica's body slumped forward, off the stool. He caught her in his arms. Her body weight landing on his arm reignited the agony in his shoulder. He yelled out and lowered her into his lap. With the knife, he cut the gag from her mouth.

He brushed aside the dark hair sticking to her face and lowered his ear above her mouth and next to her nose. No air tickled his skin. "Oh, God. Veronica wake up, please."

Pressing his index and middle fingers to her wrist revealed no pulse pushing back on his fingers. He situated his palms in the middle of her sternum. He pushed his weight onto her rib cage once, twice. Three times and he heard the pop of a broken rib. Despite knowing that a broken rib was common from CPR training he had taken in college, he cursed at the sound. Pain swelled in his own shoulder and he yelped each time he compressed her chest. He lessened the force behind each pump, imagining the broken rib puncturing a lung, but such weak presses would not reach her still heart. He pressed harder again, biting his teeth deep into his bottom lip and wincing all the while.

Blood soaked into Veronica's torn, loose-fitting shirt, pooled up over his fingers as his compressions squeezed it out from her cuts. He tasted saltiness on his lips, for the first time realizing that tears had been streaming down his face.

Pausing, he felt for a pulse again. He listened for breathing. Nothing.

Again, he pumped her chest with his palms, grunting all the while.

A memory flashed in his head of Veronica on the stage, a gold leotard against a backdrop that resembled the night sky. She leaped, floated, spun. He had clapped and smiled, proud that she was his—or, rather, that he was hers.

The splintering of wood and sound of plodding footsteps crashed through the hallway. Chris ignored it, desperate to revive the life in Veronica. He had left her, abandoned their relationship, as she'd pleaded for him to give up his obsession with underground genetic enhancements. He had told her she must be insecure about his success, about the newfound wealth that would fall on him like a blizzard. He accused her of being jealous of his time spent with Jordan, the late nights at his apartment, time spent at wild, excessive parties.

A woeful look on her face, she had responded to him that she missed who he had been before letting that monster take control of his life. He had snarled at her and accused her of wanting him to be more careless and artsy like her. His life contained no room for a hopeless free spirit. And he had left, high on anger and obsession.

Now, she lay covered in blood and no longer breathing. She jolted with each time he compressed her chest, but her eyes remained closed.

"What the hell?"

A distant voice rang hollow in his ears.

"What the hell are you doing?" A hand grabbed at his right shoulder, accentuating the pain. He grunted as he pushed.

They could take him too. He didn't care. It was his fault.

He pumped her chest.

"She's dead, Chris. She's dead."

At the sound of his name, he turned. Tracy stood behind him. She held a gun, glinting metallic in the sunlight that filtered through the cracks between the heavy curtains pulled shut around the studio. She pushed him aside. He rolled back, twisting his body to catch himself with his left hand.

Tracy knelt down. She checked Veronica's pulse as Chris had done and listened to her breathing. "She's gone." Her brow furrowed, Tracy picked up one of Veronica's feet. Her toes were bloody and without nails. "Damn it! Someone tortured her."

Chris's nose twitched and his stomach twisted.

"I wish I knew what the fuck they think they're doing," she said in a low voice, as if talking to herself. "They didn't just kill her. They wanted her to talk. What didn't you tell me about Veronica Powell?"

He stared hard at Tracy. He had seen death in prison, during the stabbings, while he himself had been in shock. Then it had not been so grisly or so personal. "I thought that he wanted to protect me. Why'd he do this?"

"Chris, how do you know Veronica?"

His eyes rose to meet hers. "How do *you* know her?"

"Don't be so stupid. I followed you here. I knew you were hiding something from me. I lost you when you came into the apartment."

"I closed the door, didn't I?"

"Yeah, you did. But remember when you told me you knew people on that list? I do. You tried to tell me later you only knew Jordan." She looked down at Veronica's face. "I searched for the addresses of the living people on that list. Found her apartment. Publicly listed. Bad decision on her part."

Chris crawled back toward where Veronica lay across the floor. "You told me you thought Kaufman wanted to protect me."

"It's not you lying in a pool of a blood." She thrust out one arm toward Veronica. "Look, he's making good on his promise. He needs to be stopped."

"It's too late. I don't care."

"Do you mean that?" Hurt flashed in Tracy's expression.

He averted his eyes, back toward a painting in the corner of the room. It had been a pristine scene of the wild, grazing horses in Assateague State Park. Now, little flecks of blood spatter tainted the image. "No."

"Look," Tracy said. "I want to know what you were doing here, but there are more pressing issues right now."

Chris turned back to her and tilted his head.

"We've got to clean this mess up. Get rid of all evidence that we were here today. Then, on our way out, we call the police. It's not going to be perfect, but we've got to scour the place as much as possible for any hair, fingerprints, everything you touched."

Hesitating, he ran his fingers through his hair.

"I know it's vile and disgusting, but we have to do it," Tracy said. "They'll be able to match your DNA since you're already in their databases. Easy first suspect, and then you're back in jail. Ben stays out here and fucks people up like this."

Chris nodded.

"Walk me through this, so I know what we need to clean up. Okay?"

Again, he nodded. He felt warmer again, his thoughts more lucid. "Yeah, yeah. Sure thing." He glanced at Veronica. Tears threatened to surge forth. He felt sick. "Oh, God."

"All right. You walked straight from the doorway, found her here and tried to resuscitate her, right? You didn't go anywhere else in the apartment today. Not her bathroom, not her bedroom, right?"

Chris closed his eyes. "Well, not today."

CHAPTER TWENTY-EIGHT

"**W**HAT THE HELL DO YOU mean?" Tracy's nose scrunched in a snarl.

Chris hesitated a moment, wondering if he should stop. "I was here yesterday, too." He looked away and thought for a moment, remembering everywhere he had been. "In the kitchen, the bathroom, and the bedroom."

Tracy's face turned red, but her words were cold. "Is your DNA inside of her?"

His cheeks flushed warm. "No."

"Right now, I'm not worrying about our relationship. Your life might be in danger and now, mine might be, too. Think about our lives. Other people that you might know. Jordan. Hell, they might come after Paul and Kristina. Before we leave here, I want to make sure that we have a head start to find these assholes. We don't want the police to arrest me," she said, her eyes narrowing, "or you while we're doing that. The police already don't believe your story about Randy, and, so far, things have just become a fucking mess. So when I ask you whether or not your DNA is inside of Veronica, I want you to be one hundred fucking percent sure."

"No. We didn't do anything."

"Even in the bedroom?"

"Even in the bedroom, we were just—"

"I don't want to know right now. I just want to focus on this."

Tracy picked up the compact pistol and slid it into a holster within her jacket.

"When the hell did you get a gun?"

"I just want to focus on this right now," she said again, but with more of an edge to her voice.

They grabbed rags from an art supply box to wipe all the surfaces that Chris thought he might have touched. Walls, countertops, tables, sculptures.

When they finished, Chris used Veronica's handheld vacuum. He wondered what evidence he might be destroying that might not just lead the police to him but also to the true killers. Tracy scrubbed the bloody footprints they had left near the scene of Veronica's death and used the soiled rag on the bottom of her shoes. Chris licked his finger and cleaned away a smear of dried blood from her face. She scowled at him but let him wipe it away.

After Tracy deemed the apartment clean enough, Chris went back to take a final look at Veronica. He wanted to pull her close, to apologize, but covering himself in more blood would be unwise. Instead, he relegated himself to stroking her forearm where less blood stained her skin. He traced from her upper arm toward her wrist, ending in a soft caress. "I'm sorry. I'm so sorry." His forefinger traveled back up her arm. It hit a little bump as it did.

He squinted and leaned in closer to the bump. It looked like a mosquito bite. As he studied it, he realized it lay right over a particularly large vein. "Tracy, come here."

Tracy appeared back at his side and examined the spot. "They inject her with something?"

He recognized the small scab for what it was. Just like when they had taken his blood in prison. The doctor had taken a sample, run it for analysis and then reused the same site for an injection. Chris had questioned the doctor, but the white coat had explained that all inmates needed to be vaccinated.

"Against what?" Chris had asked.

The white coat's eyes had narrowed, but he hadn't responded as he stuck the needle back into the spot where he had taken the blood.

Chris looked back up at Tracy. "Maybe they didn't inject anything. Maybe they took a blood sample."

She raised an eyebrow. "A sample? Seems to be more than enough blood over the rest of her and around this whole goddamned place. Why the hell would they need a sample like that?"

He shrugged. He winced and grabbed at his shoulder again. "I've had enough. You think we can go now?"

Tracy nodded and walked out back to the front door. Waiting a moment, Chris touched Veronica's wrist again, whispering his apologies. He wiped at the corners of his eyes. He imagined he felt her pulse again, weak, but throbbing. Shaking his head, he wiped away the mucus draining from his nose and walked away from her body, his head hung low.

As they left the apartment, Tracy cleaned the door handle. The doorframe near the lock was splintered, white wood sticking out like a broken bone piercing skin. Chris, willing himself to be numb, struggled to hold back from dry-heaving again.

"Careful," Tracy said. She deposited the rag in a plastic bag with the others they had used to dust and clean their traces from the apartment. After tying the bag closed, she stuffed it into her coat. "We don't need to leave any more of a mess." Her eyes went up and down the splintered wood. "Must have the deafest neighbors around."

"Probably at work." He took a deep breath.

"Speaking of work, you missed your meeting with Claire."

He glared back. He didn't want to meet with Claire or anyone else at Respondent.

"Just saying. Let's get the hell out of here. Then we're going to leave an anonymous call with the police when we get out of Fell's Point." Tracy walked tall and calm, leading Chris out of the building. "How's the shoulder?"

"Hurts."

She handed him a pill from her pocket. "Take this. It'll help with the pain."

"I think I need to see a doctor."

Tracy explored his shoulder. "No, you don't."

Chris popped the pill into his mouth. He ushered his thoughts away from Veronica, away from what he had just seen, away from what they had just cleaned up. He focused on the pill, feeling the muscles in his esophagus carry it down into his stomach. "How the hell do you carry all this around without a purse?"

Tracy shrugged. "Got to be prepared." With a huff, she gripped his upper arm with one hand and pressed down on his shoulder with the other. Chris let out an agonized yell as a sickening pop came from his shoulder. The pain throbbed on. "You should be fine after a while. It'll still hurt, but at least your shoulder isn't dislocated anymore."

Nausea swelled in him, a constant companion that day. He gulped. "Thanks."

Chris's swimming vision refocused again as Tracy led him down the stairs and out the exit of the building. He began to input a cab request in his comm card, but Tracy stopped him. "We don't need a paper trail leading us away from the crime scene. Also, you need to get rid of that coat. It's covered in splotches of blood and smells terrible."

"Get rid of my coat?" Chris frowned as he peeled the coat off and bunched it up. He held it by his side, careful to ensure no blood showed. "It's freezing out. People will think I'm crazy."

"Crazier than anyone else in this damned city?" Tracy directed him to throw it away after they had made it back to Pratt Street.

Chris threw it in a dumpster behind Philip's Seafood.

"Good choice. No restaurant likes to keep a pile of rotting crab shells around. They have to clean those dumpsters out every day."

They trudged to the Oakwoods Shopping Center in the Severn Building to buy a new coat. When they left, Tracy led them back on Light Street before she hailed a cab on her comm card. Once in the vehicle, she input an address that Chris didn't recognize. "What are you doing?"

She looked at the rear window. "Son of a bitch."

"What?"

She pointed at another cab following theirs. "We've got a tail."

Chris peered through the rear window but noticed nothing unusual. Then again, what he saw hardly matched the haunting images of Veronica that overshadowed any other of his thoughts. "We just got out of the Inner Harbor. Tourists everywhere. How do you know we've got a tail?"

"I've been watching the guy. He doesn't know I saw him, but he's been following us since we left Veronica's apartment building."

"Are you sure you weren't a PI before?"

She laughed. Chris did not. It was the first time either had exhibited any form of humor since discovering Veronica. "You know I actually pay attention to things. Don't have my head in the clouds." She jabbed him with her elbow and he winced.

"That kind of hurts, you know." He touched his shoulder. It still responded painfully to his probing.

Tracy's face contorted in an expression somewhere between a frown and a sympathetic smile.

"Where are we going?" Chris asked.

"We're going to have a drink with our new friend."

"What? After all of this? I just want to go home."

She rolled her eyes. "If we're being followed, that isn't such a great idea. Right now, we're headed to the Dragon Emporium on Emerson."

"The hell kind of place is that?"

Tracy grinned. "The kind of place where I used to go before working at Respondent. Also, the kind of place that makes carrying a gun worthwhile." She patted the spot on her jacket where the coat hid her pistol.

"Why do you still carry that around?"

"Why are you still creeping around with Veronica Powell?" She clenched her jaws, her eyes alight again. "She's that girlfriend you saw before going to prison, isn't she?"

Chris nodded. Tracy's constant fluctuations from collected crime scene cleaner to jealous lover caused him to edge up against the door of the cab.

"Still, it's strange that she's on Randy's list. You knew her and you lied to me about it. Are you sure you don't recognize the others?" She gave Chris an accusing look.

"No. Veronica and Jordan were it. I'm sorry I lied. I wanted to warn her." He waved his hands defensively. "But we didn't do anything, I swear."

"Fine," she said. Her facial features softened, but her eyes still burned with intensity. "Don't lie to me like that again. We need honesty. Especially right now."

Chris thought to press her about the gun again but decided against it. She needed honesty from him but didn't seem ready to open up herself.

The cab slowed to a stop. He opened the door, and Tracy followed him out. The face of a large dragon made of an enormous wood frame painted green and red greeted them. Steam seemed to be rising from its nostrils, and its eyes glowed red. They walked straight through its mouth and into the Dragon Emporium. Inside, projections of red and orange danced along the walls as if the beast had swallowed them into its fire-bearing belly.

"Good Lord," Chris said. "What did you ever do here?"

Tracy smirked. "Good place to meet an interesting man or two." She nodded at a couple of bald men with curling mustaches in the corner. One had brow implants and piercings that made him appear like a pink relative of the bar's namesake. The other, laced in tattoos, gulped beer from a pitcher.

Between the pain in his shoulder, the nausea in his stomach, and the guilt over Veronica, Chris felt like a weakling, waiting to be set upon by the two grisly men.

"I'm just messing with you," she said. "But, in reality, my past may not have been as clean as I'd led you to believe." Before he could follow up with a question, Tracy made a slight gesture back to the entrance of the bar. "He's still following us, isn't he?"

Chris glanced back to the entrance of the dragon's belly. A wiry man with tousled hair and a gaunt face had just entered. "The guy you saw. Does he look like a skinny little tweaker?"

"Yep."

"Then yeah, he's still following us."

Tracy walked to the back, past the two fat bald men. Music pounded through the door in the back. "Don't look back. Just keep following me."

"Is there a dance club here? In the middle of the freaking afternoon?"

Tracy smiled. "Yeah. Can't guarantee anybody's actually here, but that's one of the things I liked about this place. Party whenever you wanted."

She opened the door, and the music reverberated in Chris's chest. "I don't feel like dancing right now," he said.

Tracy prodded him up the stairs. Darkness cloaked the stairwell. "I hope our buddy back there feels differently."

The top of the stairs opened into a room that appeared too small for the music that resonated within it. The deep, reverberating bass sucked the air from Chris's lungs. Ridiculous hologram projections of dragons gallivanted through the murky fog that filled the room.

He glanced at Tracy. She gave him a mischievous look and smirked.

No other patrons suffered through the unbearable music. In one far corner, a bar stood with no bartender. Chris squinted to make out the automatic drink dispenser. Of course, no human tended the bar; working too long in that environment would be intolerable for any living soul.

Tracy pulled him through the entrance and pushed him against the wall. She gave him a quick kiss on the lips, another look filled with a strange combination of pity and slyness, and pressed herself against the wall beside him.

As if on cue, the skinny man followed through behind them. Tracy pressed the cold steel of her pistol against his head. The man shook and his lips quivered.

She grabbed hold of his collar and guided him back out onto the top landing of the stairwell and through a dark hall that led to the second-floor bathrooms. As she shoved him into the women's restroom, she locked the door behind them, the music pounding against it.

All the walls seemed to be coated in a yellow-orange grime. Tracy pushed the man down onto the toilet.

"Why are you following us?" Tracy backed up, the gun trained on the man.

He whimpered, and shook his head.

"Why are you following us?" She repeated the words with more malice, practically spitting on the man.

Again, he shook his head and refused to mutter a word.

Tracy backhanded him. As she did, Chris let out an audible gasp. She scowled at him. He straightened up and folded his arms across his chest, painting his face with a scowl to match hers.

"I don't know!" The man clutched at his face and shook.

"Why the hell would anyone send a piece of shit like you to tail us around?"

The man's hands dropped from his face as he crossed his arms. "They promised me a genie. I'm dying, okay? Muscles all out of whack. Can't buy myself a genie. I begged 'em. They wouldn't let me. Today, they called me up. Told me they got a job. I do it, I get a genie, no strings attached."

Tracy frowned. "Who told you to follow us?"

The man groaned through closed lips, already bleeding from the first blow, and shook his head.

Tracy cocked her arm back.

"I can't tell. They said they'll flay me alive."

"I'll flay you alive if you don't tell us."

Shoulders hunched, the man looked up at her. His eyelids wavered as if he couldn't decide whether to blink or not. "I don't even know their names. The two of 'em picked me up, dropped me off, and told me to watch for someone who looked like him." The man pointed at Chris.

"Why?" Tracy clenched her jaw.

"I don't know. I don't know, lady."

"Where's your card?"

"My—my front pocket, pants. I mean, no, front pocket of my jacket. Right here." He inserted a hand into his pocket.

"Don't fucking move. Chris, get his comm card."

Chris walked toward their hostage, avoiding his shaky gaze, and slipped a hand into the man's front jacket pocket. He pulled out the comm card and handed it to Tracy. She glanced at it and handed it back to him. "The number they called him from is secured, and we won't find shit on it. Break the card."

"But—"

"Break it. If they're tracking his card, they'll know where he is and where we are."

Nodding, he snapped the card in half. Tracy made the man stand up, his arms above his head, as Chris flushed it down the toilet.

"You said you spoke to these people before, right?"

The color from the man's face drained.

"Where did you meet them?"

"A friend set it up."

"What friend?"

"He's dead now."

Tracy rolled her eyes. "Of course. Where'd you meet the thugs that put you up to this?"

"Happy's Chicken."

"The fast food place?"

The man nodded vigorously. "Yeah. I gave them my ID, but they wouldn't let me get a genie until I did what they wanted."

"Great. Where's their place?"

"Their what?" The man peered up at Tracy with fright.

"Their house, their headquarters, wherever the hell they spend their time."

"I don't know!" The man's skin paled and he shook even more violently. His eyelids twitched.

"Are you telling me the truth?" Tracy thrust the gun at his groin.

The man crossed his legs. His pants turned dark with wetness and yellow liquid escaped from beneath where he sat and dripped on the ground. "Yes! I am! I swear it!" He whimpered again.

The man was clearly afraid of Tracy, frightened by the cold steel in her hands and the fury radiating from her eyes. Chris was growing afraid of her, too. He struggled to maintain his stolid composure.

"I think that's all we're going to get out of this creep for now." Tracy turned to Chris. "We're going to need to get him back to Jordan's."

"Are you insane? Why would we do that?"

"The guy's seen us and I pulled a gun on him. If we let him go, he could go to the police, ID us, and we both end up in jail. Easy target for our friend, Ben Kaufman." She glanced at the man when she said Ben's name. He didn't seem to recognize it.

"I won't go to the police. I swear!"

"If he doesn't go to the police, our friends will either flay him alive, as he says, or they'll send him after us again. And, this time, I doubt it will be under such amicable circumstances."

The man cried now.

"So, we could kill him—"

The man howled.

"Or bring him to Jordan's for a bit while we get this whole mess sorted. Who knows? Maybe we can get him whatever genetic enhancement he wants that'll help the muscle problem he says he's got when this whole thing blows over."

Chris frowned but nodded. "I suppose you're right." He turned and kicked the door. "But, damn, we don't need kidnapping charges right now."

Tracy shrugged. "Better than killing the guy outright. Besides, I'm sure your friend Jordan has means of getting rid of guys like this."

His face in his hands, the man sobbed. "I don't want to die."

"Relax," Tracy said. "I'll bet Jordan has access to things that'll knock out your memories. Can't guarantee what else it'll knock out, but at least you'll be alive."

CHAPTER TWENTY-NINE

A S THE MUSIC POUNDED AGAINST their ears, Tracy guided the scrawny man down the hall toward a door marked with a red holo exit sign. Chris followed, close enough to hear her whispering threats into the man's ear about what might happen if he tried to run. She slung her arm through the hostage's and pushed open the door to fire escape stairs that led down to the bottom of the alley. The outdoor light blinded Chris for a moment until his pupils adjusted. As the group climbed down, the rusted stairs quaked and groaned with each step they took.

"Call a cab," Tracy said to Chris without taking her eyes off their captive.

Chris held the rail and used his other hand to request a cab on his comm card. They waited at the bottom of the stairs until a taxi pulled up to the end of the narrow alleyway. Tracy kept the man in the shadows until she signaled for both him and Chris to duck into the vehicle with her.

When their captive leaned to run off, Tracy lunged. She grabbed his wrist and twisted it until he yelped. A man smoking across the street looked toward them but turned away when Chris caught his gaze. With a thrust, Tracy shoved the skinny man into the cab, and his head cracked against the window on the opposite side of the car. He sat in the seat and whimpered as she sidled in next to him. Chris gulped and closed the door after he got in.

Before inputting an address, Tracy leaned into Chris's ear. "I need your undershirt to blindfold the guy."

Chris hesitated and gave her a questioning look.

"Look, I know this is crazy, but we still don't know how dangerous this guy is. We let him go, he might go straight back to whoever sent him or he might just outright kill us. I'm not certain he's told us everything he knows."

"And yet we're going to bring him back to Jordan's."

"That's why we've at least got to blindfold him. We can lock him up in a bathroom. I'm sure Greg will help us deal with the guy."

"Fine."

As Chris took off his jacket and unbuttoned his shirt, Tracy turned back to the man. "What's your name?"

The man said nothing.

"Just give us a first name, anything we can call you."

"Todd," he said. He shivered as he spoke.

"All right, Todd. Just keep doing as you're told and everything will be fine. And if you remember anything that could help us out, it'll better for you to tell us."

Todd nodded but said nothing else, his lips quivering.

Just a couple nights ago, Chris had shared a warm bed with Tracy. With his arms wrapped around her, she had felt small to him, her eyes closed and her breathing steady. She had almost seemed delicate. And now she seemed anything but.

Tracy stared at the man like a tiger stalking prey, her gaze intense and focused. Chris could not help wondering how she had hidden this innate ferocity within her. He didn't envy Todd.

When they arrived at Jordan's apartment building, Tracy cursed. People strolled down the sidewalk toward them, scarves wrapped tight around their necks. The cab requested them to confirm their payment and urged them to exit, but Tracy waited for the group to pass by.

"We can't exactly bring him in blindfolded. That's certain to arouse a little suspicion."

"No shit," Tracy said.

For the first time, Chris saw a look of uncertainty in her eyes. It reassured him to know she didn't know the proper procedure for transporting a prisoner to an apartment. "Well, so much for all the grandstanding." She took the blindfold off him. "Don't think for a second this means I don't have a gun aimed at your gut, though."

Todd, still quivering, nodded. He stepped out of the cab, stumbling forward. For a moment, Chris thought Todd meant to sprint off and he cowered, preparing for the blast from Tracy's concealed gun.

Instead, Todd stood back up. Tracy wrapped her arm around his and led him over the marble floor to the elevators. Chris followed and hit the button on the screen for Jordan's apartment, glad that Jordan had approved him for security access. He wasn't sure his friend would have let them up if he'd known they brought a nervous hostage with them.

The elevator doors opened to the empty atrium.

"We're back," Chris called out. "Got someone with us."

No voices called back.

Chris walked to the open sitting area next to the bar and kitchen. A half-full pot of coffee sat on the kitchen counter.

"Jordan?"

His pulse quickened as he stepped into the empty library room. The holoscreen sat open on the desk, radiating a soft blue glow. Chris checked his comm card. No messages or calls from Jordan. The little red numbers projected 5:45 p.m. Jordan and Greg might still be in their labs or offices, researching and selling their equine genetic enhancements.

He exhaled and willed his heartbeat to slow. He had no idea how late Jordan might be working, so it might be normal for him to be gone at this time. His thoughts turned to Todd and Tracy out near the elevator. His friend liked hosting guests but might not be too thrilled about this particular surprise visitor.

After tapping Jordan's number into his comm card, he waited to connect. The other line rang as Chris paced back and forth. No answer. He could call Jordan's workplace, but that might not be as secure as the man's personal line. In fact, Jordan might already be headed to the penthouse, just minutes away in his company car.

Chris performed a quick search on his comm card for Jordan's company and placed a call.

A feminine voice answered, with a subtle robotic twang. "Equest Advantage. How may I direct your call?"

"Jordan Thompson, please."

"I'm sorry. Mr. Thompson is unavailable. May I redirect your call?"

"Uh...Jordan's assistant or secretary or something?"

"One moment."

Chris drummed his fingers on the edge of the desk.

"This is Margot Durand."

"I'm looking to speak with Jordan."

"Who is this?"

"This is Christopher Morgan. A friend." He wondered if he had left too many bread crumbs.

"I'm sorry, Mr. Morgan, but Mr. Thompson isn't in. Can I take a message?"

"I know he isn't in," he said, his voice snappier than intended. He tried to speak with a more docile tone. "Has he just left for the day?"

"Mr. Thompson left at lunch and never returned. I'm sorry I don't know more than that."

"Thanks." Chris ended the call, his arms limp by his side. He gazed distantly at the books on the other side of the wall, their spines blending together in a blurry mess.

Recollecting himself, he paced again. He placed another call to Jordan's comm card, pleading in his head for an answer. He stopped a moment and glanced over the words projected by the holoscreen, still open and glowing. The line rang as he bent to study the holoscreen. It appeared to be one of Jordan's stories, apparently about a truck driver from the late twentieth century that had crashed in a forested wilderness.

The ringing on the other end of the comm card stopped.

"Christopher Morgan."

He almost jumped. He recognized that cold, monotonous voice. "Benjamin Kaufman."

A slight chuckle echoed on the other end of the line. "Is that who you think I am?"

For a moment, he felt uncertain. He refused to show weakness now. "There's no use pretending you're just a mystery anymore."

"If that makes you feel more comfortable, you may call me whatever you want."

"Where's Jordan?"

"He's with us. I assure you he's alive, but I can't guarantee for how much longer if you don't cooperate."

"Yes, I know. I saw what you did to Veronica, you son of a bitch. You gave me no way to contact you, I'm ready to do what you want, and you do that to her?"

"Veronica?" Kaufman's voice sounded almost questioning. "Ah, yes. Your partner before prison, isn't that right? You've seen her recently, haven't you?"

"Stop. I'll do whatever you want. Just don't hurt Jordan." He clenched his eyes closed. "And don't touch Tracy."

"Good. That's all I need. We don't like to hurt people if we don't have to. It has come to my attention that you have discovered the samples that Randall Nee had produced."

"Yes. The vectors that I designed."

"Very astute. I just wanted Nee's notebook, along with the rest of the samples. It's that simple. Or it would have been, if you had been more willing to help sooner."

"If you'd told me sooner, I would've delivered them myself."

"Ah, I'm not quite certain of that. In any case, Mr. Thompson will serve as sufficient insurance that you can get this done in a timely manner, no?"

Chris shook his head, combing his hand through his hair. "Insurance? But I don't have those samples, or the notebook for that matter. We only have two vials now."

The line was silent for a moment. "You don't have the rest of the samples or the notebook? Then why did my men say you stole both of those items from Respondent?"

"We did take them."

"'We'? You and the Harrow girl?"

"No, I mean 'I' did take them. Just me."

"That's not true at all, is it, Mr. Morgan? Ms. Harrow did take the samples with you. Let me guess: someone stole them. Or maybe she lost them."

"I don't know."

"Mr. Morgan, you are responsible for Mr. Thompson's life. Are you willing to let him die on account of a trite lie?"

"Someone took them from Tracy's apartment. I assumed you would know about that. We left both the samples and Randy's notebook there."

"Ah, so Mr. Thompson told the truth when he said he possessed only two of the vials. I suppose we needn't have treated him quite as rough as we did."

Chris winced. "Will you let him go?"

Another drawn-out moment of silence passed. "I'm not sure about that yet. I'm going to need you and Ms. Harrow to join me first. If you can help me get everything I need, then we can talk about releasing Mr. Thompson."

He hesitated, staring around at the room filled with paper books and oil paintings, devoid of modern technologies except for the projection screen that glowed in front of him. "Fine. Where do I need to go?"

"Nowhere, Mr. Morgan. We'll come for you."

The line went dead and Chris slumped in the leather office chair. A dull pain throbbed in his head, the pressure drop before the incoming storm. He thought to tell Tracy, to warn her that Kaufman and his men would be coming soon for them. But he couldn't quite muster the strength to face her. He could envision the disgust on her face, the anger that he had given them up.

As he sat at the desk, he read the page that showed on the projection screen. The story of the truck driver, interrupted and incomplete, made him feel as if he stared at something naked. A nagging in the back of his mind warned him about reading this story before Jordan had completed and polished it. He knew Jordan wouldn't appreciate it. Did that matter? Was that what he was concerned with? Kaufman held Jordan captive and all he could think about was the slight offense his friend might take because Chris read a rough draft of a story.

He mouthed the final lines of the story to himself. "The trailer lay open, barren. Frank turned to the disheartened driver with a look of terrible sorrow. 'It is meant to be filled with your body.' The driver, confused, showed his bare forearm where the ink from prison wound in imperfect crosses, wrapped with venomous snakes biting into the man's flesh. 'But I built the truck.'"

The passage appeared to Chris incongruous with the rest of the story. The preceding paragraphs had not introduced this character speaking to the driver. Nothing before this particular section appeared as convoluted and symbolic, either. *What the hell did you write, Jordan?*

Maybe a deeper meaning hid in those sentences. Maybe Jordan had left him a clue. Did this have anything to do with the message Jordan had sent him earlier?

A sharp cry from out in the hallway quelled those thoughts.

CHAPTER THIRTY

"**S**IT DOWN NEXT TO HER." Todd, his arm shaky, held a pistol of his own toward Tracy. He had tucked hers into his pants. A slight laceration cut across her forehead, and blood trickled down, tracing her cheekbone. Her eyes wide and her lips closed tight, she no longer appeared as mean spirited on other side of a gun barrel.

Chris stood in the doorway to Jordan's bedroom, stunned.

"Come here and sit by her. Now. Sit by her." Todd pointed the gun at him and swung it back to Tracy. "Now!" His nostrils flared.

"All right, I am." Chris held his hands up and inched toward Tracy.

"They told me they just wanted you." His eyes flickered between them, making it unclear who he meant. "Now they want both of you. I do what they say. I just do what they say and it'll be okay."

"Ben Kaufman's men are coming?" Chris tried in a soft voice.

"I told you I don't know no Ben Kaufman. Don't know him. I just do what they tell me. I can get my genies." His arm shook as he held out the pistol. He used his free hand to steady the shaking arm.

"I know they're coming," Chris said. "Ben Kaufman said he'd be coming to get to us."

"I don't know Ben Kaufman! I told you." His lips curled into a delighted, sinister grin. "But, you broke the wrong card. My card. You broke mine. But I used the card they gave me." He reached into his pocket with his shaking hand and withdrew the other comm card. "See? I called them."

Chris frowned and leaned toward Tracy. "They got Jordan and now they're coming for us."

"Quiet!"

"We should've patted him down," Tracy said. "God, I'm so fucking stupid."

"Stop it. Just be quiet 'til they get here."

Todd's eyes darted between them. Chris was less concerned about Todd intentionally shooting them and more worried that the man's nervous shaking would cause him to accidentally pull the trigger. "Could you stop pointing the gun at us?"

Todd scowled. "No."

"I'm just worried that with you waving it about, you might kill us. And if you did that, I don't think the guys would be happy."

"You shouldn't be worried about me!" All the same, Todd lowered the gun and stepped back against the wall. "If you so much as try to get up, I will shoot you. In the leg, maybe. But I'll shoot you."

"We know you fucking will," Tracy said.

The slow drops of ice melting and falling against the windowsill seemed as steady as the ticking of a clock as they waited. A buzz sounded near the elevator entrance in the atrium. Todd looked back and forth between the two of them.

The entry notification system rang again.

"If you don't get that, they can't come up," Chris said.

"Fine. Stand up. Move. Move." Todd ushered them back out the door and into the hall. They congregated near the elevator door.

"You." He pointed the gun at Chris. "Answer it. Let them up."

Chris nodded and opened the security screen. The projection displayed two familiar faces. The men who had killed Randy and chased him around Fed Hill waited for his approval. For a brief moment, he hesitated, wondering if Tracy's and his odds might be better with shaky Todd.

"Do it. Let them up!"

He pressed the button for guest approval and saw the two large men walk into the entrance of the building. The elevator hummed to life, and Todd prodded Chris and Tracy to move toward a bench near the small fountain. When the doors of the elevator opened, the two men stepped out, taking in their new surroundings.

The man that had choked Chris and later chased him through the Visionary Art Museum stepped forward. His blue eyes flashed between Tracy and Chris, his gaze landing on Todd. "You found them, huh?"

Todd nodded.

The man with the blue eyes pulled out a pistol and took three successive silenced shots at Todd. Todd's eyes widened and he stopped shaking as he dropped his own pistol. His mouth agape, he fell backward into the fountain. While the spurting fountain changed colors, the water around his body turned a deep crimson as the cloud of fresh blood dispersed from the fresh bullet holes in his chest.

"You two. Get up and follow us."

Chris stood first, his head swiveling toward the coat he'd draped across the back of the couch in the living area.

The man with blue eyes stepped in front of him and scowled at him. "You won't need that."

The other man, glancing at them with his dark brown eyes, offered a slight smile. "Besides, it's warming up out there. As long as you don't go for another run, everything's going to be just fine."

Brown Eyes motioned for Chris to head to the elevator. Instead, Chris stopped. "Tracy can stay here. Kaufman doesn't need her."

"We were told to bring the both of you."

"That wasn't the plan." Chris shook his head, taking a step toward Brown Eyes. "She stays or I don't go."

His nose scrunched in a snarl, Blue Eyes grabbed Tracy by her collar and pressed the gun to her temple. "You both go or she does indeed stay."

"Don't touch her."

Blue Eyes threw Tracy at him. She stumbled into his arms. When she stood, her eyes narrowed. Chris grabbed her wrist as she made tight fists.

"That wasn't part of the deal," he said.

"Buddy, you are in no position to be making deals," Brown Eyes said. "If you don't feel compelled to join us, we can break your arms, tie you up and let you watch while we take care of her right here."

Wringing his hands together, Blue Eyes took a step toward Tracy. "She's a pretty thing, too. It'd be a shame to waste her."

"Don't you touch me!" Tracy broke from Chris's grasp. "You lay a hand on me and I'll rip your balls off."

Blue Eyes laughed and glanced at Brown Eyes. He rolled his eyes. "Let's just make this easy and go see the boss."

Grabbing Chris's arm, Brown Eyes led them into the elevator. Blue Eyes holstered his gun and put a hand on Tracy's shoulder to guide her in. She shook his hand off and spat at him. His thin lips spread wider as he gestured on the holodisplay in the elevator for the ground level. Despite the fact that Blue Eyes had holstered his gun, Chris didn't feel compelled to make a run for it when they exited the elevator at the bottom floor. If he gave chase this time, the ending might not be so favorable as before.

They led Tracy and Chris to a black sedan.

Tracy looked up at them as she ducked her head into the car. "No Corvette today? Daddy take it away?"

"Can't very well fit four passengers in a Vette, can we?" Blue Eyes pushed Chris in behind her. He joined them in the back seat and closed the door behind him. "Put your hands behind your back. Both of you."

They both did as he told them. Blue Eyes yanked Chris's arms closer together, making him wince in pain as his right shoulder stung. It didn't burn as intensely as before, but it still felt inflamed. Blue Eyes bound both their wrists, got out of the car, and moved up to the front seat with his partner as Brown Eyes entered in a destination on the panel.

"Where are we going?" Tracy asked.

"We've got a business meeting," Brown Eyes said, his gaze straight ahead.

The car took off and joined up with lines of other cars crawling between buildings during the afternoon rush hour. Lampposts, trash cans, pedestrians, and storefronts passed by. Icicles melted, and water dripped on the sidewalks. Chris saw the familiar green, red, and white awning of Il Fedelissimo and imagined the aroma of crushed tomatoes and fresh bread and pasta from within. His stomach growled, and he realized he hadn't eaten anything since he'd shared coffee with Jordan that morning.

Tracy prodded him with an elbow, and he whipped around to face her. She blinked in quick succession. He frowned, not understanding the concerned look on her face. Raising her eyebrows, wrinkles forming in her forehead, she opened her eyes wide and pursed her lips. She glanced back out at the street and back to him.

Chris shook his head.

She rolled her eyes. "Remember what we did to Todd?" She tried to speak in a low voice.

"Shut it back there."

Again, Chris frowned. He looked back out the window as they crawled along Key Highway toward the south end of Federal Hill. He could see the landmark antiquated neon orange sign above the Domino Sugars refinery on the harbor. Then his eyes widened and he looked back at Tracy, back out the window, back at her.

She nodded.

The two thugs had not bothered to blindfold them. The men might have neglected to think about it. They might be more slow witted than Chris had given them credit for. But if that wasn't true, if they didn't care that Tracy and Chris could note every street and every landmark they passed, there was one reason why they might not care—why Kaufman might not care.

Chris stared hard into Tracy's cool eyes and gulped. She nodded back.

Wherever they were going, they weren't leaving.

CHAPTER THIRTY-ONE

U NLIKE IN THE CABS THAT roamed Baltimore's streets, Chris and Tracy could not change the destination of the car without access to the front seats. Kaufman's lackeys provided a formidable barrier to the car's holoscreen. Both lazily stared out the windows as the car trolled down the street. Their broad shoulders blotted out much of the view through the front windshield.

To their left, sunlight glinted off white-capped waves between apartment and office buildings. Chris could even make out the green, bulbous dragon shapes of paddleboats in the water. He'd always scoffed at the stupid tourist trap, dismissing the idea of paying an exorbitant fee to labor oneself around a harbor smelling of fish and polluted water that stank of sulfur.

Now he envied the careless people propelling their boats through the gray water.

The views of the harbor became obscured once again by warehouses and factories, all with drab brown- and gray-hued facades. The glowing Domino Sugars sign atop the refinery stood far above them now, no longer visible through the windows as it disappeared beyond the roof of the sedan.

Tracy nudged Chris, and he turned from the window to face her. She clenched her jaw and scowled at him as if to scold him for his suspicious behavior. He straightened up and peered out of the corners of his eyes at her. Her right wrist twisted free of the nylon rope bonds.

She inched toward him, leaning slightly. Chris could feel her hand explore behind his back, tugging at the ropes that held his wrists. The sensation of a dozen needles spread in his fingers, no longer numb from lack of circulation. He wriggled his fingers to restore the blood flow.

With a subtle nod, Tracy indicated the two men in front of them. Both faced forward. Behind her back, she clenched her hands together. Chris nodded in understanding and Tracy inhaled deep. She mouthed "one, two, three."

Like a mouse trap, her arms shot around the neck of the man in front of her. Chris followed suit, just a second behind her.

The vessels in her forearms popped and bulged, her muscles tense and tight. Brown Eyes worked his fingers around her thin arms, struggling to loosen her grip as he gulped for air.

Chris used both arms to pull Blue Eyes back against the front seat. He leveraged his legs to apply extra pressure, kicking at the seat in front of him to aid his hold on the man's neck. The lackey grunted, and Chris could feel the man's neck muscles bulge out against his forearms.

With one thick hand, the man gripped Chris's right arm and twisted it off his neck.

Tracy's victim turned red in the face. He clung to her arms.

Chris's target slammed him back into his seat, and Blue Eyes reached out to help Brown. Blue delivered a powerful blow to Tracy's shoulder.

Absorbing the hit, she wrapped her arms tighter around Brown Eyes and grimaced. Chris punched Blue only to be deflected and countered by a deft chop.

Blue landed a second blow on Tracy's temple. With her grip now loosened, Brown's neck bulged. He growled as he tore her arms away. Free, he sucked in a deep breath. His face returned to its normal almond hue as he breathed, though his arms shook as he held Tracy's away from his neck.

"You think you're a strong bitch, don't you?" Blue Eyes leaned over the front seat and threw Tracy against the back of the car. Her head cracked against the rear window.

She slumped back into her seat, fuming and clutching the back of her head. Blood trickled around her fingers. She seemed more livid than hurt. Chris shrank back into his own seat, his right arm on fire and shuddering.

"Shoot 'em," Brown Eyes said.

Blue Eyes reached into his coat. Chris cowered in his seat as Tracy lunged at him, but Brown Eyes batted her away. From his inner pocket, Blue Eyes whipped out a pair of syringes. He uncapped one and grabbed Chris's wrist.

Chris flailed but could not shake the man's grip. The needle dove underneath his skin, and warmth spread from the injection site. His vision blurred as the man grabbed at Tracy's swinging arm. She kicked his hand away and sent the needle flying into the front windshield.

His head heavy, Chris blinked and reached out toward Tracy with a hand made of cement. Both Kaufman's thugs held her down now, grunting and growling, as Blue Eyes plunged the second needle deep into her arm. She lashed out at them with her unrestrained feet, kicking at their faces. Her movements slowed and faltered as Chris struggled to keep his eyes open.

At last, he slipped sideways on the cool leather of the back seat, his body falling against hers. Darkness replaced light, sounds distorted until they quieted, and his thoughts dissolved.

The harsh smell of ammonia jolted Chris awake. Blue Eyes crouched next to him, his fingers under Chris's nose. The man stood when Chris opened his eyes.

He tried to raise himself up, but his hands were secured together behind his back. He bent his legs closer to him but couldn't separate his feet. As he brought his legs up, he could see the ropes tied around his ankles. He lost his balance and fell back on his side. The side of his head cracked against concrete, but his nerves remained dulled and the pain just a distant throb. He rotated his shoulder in place. Though it ached, he felt only a sliver of the agony he had experienced before.

Water dripped in the distant corners of the shadowy warehouse where he lay. Around him, wooden crates emblazoned with the logo of a sportswear company were stacked in heaps. Metal rafters lined the ceiling like the rib cage of an enormous whale. Lights hung from above on long chains, most shut off.

"This one's awake too," Blue Eyes said.

"Good," Brown Eyes said. "Boss don't need to know we put 'em to sleep. Don't want that."

Chris craned his neck to see Tracy's eyes shoot open, her face distorting into a fierce grimace. She struggled against her bonds, and her face turned red with effort, her mouth gagged. Like a fish, she flopped on the floor, her cries muffled through the cloth strung over her mouth. Blue Eyes kicked her hard in the stomach. Chris cringed as she turned redder, her eyes narrowing to slits.

"You take the bitch," Blue Eyes said.

"Hell, no. She's as bad as a feral cat."

"You can't handle a skinny little girl?"

"Come on, man. I don't want to touch that bitch again."

Blue Eyes shook his head, bent, and picked up Tracy. He threw her over his shoulder. As they walked behind the nearest stack of crates, she stared hard at Chris and he returned her gaze with equal intensity. He wasn't sure what message she sent now, but he couldn't bear to take his eyes off her until Brown Eyes swung him over his large back.

Chris's head bounced against Brown Eyes' muscles as they wound through the labyrinth of crates and cardboard boxes. They plunged deeper into the stacks. Brown Eyes paused. The sound of a lock clicking was followed by the squeak of metal hinges. A sickening thud accompanied muffled cursing from Tracy.

Brown Eyes stepped through the doorway and stopped. He flung Chris forward and jammed him onto a cold metal folding chair. He turned to see Tracy beside him, the back of her hair matted with wet blood and a scowl glued across her face.

"Good to see you in person, Mr. Morgan."

Chris swung around. When he moved too fast, the fire in his shoulder and neck flared. "Ben Kaufman."

The man laughed. His lifeless gray eyes glowed yellow in the low light of the small office. Bookcases lined the walls. While his suit was impeccably clean and pressed, a fine layer of dust coated the paper books and windowless walls. Only the surface of the desk appeared devoid of settled grime.

"I told you: I am not Ben Kaufman. But you will meet him soon enough. Go ahead and remove the gag from Ms. Harrow's mouth. She might be helpful."

Brown Eyes untied the cloth gag and tore it from Tracy's mouth.

Tracy kicked in her chair. "Get these damned ropes off of us."

"I'm not that stupid, Ms. Harrow. I do not take caution lightly."

"Are you kidding? Caution? You left quite a mess with that girl. Blood everywhere, hung her up to die. Asshole." Tracy spat at the businessman, but her saliva fell short, splattering on the desk. "That didn't seem a bit like caution to me."

His face indicated neither disgust nor disapproval while he took out a white handkerchief from his jacket pocket. He wiped the desk clean. "That was not my mess. However, it is an unfortunate situation that I wish could've been avoided."

"I know you called her before torturing her, you sick bastard," Chris said. "And even if it wasn't you who personally killed her, you're responsible for your damned thugs."

Brown Eyes and Blue Eyes looked at each other with raised eyebrows.

"My boys are just as meticulous as I am. In fact, they'll be headed back to your friend's place later to go clean up, won't you, boys?" Both men nodded at their boss as he crossed his thin arms. "Such scenes aren't typical of our operations, I assure you. All the same, I suppose what happened is quite unlucky." He leaned forward, his cool eyes boring into Chris. "Did you have sexual relations with Ms. Powell? She wouldn't tell me during our brief call."

"What the hell business is it of yours?" Chris snarled.

"I just want to be sure we can collect our property."

"What are you talking about?" Tracy asked.

The businessman smirked but ignored her. "Answer me, Mr. Morgan."

Chris shook his head and the businessman gave a slight hand gesture to Brown Eyes. He stepped closer, pushed Chris forward with one hand, and yanked his bound wrists up.

He yelled in agony. "Yes! I did!"

The businessman nodded, and Brown Eyes dropped Chris's arms.

He sat back against the folding chair, panting. Tracy's glare burned in his peripheral vision.

"Was this recently, Mr. Morgan?"

"When we dated," Chris said between agonized breaths. "Before I went to prison."

Furrowing his brow, the businessman clasped his hands together on the desk. "But not recently?"

He shook his head, sweat trickling down his forehead and stinging his eyes. "No, no. I didn't."

"You must realize how important it is that you be honest with me, Mr. Morgan." The businessman nodded once more at Brown Eyes and he bent Chris's arms up several excruciating inches.

A drop of sweat from his forehead landed on the metal folding chair, causing a soft ping. His chest heaved and he pinched his eyes closed. "I'm telling the truth." He dropped his chin against his chest. "I'm not lying."

The businessman made another gesture to tell Brown Eyes to let go, and Chris's arms slapped down against his back. He pointed at Tracy. "Take that one away. Run the blood tests on her."

Brown Eyes indicated Chris with a nod of head. "Him, too?"

"No. I'll take care of him."

Blue Eyes and Brown Eyes picked Tracy up, swinging her between the two of them. She grunted, her eyes aflame in ferocity.

When the door shut behind the men and their captive, the businessman got up from his seat and stepped around the desk. "Now that it's just us, we can speak more freely." He knelt down by Chris's feet and looked up. "Don't try anything stupid, Mr. Morgan. I don't make idle threats." After pulling a small knife from his suit jacket, he cut the ropes binding Chris's ankles. "To be honest, I don't trust that Tracy Harrow girl, either. Never have. As you've noticed, we've two gentleman who have tailed you to protect you from, among others, her. She seems particularly volatile."

"Protect me from her? You're the goddamn monster that killed Randy and Veronica."

The businessman stood up. He rotated a silver band on the ring finger of his right hand. "To be clear, I killed neither of them. The two gentlemen you've become acquainted with did indeed kill Mr. Randall Nee, but I assure you that the man could do no more good alive. Quite a rat." He walked behind Chris, out of his vision. "No, that is offensive to rats. In fact, rats have served us much more respectably in our labs than Mr. Nee ever did. I have the utmost respect for those animals' sacrifices and none for Mr. Nee."

A couple of quick snaps preceded the nylon ropes falling from Chris's wrists. He stretched and flexed his wrists and fingers.

The businessman leaned against the front of the desk. He rotated the ring around his finger again.

Chris's eyes darted about the office, looking for weapons.

The man held up his ringed finger and pointed at the silver band. "Don't do anything rash. Among other functions, this ring monitors my heart. A sudden, prolonged surge or slowing in pulse will bring those men back immediately. I'm sure you are well aware of their gifts of strength by now and understand that you are overwhelmingly overmatched." With his hand, he brushed the surface of the desk. "Now that Ms. Harrow is gone, I might change your mind about my intentions."

"You've got Jordan hostage, and now you take Tracy too, to do God knows what with. Change my mind? You're insane."

The man's face remained stolid.

"You're a murderer, a manipulator, and a torturer. Kill me and let Tracy and Jordan go. They shouldn't even be involved in this."

A subtle, almost pitiful smirk curled the man's pale lips. "Veronica Powell is alive. She's expected to make a full recovery. It will be a long one, but she's lucky to have a LyfeGen Sustain. I've heard it called it a god organ, no?"

Chris's eyes widened. "She's alive?"

"It seems that rich parents and that expensive artificial organ had helped her survive. I assure you, Mr. Morgan, that although I did indeed try to contact Ms. Powell, I did not have her tortured, much less killed. This all could've been resolved in a much more civilized manner."

With the shock of these revelations, his mind swam. A moment ago he had felt ready to die for his friends, to die for Tracy. Now a small but persistent spring of hope found its way up through the desolate thoughts that had precipitated. "If you didn't try to kill her, who did?"

The businessman lifted his eyebrows and held out his hands. His sleeves hung from his pale, bony wrists as if the suit hung off a dapper scarecrow. "We might be able to answer that question if your friends were a bit more honest like you." The man walked his fingers up Chris's chest, pressing his index finger in front of his middle finger. "I need them to be just as cooperative as you, and I'll do whatever's necessary to convince them."

Chris resisted the urge to swat the man's hand away. "I can understand your interest in Jordan, but Tracy has nothing to do with any of this. Why can't you just let her go? I'll tell you whatever you want to hear."

"I don't want you to tell me what I *want* to hear; I want you to tell me the truth." A soft chortle escaped the businessman's throat, more a rasp than a laugh. "Mr. Morgan, now that it's just you and me, I will ask this once more. *Only* once more." The businessman snapped his fingers, and a projection display lit up across the surface of the desk, illuminating blue dust motes that floated in the musty air. As the image cleared, Jordan Thompson appeared, kneeling on the ground, his hands behind his back and his face cranked toward the ceiling. An arm stretched from beyond the vantage point of the display with a gun pressed against Jordan's skull. "Did you have intercourse yesterday morning with Ms. Powell?"

"How do I know that you haven't already killed him? That this isn't just video footage from earlier?"

The businessman reached into his suit jacket pocket again, revealed his comm card, and whispered into it. "Make Mr. Thompson wave."

In the projected display, the gun jerked at Jordan. He appeared to respond, but the sound was muted. The gun jerked again and he lifted both his arms. Chris resisted the nauseating urge to vomit. Jordan's fingers clenched and unclenched on his right hand, but his left hand hung, bent in his forearm where no joint existed.

"What did you to do him?" Chris asked.

"Mr. Morgan, did you have intercourse with Ms. Powell?"

Chris shook his head. The businessman brought the comm card up to his mouth and stared at him. The citrus scent of Veronica's perfume and the touch of her naked porcelain skin against his flooded back from the day before. He had given in to her, to his emotions, and their conversation in Veronica's studio had seemed so familiar that it had felt as if they had never been apart. Their teasing jokes and stories had escalated into a stolen touch, a passionate kiss, and then that moment when repressed desire erupted between the two of them in her bedroom.

Holding out both hands in a pleading gesture, Chris shouted, "Yes! I did!" He hung his head. "I did."

"That's what I suspected. Ms. Harrow will be rather upset to find all this out, won't she?" The businessman smirked.

"I'm not worried about that right now." Chris scowled. "How do you know Veronica's alive?"

"I maintain a useful network of medical professionals in the area who can be easily persuaded. Quite necessary for our business here." His eyes narrowed, and he pointed at Chris. "In fact, you met one of these individuals when you first went to prison."

Chris racked his brain thinking about the officers and guards he had met in various stages of the commitment process when he began his sentence. Nobody stuck out as strange, though. He massaged his wrists. Ligature marks reddened the skin where the cords had been. Then a realization hit him as he considered the businessman's interest in his relationship with Veronica. He recalled the strange injection site on her arm. Jordan's writing, too, flashed in his mind. The truck and trailer, built by the driver, but the driver's body was the cargo.

Shaking his head, Chris scowled and rubbed the red marks on his wrists as if to smudge them away. "You never cared about the samples that Randy produced, did you?"

The businessman's expression remained as cold and straight as ever. "We did. But they were a secondary concern. A bonus of having you work with us." His lips twitched, forming a controlled but evident smirk. "You're smarter than I initially thought."

"It was the doctor," Chris said. "That's what this is all about? When I first went to prison, he injected me with something." He thought back to Jordan's peculiar ending to the story sitting on the projection display in the office. "Jordan thought he figured it out, didn't he? You wanted me alive because whatever you need from me, it's already inside of me."

CHAPTER THIRTY-TWO

"**V**ERY GOOD." THE BUSINESSMAN CLAPPED. "Very good, indeed."

"Why would you do that? Why me?"

The thin, suited man stood up and moved behind the desk. He paced back and forth before leaning on it. "Let's see if you can figure this out. Mr. Morgan, before, I thought you were dispensable. Over the course of the past few months, I've realized you are more technically gifted than I initially supposed. I want to see if there might be a place for you within our organization."

"I'd never work for you."

"You already have."

"Not by my own free will."

"I gave you an offer. Nothing bound you to that offer, but you took it."

"You threatened me," Chris said. "I couldn't find another job. Didn't have another choice."

"But you did have a choice." The businessman played with the silver ring on his right hand. "Now, I might give you another. However, I want you to be well aware of what you would be getting yourself into. It might change your interest in these matters."

When Chris had first entered the black-market enhancement trade, Jordan had said something similar. He had warned Chris that once he sold his genetic enhancements and delivery systems on the black market, he could never go back. He could never remove the genes from the people that bought the manufactured enhancements. They would be permanently changed. Just as Chris would be.

"Even if I wanted to go back to manufacturing your damn genies, I wouldn't work with anyone who hires goons like that Todd character."

The businessman sighed, his yellow-gray eyes rolling in disgust. "Neither would I. I asked the men that followed you to bring in Mr. Thompson and his friend while they went out to lunch. My men made the unfortunate decision to convince a former client in your area to tail you and Ms. Harrow as they caught up to Mr. Thompson."

"Not bright men. That doesn't inspire confidence for your organization or whatever the hell this place is."

"I can understand your reservations, but that's an issue I'll be addressing when my time with you is up. Regardless of your confidence, you're now at the point where I'll be able to dispose of you or you'll work for me. It's safe enough for me to tell you that I work with Ben Kaufman. He's the technical side and the investor, if you will. I do the legwork, the human relations." The man stood and paced back and forth. "You can either work with us or we can kill you. I understand it may be a difficult choice, but I'm not giving you weeks to make the decision again."

"I want you to answer my questions first."

"Very well. I suppose any potential employer allows a prospective employee the opportunity to ask a couple questions." He sat down behind the desk again.

"What did you have injected in me?"

"An appropriate initial question. You've been infected with an inert, nonlethal, nontransfective viral vector that contains the genetic data necessary for improving the function of efferent nerves, along with increased motor neuron activity."

"All this to improve strength," Chris said.

"Yes, yes, that's right."

"Why not increase muscle mass and size?"

"Our genetic enhancements may be utilized in conjunction with enhancements like that if the end user so desires. On the other hand, think of the people who might wish to have concealed strength. Improving neuron motor recruitment capabilities might offer an individual more strength while providing their opponent little insight into their true potential. Or certain organizations may value a stronger soldier, a more powerful grunt that takes up less cargo weight." He winked.

"You mean the government is interested in your crap?"

"Not mine. Ben Kaufman's. Kaufman is associated with certain companies that have access to government contractors."

"But you would still need proof that this works in humans before the army or anyone purchases anything," Chris said.

"It's also much easier to run a successful clinical trial after you've already performed human trials."

"Human trials? What group approved those?"

"My group did. Most companies spend several years developing a whole slew of enhancements, years on animal models, and then too many years on clinical trials in humans before they realize it doesn't work."

"Yes, I know that. That's just the typical FDA approval process. Every company spends at least a decade or more to develop anything new." Chris inhaled. "Unless you jumped straight to human trials."

"Correct. It's much easier to test the enhancements on humans first, pick which works best. We've been able to do just that. Human trials were a resounding success. It's especially easy to select volunteers when those volunteers are paying you for black-market enhancements." The businessman smirked.

Chris raised an eyebrow. A bead of sweat rolled down his forehead, staying on his lip. He brushed it away. "But something went wrong, didn't it? Why aren't you and Ben Kaufman busy forging your animal trials and applying for FDA clinical trials with his contractor friends?"

His shoulder dropping, the businessman gazed toward a corner of the office. "Others interested in similar technology compromised our operations by tipping off federal investigators. We disbanded for a while."

"And you couldn't risk any evidence linking you to your new genetic enhancements or your human trials. You destroyed your labs, but you couldn't afford to destroy your DNA." Chris massaged the red marks around his wrists. "I don't understand why you didn't just replicate the DNA from your bioinformatic records when you started over."

The businessman turned away, momentarily silenced, and let out a long sigh. His expression appeared grim. "Mr. Kaufman is protective of his property, particularly his intellectual property. We kept no electronic copies of the makeup of the genes themselves. Between government agencies, amateur hackers, and our competitors, such electronic formats are more of a liability than a safeguard."

"So, the records were all on paper?" Chris said, his thoughts clicking together. "Does this have anything to do with the outbreak of arson incidents in the area a year ago?"

The man nodded.

"Your competitors burned down your labs before you could remove everything yourselves, right after you got word the police had received a warrant for the facilities."

Again, the businessman nodded.

"They played you, didn't they?"

A crimson hue spread across the man's face. His lips remained tight and his eyes narrow. "That they did. The only people that remained from these attacks were Mr. Kaufman, myself, and a couple other men that we could trust."

"You mean to tell me this whole operation—the genetic development and testing—was run by just the four of you?"

"There were more of us."

"What happened to them?"

The businessman stared hard with narrowed eyes but did not answer. He loosened his tie.

"The DNA, though. You saved a sample of it in your viral vectors. Injecting it in people seems a bit...unnecessary...to store it." Chris's eyebrows wrinkled together.

Now the man's pallid lips curled again. "Not just store it, but produce it—let it replicate. We couldn't let years of developmental work go to waste. We didn't want to risk losing the last vial that we had left. Besides, the viral vectors we found available could passively replicate without genetic transfection in live animals. Without our lab space, we didn't have access to the usual small mammals, and these particular viruses thrive best in a human host anyway."

"I can't believe it. You persuaded the intake physician at Fulton to inject it into random prisoners." Chris shook his head, thinking of Vincent's list. "No, they weren't random. They all shared connections with the enhancement trade, didn't they?"

"That's correct. A few were former employees of mine stupid enough to get caught. Others were small-timers, like you."

"You wanted to use that to your advantage, to manipulate us all while the virus replicated inside us," Chris said. "We served as living bioreactors. Just vessels to replicate your vectors until you could collect us, collect the genes, and sell them." Images of Vincent's notebook, the lists, and Lash's eyes flashed before him. "You needed to keep us alive, but your lackeys failed you. You almost lost all of it."

The businessman pursed his lips. His tie wrinkled as he folded his arms over his chest. "Almost. Our competitors tried to destroy our product."

"I don't understand why you didn't just inject the viruses into your own body."

"Mr. Morgan, did you ever inject your own experimental products into yourself?"

Chris shook his head. He never had.

"Just like a good narcotics dealer refuses to enjoy the very product he is distributing, we refused to affect ourselves."

Pressure pulsed behind his eyes as he pictured Veronica among her ruined art. He pinched the bridge of his nose. "My God. The virus you've used to house this DNA—it can be passed on with bodily fluids, can't it?"

"That is a flaw in its design."

"So these rivals of yours found out about me and the others, and they've followed me ever since?"

"I suspect that's the case." He clenched his hands together on the desk. "However, my men never spotted anyone following you around. Mr. Nee grew cocky, though, trying to raise the price for the supplies and delivery technologies he procured. Obviously, someone whispered into his fat little ears—their eyes once again on our technology and, I suspected, on you." The businessman gritted his teeth, his nose scrunching in a snarl. "Mr. Morgan, you've proved yourself adept at understanding this complicated situation. Would you mind putting this last piece of the puzzle together? Who possessed the knowledge, the connections, and the capability of stealing this technology from us? Who do you think took Veronica Powell's blood? Who knew about your relationship with her? And who knew what you and Ms. Harrow were up to?" He leaned back in the creaking office chair. "I think this is quite a simple puzzle."

The small projection display on the desk glowed blue. Jordan Thompson knelt on the ground. No pistol pointed at him. Blood trickled down his forehead.

"Mr. Morgan, you know that we both have vested interests in finding Veronica Powell. I cannot let this technology fall into the wrong hands, and you two are involved in a rather personal relationship. I want your help."

Chris nodded.

"Mr. Thompson refuses to speak to us. You know what you must do."

Gulping, he closed his eyes. "Then you will let Tracy and me go, right? You can take enough blood from me to isolate your virus, but I want to know that we'll be free."

"I can't promise you anything right now." The businessman leaned forward. From his sleeve, he drew the knife he'd used to cut Chris's bonds. "But I believe Mr. Kaufman will be much more merciful if you can convince Mr. Thompson to cooperate. He may even let you have that permanent position with us."

CHAPTER THIRTY-THREE

"**P**LEASE, JUST TELL ME WHERE Veronica is." Chris knelt in front of Jordan.

Blood pooled in one of Jordan's battered eyes from a burst vessel. Bruises appeared black on his dark skin. His shirt flapped against his body in tatters, soaking up sweat and blood. Chains clinked against the tile floor as Jordan shuffled on his knees. "I don't know. I've told them: I don't *know!*" A sheen of wetness glazed over his eyes.

Chris stood up and pressed his eyelids closed, clenching and unclenching his hands. His pulse quickened, his heart pounding against his rib cage, his headache beating in the same rhythm. He took a deep breath. The sterile smell of cleaning chemicals mixed with the aroma of foul body odor and the metallic scent of blood. A stainless steel table stood at one end of the room. An open container of sterile gauze sat next to an array of scalpels, forceps, and assorted blades.

In the opposite corner of the large suite, an armed guard stood near Greg. His wrists were tied in front of him, and he sat on a stool. His shirt lay in a sopping pile on the floor next to him. He appeared to have no broken bones. Even so, his head hung against his chest, and lacerations along his bare skin dripped with blood.

Chris stepped over the chains connecting Jordan's ankles to the heavy examination table. "Please, just tell me what you did with her."

"I didn't do anything." Jordan quaked. He struggled to his feet. "They're brainwashing you. I don't care about their enhancements or what they're doing with them. I'm not in that business anymore."

Chris's nostrils flared. He pointed at Greg. "What about him?"

"He hasn't left my side the entire weekend." He coughed and spat a mass of saliva and blood on the floor in front of him. "I trust him with my life."

Facing toward Greg again, Chris caught his eyes. The green in them shone bright despite the pallor in his cheeks. Greg's eyes shied away from Chris's gaze and landed on Jordan. A pitiful expression spread across his face.

"I don't know what to believe," Chris said, looking at the ground. He toyed with the knife that the businessman had given him, passing it back and forth between his hands. "You killed people before, when we worked together, and never told me. How am I supposed to believe that you didn't try to have Veronica killed and harvest the DNA from her for yourself?"

"Stop being so weak." Jordan's voice rose, more venomous than Chris had ever heard it before. "I warned you: if you think these people will let you live, if you think they will let any of us live, you are more ignorant than I could've ever dreamed. You trust these people over me? I may not have been completely honest with you, but I never lied. If you had asked me if I'd had people killed before, I would've told you. I regret every action I took in that business, and I wish I could change it. It took you going to prison for me to wake up." He coughed again, falling to his knees. After the fit subsided, he looked up at Chris, his bloodied eye dilating uncontrolled. "Torture me, kill me. Do whatever you want with me. It won't change the fact that you're going to end up dead, too."

He coughed again and spat a slimy combination of mucus and blood onto the cold white-tiled floor. "I warned you. I told you to let this go."

Chris eyed the guard standing beside Greg. At the door, another guard stood, his arms folded and a pistol holstered in his belt. He guessed the businessman was still watching, waiting. He had to act. With a sudden swipe, he backhanded Jordan. He spun behind him, pressing the blade of the knife against Jordan's throat.

"Stop!" Greg jumped to his feet, and the guard slammed him back onto the stool. Both guards now stared at him.

With a quick glance, Chris caught Greg's eyes and nodded subtly. He leaned in close to Jordan's ear. "Get ready."

Greg tried to stand again, yelling. The guard at the door strode across the room to help subdue him, bringing with him a length of nylon cords.

As the guard walked by, Chris slashed at the back of the man's knee with the knife. The blade dug deep into the man's skin, and the guard crumpled, crying out in agony. The other guard jumped at the cry and, in that brief moment, Greg stood up with enough force to knock the guard against the wall.

With his wrists still bound, Greg wrapped his arms around the guard and strangled him. Chris took the nylon cord the other guard had dropped. The man reached for his pistol. Jordan kicked at his hand and crunched the guard's fingers.

A large thud echoed from the corner as Greg dropped the unconscious body of one of the cronies and stepped toward the other, who was writhing in pain next to Chris and Jordan. Greg delivered a couple of kicks to the guard's head, leaving the man with a crooked broken nose and blood bubbling out of his nostrils. He cocked his leg back again but stopped when Chris placed a hand on his shoulder. The man lay unconscious.

Chris cut the cords wrapped around Jordan's wrists. "They've got a camera in here, so we've got to get moving." He stood up and cut Greg's ropes loose.

Rubbing his wrists and flexing his fingers, Greg walked over to the examination table and tugged at the chain connected to Jordan's feet. It wouldn't give. He looked around the room, searching through the surgical tools and drawers, while Chris took off his own shirt. He fashioned the shirt into a sling for Jordan's arm. When he finished, he tucked one of the guard's pistols into the waist of his pants. He retrieved the other gun from the guard slumped against the wall and gave it to Jordan.

"I can't find anything to take care of that damned chain." Greg threw a drawer across the room, and its contents spilled out, plastic syringes clattering across the tiled floor.

"Does one of the guards have a key for the lock on his ankles?" Chris asked. "We need to get the hell out of here fast."

Greg shook his head. "The man in the suit took it."

His knees shaking, Jordan stood up with one arm on Chris's shoulder.

"You think you can push that thing out of here?" Chris asked, indicating the examination table that Jordan's chains were secured to.

Greg smiled. "Hell, the sled in college was heavier." He kicked the little metal levers on the wheels of the table to unlock them. "Plus, this has wheels."

"The sled?" Chris cocked his head.

Jordan smirked through his bruises. "He played football in college. He's talking about the training sled."

"Great. Let's get out of here."

Greg led them out, grinding his feet into the floor as he pushed the table through the doorway. Jordan limped out after him with Chris's help.

"We've got to find Tracy," Chris said. "Do you have any idea where she is?"

"I'm not sure, but I thought I saw other rooms like this in the direction we came from." Greg pointed down the hall where it took a sharp corner.

Clicking the safety off on his pistol, Chris looked behind them. "Where the hell is everybody?"

"Strange," Jordan said, through gritted teeth. "But I don't recall seeing many people on our way in. In fact, I only saw those two guards and that man in the suit."

"I know there are at least two other guys around here," Chris said. "They brought Tracy and me here. I think they're running a smaller operation since the fire."

Jordan rubbed his red eye with the back of his good hand. "Fire?"

"It's a long story."

Jordan managed a grin. "Maybe it'll be enough for a new book, huh?"

They continued down the corridor, and Chris explained as much as he could to Greg and Jordan. They passed windows that revealed rooms vacant of people but full of equipment. Machines shined and glimmered, metallic surfaces glinting in the bright lights. There appeared to be a large bioreactor, several incubators, PCR machines, and microscopes scattered in one of the rooms. Another housed shelves of empty cages suitable for rats or mice. Few machines appeared to be on.

Huffing, Greg turned around again as he pushed the table down the hall and navigated it around the corner. "We need to get this chain lock off."

"I might be able to help you out."

The three of them turned around. Behind them, the businessman stood with a pistol aimed at Chris.

"Mr. Thompson, Mr. Morgan. Please, drop your pistols and kick them over to me."

Frowning, Greg caught Chris's eyes and glanced at the businessman. Chris shook his head, dropped his pistol, and sent it skittering along the floor at their captor. Jordan followed suit, using his good hand to retrieve the pistol. He dropped it and kicked it toward the businessman.

"Good." For a moment, he stood silent, poised with the gun pointed at Chris, Jordan, and Greg. His eyes appeared vacant and distant. "I'm wondering if it's worth leaving all three of you alive." Keeping the gun pointed at them, he knelt and picked up the two other weapons. He stowed one in his belt and tucked the other away in his suit jacket. A wide grin spread across his face. "Maybe we can try another strategy to squeeze out the information I need, in which case, you'll be more use to me alive." He pointed down the hall. "Keep on that way. You'll see Ms. Harrow again soon. But if one of you even turns to look at me, I won't hesitate to gun you down where you stand."

They passed by more long windows that opened up into various rooms. Chris would not so much as glance to see what they contained. A bead of sweat rolled down his forehead, and he kept his eyes forward. They trudged toward an open door at the end of the hallway. Two men stood outside the room and nodded at the businessman as the group approached.

"Go in there," the he said, pointing through the doorway. He withdrew the two guns that he had taken from Greg and Chris and handed them to one of the men guarding the room. "Take these upstairs and send Mr. Kaufman down here."

Chris walked into the room first. In the center, Tracy sat on a chair designed for donating blood. Straps secured her wrists and ankles to the chair. A length of silicone tubing stretched from an IV needle in her forearm to a plastic container and pump that collected her blood. Her eyes lit up when they entered. "Chris. Can you get this shit out of my arm?"

When the businessman came in behind them, her expression dropped. "Now, now, Ms. Harrow. We need to retrieve as much of your blood as we can."

She glared at him. "You keep taking it from me and I'll end up dead."

"No matter to me." He shrugged. "Mr. Morgan, you'll find a box of individually wrapped syringes in the second drawer to your left. Please remove three of them for me."

Chris steadied Jordan against the examination table that Greg had pushed in.

As Chris searched through the drawer, Greg stepped between the businessman and Jordan.

"Now, now. Don't do anything rash." The man pointed his gun at Greg until he stepped back up against the wall.

Chris found the sterile syringes in a white box and took out three of them.

"You'll find a glass bottle in that shelf-top refrigerator. Fill each syringe with five milliliters from that bottle." The businessman squinted at Greg. "I take that back. Fill two of them with five milliliters and the third with seven milliliters of the solution."

Chris opened the small refrigerator. Ten little glass bottles with rubber tops, labeled identically, rested on a shelf. He took one and plunged a needle in. As he retracted the syringe plunger, the liquid surged up into it to the 5 ml mark. He filled the other two and turned back for further instructions.

"Inject Mr. Harding with the seven-milliliter syringe," the man said.

"What's in it?"

"Give Mr. Harding his shot." He waved the pistol at Chris.

Chris stepped toward Greg, the syringe shaking in his hand. "I'm sorry."

"It's okay," Greg said, holding out his forearm. "Do what you have to."

Taking Greg's wrist in his, Chris steadied the syringe in his other hand. He inserted the needle into Greg's flesh, plunging it into a vein. The clear liquid swirled as he pushed down on the plunger.

As Chris withdrew the needle, Greg stumbled back, losing his balance. His eyes rolled up into his head so that only the whites showed. Then his eyelids jerked closed and he fell.

"Greg!" Jordan knelt at the man's side and checked his pulse.

Greg's barrel chest still rose and fell. He was deep in the throes of unconsciousness.

"Perfect," the businessman said. "Mr. Thompson goes next."

Lowering himself beside Greg, Jordan grimaced. He placed his good hand on top of Greg's. "Go on." He closed his eyes and sat with his head against the tiled wall.

Chris steadied the cold needle against Jordan's skin. He hesitated and used his undershirt to wipe the blood from

Jordan's forearm. Using his fingers to better isolate a vessel, he inserted the needle and pushed in the plunger. Jordan's breathing slowed as his head tilted toward Greg.

The businessman picked the last syringe up from the table. He tapped it, releasing the bubbles that clung to the sides, and held the needle upright, pressing the plunger to clear the trapped air. "Your turn, Mr. Morgan."

"Don't let him do it." Tracy struggled against the straps holding her in place. The chair rattled.

The businessman pointed the gun at her. "Go on." He handed the syringe to Chris.

Choosing a vessel in his forearm, Chris clenched his hand and lowered himself against the drawers. He plunged the metal needle in and felt a sharp pain. As he pushed on the plunger, a cold jolt erupted in his arm. It spread as his blood carried the liquid through his body. He blinked, lightheaded, as the lights around him appeared to dim. Tracy's eyes turned into black beads before the rest of the lights disappeared, swallowed by a dark void.

CHAPTER THIRTY-FOUR

"**W**E'LL BE THROUGH WITH HER in about half an hour or so."

"Good, good. You don't think we should let her live?"

"Not at all. I think that would be unwise given the trouble that she's caused with Mr. Morgan. We'll have more than enough of the recovered virus to start replicating the DNA. We've recovered what we've hidden, and she'll be no use to us anymore."

"What about him?"

"I would like to keep him around until we can find Ms. Powell. We may be able to use him as leverage to get Mr. Thompson to talk. I believe using Mr. Harding may be effective."

"Thompson's been pretty stubborn, huh?"

"Yes. He's been most regrettably stubborn."

"Fuck you both."

"Now, now, Ms. Harrow."

A stubborn urge to gasp for air sent an electric pulse through Chris's nerves. He repressed it in an effort to stay unnoticed. His eyelids were heavy, and he struggled to open them. His pulse beat in his ears, and he wondered if anyone else noticed the heavy thudding. With careful, deliberate effort, he maintained his breathing, hoping that it sounded as if he still lay unconscious.

He had managed to squirt out most of the liquid from the syringe onto his skin before inserting the needle into his arm. It had been risky, but he could not stand to be put into an induced sleep again.

As he raised his right arm, it met with a slight resistance. The effort caused a flash of pain in his injured shoulder, but he prevented himself from grimacing. He lifted his left wrist and felt the same resistance. Leather straps secured both arms, similar to the ones he'd seen on Tracy's wrists. When he risked a peek, his eyelids quivered as he kept them open just enough to let the bright lights of the room burn into his unprepared pupils. As his eyes adjusted, the silhouettes of two men appeared hovering over Tracy.

He recognized the businessman in his suit. The man's tie hung loose, and the top of his shirt splayed, unbuttoned. Another man standing next to him shared the same sharp nose and pale white skin. This individual wore a white T-shirt and dark denim jeans. He clapped the businessman's back. "Good job, Lawrence."

"Enough of your bullshit." Tracy tried to spit at them. Her face appeared paler, sicklier than before. "You'll pay for this. For all of this. I'll kill you both."

The man in the white T-shirt laughed. "You're so feisty. I love it!" He clapped his hands and rubbed them together. "I can't wait to get a look at that blood. I've missed working with my little babies!" He picked up the plastic canister filling with Tracy's blood. "Are you sure I have to wait until she's dried out? I'd like to start now. Isolating the viruses is going to take long enough. Then I have to lyse them and parse out the DNA, sequence it, and send it through the replication process. I want to have working samples to send out to NanoTech as soon as we can."

"Just be patient. A few more minutes won't kill you," Lawrence said.

"It'll kill her, though." The man in jeans laughed.

"Exactly."

Tracy rattled the chair again. "Let me go!" A vessel in her forehead throbbed as she lashed forward at the man in jeans. He jumped back in surprise.

Standing up, he put his hand on Lawrence's back. "What do you say? Should we let her go?"

Lawrence glared at Tracy, saying nothing.

Again the man in jeans laughed, holding his sides. "Of course, we won't!"

Tracy lunged forward again, pressing her wrists against the bands. The man in jeans laughed but then stopped when a tearing sound came from the straps on the arms of the chair. In a flash, Tracy tore from her restraints and pounced on Lawrence. The IV needle ripped from her arm, a spray of blood following it.

She wrestled with the businessman and pulled his gun from his jacket. Pointing it at his head, she pushed him against the floor. She squeezed the trigger until a deafening report echoed against the walls. Lawrence's gray eyes turned lifeless. A mess of blood and red tissue splattered around the floor and onto Tracy.

The man in jeans shrieked. Running out of the room, he closed the door behind him.

Chris's eyes shot wide open as Tracy jumped after the man. She yanked the handle of the door, and the metal groaned. The color in her cheeks rose as she settled back against the chair where Chris was restrained. She turned to him and steadied herself. "Goddammit. I need to eat. They took too much blood." She pulled at his wrist straps, peeling them from the chair in a single effort. "Glad to see you awake."

Shaking, Chris sat up. He pulled the IV needle from his skin and pressed his hand over the insertion point to stop the bleeding. "How did you do that?" His head still felt light, and he found it difficult to believe what he saw.

Her gaze appeared distracted as she ignored his question. "I didn't want them to know about me, but I needed to get out of there. I had them both...but he got away. Dammit."

"I don't understand."

Tracy tore the straps from Chris's ankles. She gripped his left shoulder and pulled him up straight, supporting him with one arm. He winced at the pressure. "You think you can stand up on your own?"

He blinked the haziness from his eyes. "I think so." He tottered up and leaned against the wall as the blood drained from his head. After the lightheadedness cleared, he looked around. Jordan and Greg lay unconscious against the wall. Chris went to the drawers, scattering the contents of each as he searched for smelling salts to wake them up. He found a small packet in one of the drawers next to extra coils of IV tubing and boxes of bandages. "Can you find anything to get that chain off Jordan's foot?"

Peering out the window in the locked door, Tracy turned and nodded. She took the gun out of her belt and pointed at Jordan.

"What the hell are you doing?"

She fired, and the lock on the chain securing Jordan's ankle burst with metal shrapnel. "Happy now?" Tearing at the broken metal, she released the chains and threw them aside. "We need to find Ben."

His mouth agape, Chris glanced from the torn lock to Tracy. He cocked his head, a fog still hanging over his mind. "Ben?"

"Ben Kaufman. The other man that was here." She kicked the businessman in the ribs. "This asshole's brother."

"Brother?" Chris stood in front of her, dumbfounded.

"Yeah, they're in business together." She looked down at Lawrence's body. "Or, they *were* in business together." She slammed a fist down on the top of the metal drawers where Chris had retrieved the syringes. The top of the drawers dented inward.

Chris knelt in front of Jordan. He tried to calm his racing heartbeat. Pinching his fingers together, he waved the smelling salts under Jordan's nose.

Jordan shot awake and looked around. "Are we okay?"

"I don't know." Chris woke up Greg and turned back to Tracy. "What do we do now?"

"We need to get the hell out of here."

"They're going to need this," Chris said, indicating the container of blood. "The virus, all the DNA, is in here, and we're stuck in here. Ben will have to come back."

Tracy paced in front of the door.

"You should sit and relax. You'll faint with all that blood loss."

Her face turned up in a growl. "I'll be fine." Her expression softened. The fire in her eyes subsided. She threw her arms around Chris. "Dammit. I'm sorry." She pressed her cheek against his. Her skin felt feverishly warm. "I'm so glad you're okay. I'm so happy you're alive." Drawing away, she gripped his sides. Her eyes seemed wet with tears. "I thought they killed you."

"I'm fine," he said. "I'm sorry I dragged you into this. All of this. Please, sit down a minute. We'll see if we can break this lock, but you need your strength. You lost too much blood."

Greg struggled to his feet and lumbered to the door. "Yeah, Chris is right. Let him and me get us out of here." He tried pulling on the handle of the door, but it didn't budge.

"Wait a second," Jordan said. "Check his pockets. Maybe he's got a comm card we can use to call for help."

Tracy's brow wrinkled, but her expression grew complacent again. "Good idea." She let Chris go and knelt by Lawrence's body to check his pockets. "Got it." Brandishing a comm card, she tapped on it. She gestured in a couple of commands as the card projected a blue, winding image that turned red. "Shit, shit. It's locked." Her nose scrunched in a snarl, she broke the card in half and tossed the pieces toward the sink. The shards of the card fluttered and landed harmlessly on the tiled floor.

Eyeing her, Jordan coughed and wiped his mouth with the back of his hand. "Surely he'll be back with help to keep you both from getting away. You both are too valuable to him."

"Then we need to be prepared." Greg dismantled the IV pole that, minutes ago, had held the tubing draining Tracy's blood. After swinging the pole around to gauge its weight and balance, he bent down and picked up the container with Tracy's blood in it. "He's *got* to send someone back."

Chris opened his mouth to mention that someone on the outside, Veronica, possessed the DNA they needed. If Kaufman found her, he wouldn't need them. He could leave them to starve and rot in the whitewashed examination room. But he decided against saying anything, snapping his mouth closed again.

Sitting on the examination bed, a laceration on his head still bleeding, Jordan erupted in another coughing fit. Greg wrapped one of his large arms around Jordan, dwarfing the man, and held him steady.

Distant sounds of raised voices penetrated the door. Chris walked over to Tracy, her eyes transfixed through the reinforced rectangular window. "We've got to get help," he said. "Jordan needs a hospital."

"We need to catch Kaufman." She watched out the window like a guard dog waiting for a burglar.

"Jordan's going to die if we don't get him out of here."

Red flames burning in her eyes, Tracy glared at him. "I've got to get to Kaufman. You can save your friend."

Chris backed away, setting his jaw, but said nothing. He went to the drawers, leveraging his body weight to open the one that Tracy had dented inward. Amid the scattered cardboard boxes, he squeezed out a box of medical tape and several packets of sterile gauze infused with antibiotic nanoparticles. He scooped up the supplies with one arm and grabbed a brown plastic bottle of rubbing alcohol from next to the sink with his free hand.

One of Jordan's eyes had swollen shut, caked with dried blood and black with bruises. Chris squirted a stream of alcohol across Jordan's forehead and dabbed at it with a cotton swab. Jordan winced but made no sound as Chris cleaned up the wounds.

Greg watched with cautious interest as Chris finished cleaning the lacerations and blood. He applied gauze patches over the torn skin.

Outside the room, a muffled pop sounded. Chris whipped his head toward the door, the quick movement sending a flash of pain in his still-tender neck and shoulder. "What the hell was that?"

Tracy seemed to grin. "Gunfire."

"What the hell are you so happy about?" Greg said, his voice shaking.

"Gunfire means problems for Kaufman," Tracy said.

Ripping a piece of medical tape with his teeth, Chris paused. "Trouble? You think the police are here?"

Her eyes narrowed and turned back out the window. She lowered her voice. "Not likely."

"Who, then?" Chris cocked his head, the medical tape still in his hands as he lined it up over another patch of gauze. Tracy shook her head and remained staring out the window as Chris pressed the gauze over and across Jordan's cheek.

Jordan recoiled, pinching his lips tight until they drained of color. He relaxed after Chris stopped applying pressure.

Tracy seemed distracted and distant. Chris frowned, wondering what she meant, as she peered through the window.

Greg leaned in to Jordan, tracing the man's cheek with his index finger. "I think it's fractured."

"You think, doctor?" Jordan poked his cheek with a light touch, probing at his jawline.

"Tracy, you don't happen to have any of those pain pills on you?" Chris asked.

"No, they took everything I had on me."

"You know what they did with them?"

She glowered. "Jesus, I guess I forgot to ask."

"I'm just trying to help the poor guy out."

Tracy's expression softened again. "Sorry." She left her post at the door and placed her hands on Chris's shoulders. "Thanks for trying to save me."

"You didn't need too much saving." He held her close, inhaling the scent of lilacs from her hair. In spite of everything, that persistent scent still clung to her. He kissed her on the cheek and then pressed his cheek against hers as they embraced. "Turns out I gave you a bit of these genes they had me carrying, huh? God, I'm sorry for getting you into this mess."

When he pulled his head back to see her face, she wore an odd, almost pitiful expression. "Don't be sorry. It's my fault."

"I don't see how you can even say that," he said. He kissed her, the hint of a metallic taste lingering on her lips.

Before Tracy could say anything else, the clatter of metal against metal sounded outside the room. Heavy footsteps drew them from their embrace and back to the window. Greg tensed, stepping in front of Jordan to protect the injured man from whatever lay in wait for them outside the door.

CHAPTER THIRTY-FIVE

A HAND PRESSED AGAINST THE NARROW window of the room, obscuring Tracy and Chris's view out the narrow window. Greg cocked back the IV pole, ready to strike as he stepped forward. The door swung open, Tracy and Chris jumping back, and Kaufman, his white shirt soaked with sweat, stepped in.

"You need to follow me right now." Kaufman held a pistol in his right hand but didn't point it at any of them. Instead, he stared down the hallway.

Tracy and Chris looked at each other. Greg began to swing the IV pole at Kaufman when Blue Eyes entered and pointed a handgun at him. "Drop it."

Greg released the pole, and it bounced on the floor with a clang. Brown Eyes stepped in. His skin was ashen and he clutched at his right shoulder even as he brandished a submachine gun.

As Tracy reached for the pistol tucked against her waist, Brown Eyes glared at her. "Get your hands away from that." He let go of his shoulder, revealing a long tear in his skin, evidence of a slicing knife or grazing bullet. Blood oozed from the wound as he plucked the pistol from Tracy and slipped it into the waist of his pants. Through gritted teeth, he said, "listen to Kaufman."

Kaufman's nostrils flared. He leaned out the door again, his head swiveling to look down either end of the hallway. With his hand, he motioned for everyone to follow him. Tracy and Chris filed out behind him, and Greg hoisted Jordan up, allowing Jordan to lean on him for support. The two thugs followed behind. They rounded the corner where Chris, Jordan, and Greg had escaped earlier. Kaufman led them onward, breaking into a hobbling jog.

Her eyes narrowed, Tracy stared at the back of Kaufman's neck. She flexed her hands at her sides. Chris reached down and grabbed her wrist. When he did so, she looked at him and he shook his head. "Not now," he whispered. "Not now."

Kaufman used his comm card to unlock a door that led to a flight of stairs. The winding stairs seemed to spiral up into dark shadows, with no lights to illuminate their way.

She turned forward again. "What the hell is going on?"

Kaufman turned back to them. "We've got unwelcome visitors."

Tracy flashed a quick grin. "Not the police, are they?"

Without saying anything, Kaufman turned back and glared at her. "Too bad I still need to keep at least one of you alive. I don't need them, though." He stopped and pointed at Jordan and Greg. "Take them down."

Tracy lunged at him, gripping the arm that held his pistol, as his two lackeys leveled their guns at Greg and Jordan. Before either could pull the trigger, Tracy tore the handgun from Kaufman's hand and pressed its muzzle to the side of his head.

"Don't," Tracy said.

The two lackeys froze, their guns still pointed at Jordan and Greg. They looked to Kaufman for guidance.

"Drop 'em," Tracy said.

They didn't respond.

"Do what she says," Kaufman said.

Both men bent and placed their guns on the cement floor. Tracy motioned for Chris to pick them up. He retrieved the weapons, examining them as he did. With little experience in firearms, he put the strap of the submachine gun around his left shoulder and held the pistol in his hand. It, at least, felt more comfortable than the larger, cold metal grip of the other gun.

Heavy footsteps echoed down the halls. Tracy prodded Kaufman with her pistol. "How many more do you have besides these two buffoons?"

"I don't know," Kaufman said.

"What the hell do you mean?"

"There were at least four others on our side in the firefight. It didn't last long, but I didn't stay to check for casualties, either." Kaufman's nose scrunched in a snarl again. "I have no idea how they found us."

"How many of you were there before the attack?"

Kaufman didn't respond.

Tracy pressed the gun against his head harder, the skin turning red where the metal touched his temple. Her voice rose. "How many?"

"Nine of us in total. Including me and Lawrence."

"Your brother?"

Kaufman nodded.

The sound of doors slamming open and voices yelling grew closer. A grim sneer spread across Tracy's face as she choked Kaufman with her arm.

Blue Eyes lunged. Tracy fired three shots at his chest. The bullets knocked him backward. He clutched at his chest, evidently protected by a bulletproof vest, and groaned. Tracy leveled her pistol at Brown Eyes. He ducked, but Tracy's aim followed. Another three shots exploded from the gun barrel. One hit him, piercing his skull and causing him to collapse into a messy heap at the bottom of the stairs. She pulled the trigger once more to finish off the other man.

The voices down the hall rose up in response to the shots, the door slamming ceased, and the clatter of shoes against the floor grew louder.

CHAPTER THIRTY-SIX

"**W**E'VE GOT TO MOVE!**" CHRIS jumped up the steps toward Tracy. He grabbed Kaufman's collar, stretching out the cotton fabric until it ripped. "Hand me your comm card."

Kaufman's lips drew tighter, and he made no move to comply.

Chris patted the man down and reached into a pocket. Kaufman kicked at him and struggled in Tracy's arms until she tightened her grip around his throat. Chris pulled out the comm card.

Tracy dragged Kaufman up the stairs, her face red. "Don't call the police."

The din down the hallway grew more pressing. Greg lugged Blue Eyes's body out the door next to that of Brown Eyes and threw the door to the stairs shut. The lock clicked shut. They plunged into darkness, with only the narrow window of the stairwell door providing meager illumination.

"We need to move," Greg said, helping Jordan up the stairs. "Let's get the hell out of here."

"There's no need." Tracy pushed Kaufman forward. "If they're his men, they won't hurt us if we have him hostage."

Chris glanced at Kaufman and then back at the door. "What if they're not his? What if it's the group that attacked Kaufman, the one that tried to kill Veronica?"

Creases forming across her forehead, Tracy jutted her head forward. "What do you mean they *tried* to kill Veronica? She's dead." Her eyes narrowed to dark slits.

"No, she's not. But we will be if we don't move."

Without a word, Greg stepped past with Jordan limping beside him. Tracy followed with Kaufman in tow, overtaking them, and Chris brought up the rear. He glanced at the strip of a window once more to see shadows looming down the hall as unidentifiable pursuers came searching for them.

Chris froze on the stairs. "Why don't you want me to call the police?"

Stopping half a flight above him, Tracy turned. "You know what the police think about your involvement with Randy. If you introduce this whole mess, you're landing back in Fulton."

Looking down from Tracy, Chris toyed with the comm card in his hand. "Jordan's in rough shape, we have who knows how many other people after us, and we just uncovered a goddamned illegal genetic enhancement conspiracy. If I end up back in Fulton because of that, so be it. I can't stand for anyone else to get killed."

"You're making a mistake," Kaufman said. "You can just let me go, and we can forget about all of this. About all of you."

"No," Jordan said, his voice gruff. "Call the police."

Chris tapped at the comm card with his hand. The card was locked, requiring its owner's thumbprint. He grabbed Kaufman's wrist and pressed the man's thumb against the card. The screen lit up green. As he dialed up emergency services,

Tracy threw Kaufman down the stairs at him. He dropped the pistol he held in his other hand, and it clattered down the stairs. Grabbing at the rail to stay upright, he dropped the comm card. Kaufman tumbled down the stairs and crumpled into a heap.

"What the hell was that for?"

Tracy pushed past Chris, pressing him against the railing, and fired four shots in quick succession at Kaufman. The bullets smashed into him, the blast of the gun ricocheting in the enclosed stairwell.

Chris clapped his hands to his buzzing ears. Tracy turned back up, leveling the gun toward Jordan. Greg charged down the stairs. The muddled sounds of Tracy's yells and Jordan's words crashed as Greg leapt at her. She blasted two rounds into his chest. Greg's body crashed into her. The two bodies intertwined, rolling back down the stairs to lie motionless on the shadowed floor.

Chris took a single step down as the ringing in his ears faded.

"She's not on our side." Jordan's raspy voice drew his attention. "She called someone. Them, I think." Jordan pointed at the door, his chest heaving. Drawn by the gunfire, shadowed faces peered in, squinting into the dark recesses of the stairwell. Fists pounded on the door, and it sounded as if someone hammered on the locking mechanism on their side. "I saw her use the comm card. She sent a message. I barely saw it, but it said where we are. Who we were with." He glanced at Kaufman's crumpled form and at Greg's limp body.

"No, that's not right." Chris shook his head. "That's impossible."

"I'm afraid it's true. Don't you see? She's not strong because she has the same virus with the same DNA you have. You'd be just as strong. No, she's an enhancer. She works for them. Everywhere you go with her, there's a wake of destruction."

"She wouldn't do that. They broke into her apartment and stole the samples."

"Who broke in?" Jordan put a hand on Chris's shoulder, his voice rising. "It wasn't the Kaufman brothers. They tortured me to find out where those extra samples were. I can see in your eyes you know they didn't take the samples."

"She staged it?" Chris cocked his head, furrowing his brow, and took a step back. He didn't want to believe it and tried to conjure an argument that would contradict Jordan's allegations.

"She killed Greg, and she tried to kill me." Jordan's good eye filled with pitiful sorrow. "We've got to go."

Chris took up one of Jordan's arms and helped him to scale the stairs. As they rounded the first landing again, a heavy thud sounded from below them. Tracy emerged from beneath Greg. A cut on her head bled. She wiped it with the back of her hand, studied the blood, and wiped her now-empty hands on her torn slacks.

"Stop!" She stood at the bottom of the stairs, her hair tangled around her face, as a trickle of blood dripped from her nose. "I've had enough of all this. You've got a choice." She glanced at the door, which several people still struggled to open, and looked back at Chris. "Jordan's not wrong. I'm leaving with those people. You can come with me, too. All I wanted to do was find the Kaufman brothers. They were dangerous and needed to be stopped. Can't you understand that?"

Chris's chest heaved, his heart thumping against his rib cage. "How are you any better than them?"

"You know me. I can protect you. Hell, we could use a guy like you."

The words sounded too familiar. "I'm not going to be a part of that."

"Don't act like you're better than me. You were a part of this business before with that amateur." She pointed a shaking finger at Jordan. "Join me. You're smart. Think about what you could do with us. If we take the DNA you and I both have, we could expand our business. We could find a way to sell it to NanoTech like these idiots were trying to do."

Chris took a step down the stairs, the submachine gun still hanging from his left shoulder. It clanged against the railing. "I'm not interested. I gave all that up."

"Why? You couldn't stand working at Ingenomics. All your efforts, your inventions, belonged to them. Isn't that how you ended up in this business? Don't you want to be rewarded for your work?"

"Rewarded like Randy?"

"He was a fucking idiot. Tried to start a bidding war between us and the Kaufmans. Hell, he was going to try to sell *your* delivery system. You saw his notebook." She stretched a beseeching hand, the vessels in her arms dilated and pulsing.

"I won't work with...with whatever group you're with."

Tracy sneered at him, shaking her head, her tangled hair whipping. "Where do you think you're going to go? You've got nothing without me. You were going to lose your job today, too. Since you lost Randy's protection, Claire was going to fire you. They know what you are now. So answer me this: Where will you run to?" She threw her hands up. "You've got nothing." She lowered her voice, the red from her face draining, her natural skin tone returning. "Besides, we make a great team."

Chris took a step forward. "You lied to me."

"Not about everything." She held a hand out to him, palm up.

He took another step forward.

Grinning, Tracy motioned for him to come closer. "See? You're like me. You can do this too."

He pointed at Greg's body. "I've never killed anyone. I couldn't do that." He bent down toward the comm card that had flown from his hand as Tracy scowled. "You're the one that led them to Veronica, weren't you?"

"Don't," she said.

As Chris bent to retrieve the card, Tracy jumped for the pistol that had come clattering down the stairs when she had knocked past him. She picked the gun up, swinging her arm up past him. Toward Jordan.

Chris fumbled with the submachine gun, shouldering it and aiming it toward Tracy. She fired up at Jordan and Chris pulled the trigger in response.

The recoil sent the barrel flying upward, the stock of the gun slamming into his shoulder, and he fell back, cracking his head against the stairs. Again, his ears rang and his vision swam. He grasped the back of his head. Warm liquid smeared onto his hand. No more gunshots, no more cries, no yells. Shadows danced at the narrow window of the stairs, wilder than before, jumping about like hyenas on a dead gazelle.

He reached out to the metal railing and hoisted himself up with his left hand. At the bottom of the stairs, Tracy had fallen over Greg, one arm flung across Kaufman's back. The pistol rested at the corner of the stairwell, glimmering as light hit it, reflected from the door's window.

"Chris."

Spinning around, Chris scooped an arm under Jordan. He felt a new warmth run over him as he lifted his friend. The hotness spilled from Jordan's side and the man groaned. He was bleeding heavily.

"Chris. The comm card."

The card lay on the stair again and Chris bent to retrieve it. He dialed for emergency services.

"What's your emergency?"

He stammered, unsure. "Shot. Dead." He shook his head and he looked at Jordan. "There's someone hurt. He's alive. I need an ambulance. The police."

"May I use your current location according to your comm card's GPS?"

"Yes."

"Thank you, sir. Please remain where you are and with your comm card. Help is arriving."

They'd escaped. Help was coming. It would be all over.

The pounding against the door ceased. The whine of metal against metal, the purr of a drill echoed in the stairwell.

Jordan gripped Chris's shoulder. "We have to move."

They powered up the stairs into darkness. No emergency lights illuminated their way or declared a safe exit above them. These stairs must have been obscured, hidden for such an escape. Adrenaline surged through him once more. Jordan winced with each step as Chris reassured him.

Below them, the sound of the drilling ceased. A crack echoed up the stairwell followed by a crash. Voices rose up around them as they carried on.

Footsteps echoed up the steel stairs. Chris's heart pounded faster and harder. He pushed on.

A dozen tiny white lights shone ahead. He reached out toward them, but something cool and hard blocked his way. When he pressed forward, it gave away. A glass window, a door. It let them out into the freezing night air onto a walkway bordering the water. Small waves splashed against the side of the causeway where they stood and stars dotted the sky.

They hobbled toward the end of the walkway along the massive warehouse toward the street.

Blue and red lights, appearing distant, grew closer. Lights flashed and sirens became louder. Jordan grappled Chris and pulled him into a hug with his good arm. "We made it."

He did not reciprocate, standing frozen. "I killed her." His eyes gazed off, back over the water. Wave tips caught the light of the moon, the light of the city, throwing it back into the air, back at him. He stared at Jordan's battered face. "I killed her, Jordan." His bottom lip shook.

"You did what you needed to do. You did the right thing."

But Jordan's words fell across Chris with as much effect as a pebble thrown into the ocean. "It doesn't feel right."

CHAPTER THIRTY-SEVEN

T HE FUNERAL WAS HELD TWO weeks after Randall Nee's.
This time, Chris went with Jordan. They arrived together in
Jordan's sedan at the white-domed First Unitarian Church
of Baltimore. Chris had not anticipated the sheer number of
people he saw at the memorial service, shaking hands and
introducing themselves as friends or family members of Greg's.
He followed Jordan through the mass of people congregating
near the altar. As they grew closer, the open casket became
visible as people passed and hugged, cried and laughed. Stories
of Greg's exploits as a child, as a colleague, as a friend drifted
throughout the gaggle of voices.

Jordan embraced a wrinkled woman wearing a scarlet dress
that shone bright against the other mourners clad in muted,
dark tones. Its folds draped her skinny frame and hung around
her like a windless sail from a mast. Tears intermittently
escaped her eyes, yet she wore a quivering smile. When Jordan
approached her, she broke down and he stooped to embrace
her. They clung together, her hand rubbing Jordan's back.

Releasing the woman, Jordan motioned to Chris, clasping the woman's hands all the while. "This is Greg's mother, Mrs. Harding."

She released Jordan and grasped Chris's hands. Her palms felt dry and warm, her knuckles swollen with arthritis. "Call me Jeanette. Were you a close friend?"

Chris thought to respond that he wasn't. That he had only known Greg for a couple of days. He remembered watching Greg read a book while he, Jordan, and Tracy had discussed the unraveling of a conspiracy, the untangling of a mess that Chris had dove headfirst into without considering the depth of his plunge.

Instead, he nodded. "Greg was a wonderful man." He opened his mouth to say more, to express something, anything, but he pressed his lips closed again and offered Jeanette a smile that he hoped appeared as sincerely sympathetic as he felt.

"Thank you for coming," she said, letting go of his hand and smiling back at him with an expression of sorrow. Chris could tell that expression was not just sorrow for the loss of her son, but it was an expression of her own condolences to *him*.

Once again, he followed Jordan into the small line in front of Greg's casket. A window composed of intricate, curling patterns above them let in a golden glow above where Greg lay in repose. Chris gazed up, avoiding the casket. His eyes darted among the ornate carvings in the arching ceiling, protruding square shapes, each with a circle in the center like eyes watching the service from above.

A tide of dizziness swelled up in him and he started for the pews, but Jordan grabbed his arm. Chris opened his mouth and closed it again, his eyebrows arching. The words he wanted to speak would not come.

"It's okay." Jordan squeezed Chris's arm. On Jordan's ribs, a long gash healed with the help of dermal tissue wraps. The engineered cell populations in the wraps rejuvenated his skin, minimizing the formation of scar tissue while preventing infections. A dark ring encompassed his left eye. Stubble sprouted from his head as his tight curls of black hair grew back in from where the nurse had shaved it to better glue up the cuts on his head. His left arm was slung in a cast. On his foot, he wore an oversized boot secured in place with Velcro to stabilize the healing fractures in his ankle. He insisted on the walking boot and refused to use a crutch to support his weight. The doctor had told him he could walk on the fracture and that he was lucky to have such relatively minor injuries. But Jordan had told Chris he had not felt lucky. What he had lost that day had nothing to do with his own body.

"Thanks." Chris closed his eyes and breathed in slowly.

As they approached the open casket, he traced the dark-stained wood that marked the top edges, brushing his fingers along it. Jordan bent to kiss Greg on the cheek. Chris bit the inside of his cheek, willing himself to remain stolid.

Jordan whispered something to Greg, closed his eyes briefly, and then turned. "Your turn."

Greg seemed relaxed. His lips curled slightly, hinting at a smile that would never see fruition. His hands were clasped together on his chest in repose over a royal blue tie. The black suit jacket curved over his rounded shoulders and narrowed as it disappeared into the casket. Now, more than ever, his cheekbones struck out from his face and his pointed chin jutted out.

This man had never sought to solve a murder or concern himself with chasing down a vicious illegal genetic enhancement organization peddling its wares to street users and government buyers alike. He had never expressed interest in connecting a rash of prison murders to organizers on the outside. Yet he had given his life when Tracy threatened to take Jordan's. And Chris could not shake the thought that all of this was because of him. Because he had been stubborn, tried to play amateur detective, manipulated both by the businessman and then by Tracy.

No, not manipulated. He had made his choices. No one else could be held responsible. He wiped his eyes with the back of his hand. He placed that hand on Greg's chest, let out another long breath, and then joined Jordan in a pew.

With no destination in mind, Chris and Jordan meandered along the Inner Harbor. Both admitted they did not feel inclined to spend the rest of the afternoon in either of their homes. Tomorrow, they would be interviewed by Baltimore PD detectives yet again. Chris would undergo another round of modified dialysis so the PD's Bio Unit could remove and analyze the viruses and gene samples from his blood to help them in the investigation against the Kaufmans' group and Tracy Harrow's as-yet-unidentified organization. His willing cooperation and the use of his blood as evidence enabled him to eliminate his remaining time on parole. Still, at the remaining interviews, there would be questions, untold scrutiny, and little rest.

Today, there was nothing.

A chilling wind blew in from the harbor, imploring Chris to hold tight to his coat. He shrank his neck into the coat's collar. Jordan limped along, gritting his teeth with each step but refusing to complain. Despite the cold brought on by the wind, the sun shone brightly. The calm waters of the harbor mirrored the clear blue sky and reflected blinding light onto them as gentle waves curled up.

They walked west along the Harbor Bridge. A family with two screaming toddlers passed by as Jordan and Chris pressed themselves against the low wall of the walkway.

They paused in the middle of the bridge between the piers. A massive cruise ship embarked in the distance, blasting three low calls from its horns to mark its departure.

Chris wrapped his gloved fingers around the steel bar and swung his head up to the sky. He inhaled, sucking in the mix of salty air from the harbor and the pungent smells of the city. "I can't believe I let her manipulate me."

Raising an eyebrow, Jordan said nothing.

Chris opened his mouth to let out the protest dancing on his tongue, the excuses and the cruelties that Tracy had inflicted on him. He stopped. "No, you're right. I was blind. Stubborn."

"You see what you want. You've always been that way."

Jordan did not need to remind Chris about his initial arguments for dealing in black-market genetic enhancements. As he looked back at Jordan, the man's left eye still yellow from healing, he recalled his disdain for working at a life-sucking company that owned his inventions and profited from his efforts. And, when the company reported its latest innovations to investors or celebrated its quarterly earnings, the investor briefings and press releases never acknowledged Chris's part of the work. He had carried them—he and an army of other scientists and engineers who worked tirelessly and without recognition. The company constantly reminded them that they toiled for a greater good, distributing images of the children whose lives had purportedly been saved by their technologies. But of course, the company turned a hefty profit in the meantime.

"I was immature, wasn't I?"

Jordan closed his eyes and chuckled. "Yes. You were. Probably still are." He smiled. "But I'm not claiming to be any better."

They both turned back to the bay. The cries of circling seagulls accompanied the scraping of the wind against their ears.

"I'm sorry, Jordan. I truly am." He placed his hand on Jordan's back.

"What will you do now?" Jordan asked.

"I don't think I could've gone back to Respondent even if they had kept me on, and I'm not sure that I'll be an easy hire anywhere." He laughed, shaking his head. "I'll figure something out."

"At least you've got time. Will you stay in Baltimore?"

Shaking his head, he shrugged. "I'm not sure that it's safe here for me anymore, but I'm not ready to leave."

"Yet you're too stubborn for witness protection."

Chris's brow wrinkled up as he frowned. "I'm not going to hide from my problems."

"It's your life."

"I know," he said and let out a sigh. "As corny as it sounds, I won't give up who I am and everything I've done. All the choices I made were mine. You were right."

"That's fine, but it doesn't mean you need to risk your life."

"I already have." He locked eyes with Jordan. "I risked yours, too. Greg's. Veronica's."

"What are you going to do about the girl?"

"Veronica?" Chris raised an eyebrow. "She's no girl."

Jordan held up a hand in self-defense. "Pardon me."

"She hasn't returned my calls. Her parents wouldn't tell me where she is." He turned away for a moment. "Rightfully so, I suppose."

"You want to see her, huh?"

"Of course. I need to apologize to her. Out of everyone, she had the least to do with any of this. I want to make things right."

"If that's the case, maybe you should let her go. Let her take care of herself. Like you said, she's not just a girl, and you might reintroduce her to a world of trouble."

Neither of them said anything while they watched the gulls circle and dive above them. Jordan motioned for them to continue walking toward the aquarium. They dodged through crowds as the cold ate through Chris's coat and settled in his skin. He could feel goose bumps sprouting on his arms and shivered. They passed the *U.S.S. Constellation* docked nearby. Despite his discomfort, he admired the old three-masted sloop. It was more than two hundred years old, yet it had withstood the seasons and the storms to remain a permanent fixture in the Inner Harbor. He could not help but imagine what it had looked like with billowing white sails delivering it across the Caribbean in pursuit of slaver ships. The ship and its history captivated him, and Jordan tugged on Chris's shoulder to prevent him from running into an equally transfixed tourist.

"Thanks."

"I'll look out for you," Jordan said. "Like I said before: if you need anything, I'll be there."

"I know." He took a final glance at the *Constellation* before they crossed Pratt Street. Its image reminded him of his own amateur attempts to capture a three-masted sailing ship in one of his prison charcoal drawings. "There's still so much about all of this I don't understand. Like, how did Vincent know about Ben Kaufman?" A shiver went down his spine.

"Maybe he was one of the former employees Lawrence mentioned?" Jordan shrugged as they crossed the street, winding between cars stopped in traffic. "Besides, I would've hoped you'd learned not to worry about those kinds of questions now. It might be safer not to know."

Sighing, Chris nodded.

"Remember, you can always take up that witness protection offer."

A cool wind rustled the branches of a tree growing from one of the planters that lined the sidewalk. Spring would come soon enough. The mercurial weather blowing over them and eastward toward the Atlantic would cease its fluctuations, replaced by a humid heat and intermittent, warm showers. The dirty, melting snow would be cleansed from the city, and Chris would still be here to soak it in.

Alive.

He was alive.

Maybe he should listen to Jordan, leave it all behind. Start over again. Only this time, he vowed to get it right.

EPILOGUE

INSTEAD OF MOVING AWAY AFTER the Baltimore PD's investigation concluded, Chris stayed in Baltimore. He applied to a couple of companies in passing while he lived off his remaining savings and the severance pay he'd received from Respondent. If money ran out, he could always go to Jordan.

Jordan would gladly host him in his penthouse, which Chris imagined seemed even lonelier now than ever before.

But he couldn't do that. He couldn't be reminded of the loneliness brought on by his actions.

Most companies did not bother to respond to any of his applications. He would have been inclined to believe that they were adamant to avoid a convicted felon, along with a man who had become momentarily infamous for his involvement in bringing down two underground genetic manufacturers. While a few news streams seemed to laud him for heroism, others took the opportunity to resurrect his past and use it to incriminate him in a deeper scandal. They suggested that he was still involved in the illegal genetics manufacturing economy and had been granted amnesty for blowing the whistle on the Kaufman brothers and their rivals.

Frustratingly enough, no news organizations seemed to implicate any governmental interest in these technologies, nor did they accuse companies like NanoTech that Ben Kaufman had suggested would be serving as launderers for the neural strength enhancements.

When he wasn't applying for jobs, he read Jordan's draft manuscripts. He tried to assure Jordan that he would be of no use when it came to critiquing the man's novels. But Jordan felt certain that Chris owed him a favor or two and that reading his works-in-progress would be recompense enough.

As he reread the story about the truck driver, a soft knock came from his door. At first, shaken out of the story, he cocked his head, unsure if the sound had come from elsewhere. The soft patter sounded again, and he pocketed his comm card, the manuscript projection shimmering closed, as he stepped toward the door.

Without checking through the peephole, he swung open the door. Before him, a woman with cropped, raven-black hair and crisp blue eyes looked up at him. Her heart-shaped face and knowing smile set him at ease.

"Veronica." He could say no more.

She let herself in, brushing past him. "How are you?"

Chris closed the door and locked the deadbolt for good measure. "I'm fine. What about you?"

Veronica smiled her characteristic, toothy grin. The goofy smile contrasted her litheness when she danced, especially when she convinced him to join her on the dance floor, pretending to let him guide her through crossovers, spins, and twists. In reality, she had led Chris. She unbuttoned her jacket and pulled down her shirt collar to show the small, pink scars. "Doing better."

"Why didn't you get dermal patches to heal those up?"

She scoffed at him. "Did you?"

He patted the scarred ridges in his side. "No, but I didn't have a choice. Prison medicine isn't exactly about aesthetics and, frankly, fixing a couple scars was not a priority when I got out."

"I never wanted to forget," she said, her voice dreamy and strangely uplifting.

"Your dancing, though."

Veronica laughed. "Choreographers don't seem to be so worried about a couple of scars." She pursed her lips. "I think, in a weird way, a few of them like it."

"So you've been performing? Is that such a good idea right now?"

"I've been dancing with a company, but I haven't performed yet. Why don't we sit?"

Before he could answer, she gripped his wrist and pulled him down on the couch. She draped her legs over his coffee table and leaned against the armrest on her side. Chris sat on the opposite end, his posture bent and stiff.

"No one has bothered you, then?" he said, his face contorted in worry.

Veronica's grin evaporated. She closed her eyes and shook her head. "Not since that day."

He reached a hand across the couch but restrained himself from touching her. "I'm sorry." He pinched his eyes closed. "God, I'm so sorry."

"I should've listened to you and left as soon as you told me to go."

"No, don't even pretend like it's your fault. Don't do that." He exhaled a long breath. "I thought you had died. Seeing you on the floor, I've never felt worse. Hell, it's selfish of me to tell you how I felt." He restrained himself no longer and hugged her.

Veronica recoiled but then placed her arms around him. At first, she bent her arms at stiff angles. She relaxed. Her breath tickled his ear. "The doctors said someone had tried to resuscitate me. Without that—without any forced pumping— even the Sustain wouldn't have saved me."

"I didn't save you." Chris pulled away, his hands on her shoulder. "I almost killed you." He let her go, but she held onto his hand.

Veronica played with his hand, threading her fingers between his. "What will you do now?" She was no different than Jordan. Asking him about his future. Asking him about what he would do now that it was over. It would never be over.

Chris turned her wrist over in his hand, massaging her palm with his thumb. He did not look into her eyes. "I'm not sure yet." He held her hand as his eyes explored her pale skin between the white scars. A vessel in her wrist protruded, reminding him of its hidden contents. "I think I might start my own business." He looked up at her, a new light in his eyes. "Yes, I think I'll give it a go as an entrepreneur."

He sat up straighter and grinned. "Jordan mentioned that he would be willing to invest in me." Shaking his head, Chris chortled. "I don't know why the man has so much faith in me, but I'd like to think it's for a good reason."

Veronica smiled again. The jubilant innocence returned to her face. Her cheeks flushed with a red warmth and her teeth appeared to shine. Her face, small scars still evident on her cheek and high up on her forehead, appeared beautiful, optimistic to him.

"What did you have in mind?"

Chris took both her hands in his. He'd never told Jordan or the police what he had told Ben Kaufman. The police, of course, knew Veronica had been tortured but had fallaciously connected it with efforts by Tracy's group to find out if he had told her anything about the Kaufman brothers and their whereabouts.

But no one, not even Veronica, knew of the advanced genetic technology coursing through her arteries, pumped by her heart, and returned through her veins. The vectors replicated, nascent and innocuous to Veronica. With reverse engineering and a bit of modification, Chris could manipulate the genes. He could make them seem new, different from the samples from his own blood. He could make them his.

"I've got a couple ideas," he said. He smiled at her, hoping he did not appear too gleeful or happy. After all, he should be stricken with guilt, bedridden by depression. He forced his grin to dissipate. His lips became tight, his eyes narrow. "You know, nothing can be the same now. Not between us, and not here in Baltimore."

For a moment, he saw Tracy's hazel eyes and her dirty blond hair. He felt her solid grip on his arms, the way she embraced him, pushed the air out of him. He heard the brashness in her voice, the determination and fierceness. She was not so different from him. She had wanted what he wanted.

She had killed someone, multiple people, to prevent them from getting in the way of her succeeding in her black-market business. Chris had never killed anyone before that day.

He thought for a moment, reminding himself of what Jordan had done. People had died for Chris's manufactured enhancements and vectors. People had died because he had stubbornly pursued his enigmatic businessman, refusing to comply with the man and give himself up without a fuss.

Maybe he had not pulled the trigger, but he could not claim complete innocence. Had Tracy wanted anything different than he had? After all, she had offered him the opportunity to stand by her side. In the end, he thought she had been the most honest. She could have killed him. She'd had everything she needed within herself, if she wanted. Instead, she'd waited. She'd asked Chris to leave with her. And he had killed her.

He shook the thought away and gave Veronica's hands a gentle squeeze. He recalled the hurt on her face when he had first pushed her out of his life, remembered her virtually lifeless body in her apartment. "We can't just go back to the way we were before all of this, before I went to prison."

"I know," Veronica said. "I know. I didn't come back here for you. I came back for me. For closure."

Chris nodded. He would let her go. He would let her go with those genes inside her. He had taken enough from her, and he would take no more.

THANK YOU FOR READING

Dear Reader,

Thank you for reading *Enhancement*. I sincerely hoped you enjoyed taking a ride with Chris in the world of illegal genetic contraband. But Chris isn't free from the world of *Black Market DNA* yet. If you're interested in future releases in this series and other works of mine, please consider joining my mailing list. I won't spam you and I won't share your email: http://bit.ly/ajmlist

Or, drop me a line at my website http://AnthonyJMelchiorri.com to stay in touch and see what else I have out. I also enjoy interviewing other authors and talking about both science and books on my blog there.

In any case, as an independent writer, your feedback and support is crucial to my craft. If you've enjoyed the story, please consider writing a review (as long or short as you like) on Amazon at http://bit.ly/ednarev. Reviews help independent authors like me spread the word so others might experience our stories. I greatly appreciate any and all honest feedback. Every review is important!

ALSO BY ANTHONY J MELCHIORRI

The God Organ

Brilliant biomedical scientist Preston Carter introduces an implantable artificial organ designed to grant its recipients near-immortality. But many of those recipients are suddenly dying. With the organ already implanted in his own body, Carter must uncover the truth before he's killed by his own invention.

Buy it here: http://amzn.to/1yjmMGF

The Human Forged

Former Army Specialist Nick Corrigan is abducted and unwittingly becomes embroiled in a biotechnological nightmare. He embarks on a dangerous adventure to return home. The only person that might be able to help him is a man Nick never knew existed—his clone.

Back in Washington, CIA analyst Sara Monahan makes a startling discovery while tracking the use of biological weapons in an ongoing war in Africa. She races to uncover a global conspiracy that may shake the very essence of what it means to be human.

Buy it here: http://bit.ly/thf14

ABOUT THE AUTHOR

Anthony J Melchiorri is a writer and biomedical engineer living in Maryland. He spends most of his time developing cardiovascular devices for tissue engineering to treat children with congenital heart defects when he isn't writing or reading.

Made in the USA
Monee, IL
10 December 2019

18327512R00164